THE PARSON'S WIDOW

Originally published in Finnish as *Hänen olivat linnut* by
Otava Publishing Company Ltd. (1967)

Library of Congress Cataloging-in-Publication Data

Vartio, Marja-Liisa.
[Hänen olivat Linnut. English]
The parson's widow : a novel / by Marja-Liisa Vartio ; translated
from the Finnish by Aili Flint and Austin Flint. -- 1st English
translation.
p. cm.
Originally published: Otava, 1967.
ISBN-13: 978-1-56478-483-4 (alk. paper)
ISBN-10: 1-56478-483-5 (alk. paper)
I. Flint, Aili. II. Flint, Austin. III. Title.
PH355.V37H3613 2007
894'.54133--dc22

2007026646

FILI—Finnish Literary Information Centre has supported the translation of this book.

Partially funded by grants from the National Endowment for the Arts, a federal agency, the
Illinois Arts Council, a state agency, and by the University of Illinois, Urbana-Champaign.

WWW.DALKEYARCHIVE.COM

Printed on permanent/durable acid-free paper and bound in the United States of America

THE PARSON'S WIDOW

MARJA-LIISA VARTIO

*Translated from the Finnish
by Aili and Austin Flint*

Dalkey Archive Press

Champaign · London

*I*NTRODUCTION

When *The Parson's Widow* was published in 1967, one year after
Marja-Liisa Vartio's untimely death at the age of forty-two, Finnish critics declared it the best of her five novels, predicting that
it would be regarded as a classic of modern Finnish fiction. This
judgment proved to be on the mark, for despite changes in literary
fashion, the book has remained in print during the forty years since
its publication, and it continues to elicit thoughtful and deeply felt
responses from general readers as well as from critics.

Vartio's early years gave little indication that she would become
one of Finland's most highly regarded novelists. After completing
studies in art history, world literature, and folk poetry at Helsinki
University, she chose not to pursue any of those fields profession-
ally but instead turned to writing poetry. Though her poetry never
attracted a large following, she enjoyed early success; two of her poetry collections, *The Wedding* (1952) and *The Garland* (1953), were
published while she was still in her twenties.

Her first work of fiction, a collection of short stories entitled
Between Land and Water (1955), did not represent an abandonment
of poetry but rather the application of a poetic sensibility and
technique to her short fiction. She did not yet call these stories
prose poems, but several of her briefest pieces from this collection
could belong in that category. Many of the stories have little or no
plot; their impact comes from striking visual imagery and a sur-
real, dreamlike quality. The physical objects Vartio describes may be

familiar, but they are seen through a distorting lens. In "The Rose," we are told that "The room was like an object floating in space, like a piece cut out of space and set inside walls. The ceiling and floor were slanted in the same direction, as if the room were tilting, and all that was in it seemed to be floating or touching the surface underneath it very slightly."

Dialogue from the same story is also disturbingly off-kilter. A woman wearing a "white coat like a doctor's" takes up a piece of chalk and begins to draw the picture of a rose on a blackboard. A woman asks her, "I can see that it is a rose, and a beautiful one. But why did you leave the center empty? Why have you drawn only its petals?" The woman in the white coat answers, "I have been asked to tell your friend that she will understand, when she thinks about it, why the rose only has petals, why the rose has been made crumbling and hollow."

A decade later, in the prose poem "Underground" from a collection entitled *Poems and Prose Poems* (1966), her first-person narrator says, "I went underground. I was looking for my brother's grave, and I saw him lying under a transparent slab of marble. His face was like gold, death had passed from it, and I knew I no longer mourned him."

It is in "The Vatican," the longest and most remarkable dream story from *Between Land and Water*, that one can most clearly discern the roots of the narrative method Vartio employs in *The Parson's Widow*. As in her other stories, she presents moments that convey a strong visual and emotional impact, but here she weaves those moments into a more extended narrative. The story is told from the point of view of a simple farm woman who suddenly and without rational explanation finds herself amidst a group of other farm women on a pilgrimage to the Vatican to obtain a blessing from the Pope. This is no usual procession of pilgrims, for the women are in tattered clothes and look as if they had "taken off right in the middle of their laundry or baking chores." Their aprons are dirty and one woman's arms are covered with dried dough up to her elbows. The strange events that unfold are especially powerful because Vartio describes the pilgrims' trek, first through a rural landscape and then on to the splendors of the Vatican, in vivid detail yet with a tone of detachment, as if these peculiar occurrences were the most natural thing in the world.

With her increased focus on narrative, it is not surprising that Vartio was then ready to embark on longer fiction. Within the space of five years (1957–1962) she published four novels: *This Then Is Spring; Any Man, Any Girl; All Women Dream;* and *Emotions.* Finnish critics generally agree that the first of this group is the best, surpassed in quality only by the posthumously published *The Parson's Widow.*

While Finnish critics regard *The Parson's Widow* as Vartio's finest literary achievement, many have also expressed surprise at its continued popularity. For all the sophistication of its narrative method, perhaps influenced to some degree by the French, the novel is set not in the contemporary world but in a rural Finnish village at an unspecified time in the past, probably the first half of the twentieth century. The characters Vartio portrays are trapped in a claustrophobic world far removed from the Finland of today. The villagers' mores, assumptions, ways of dealing with and even of addressing each other can seem as archaic to contemporary Finns as they do to a foreign reader, but if one looks beneath the surface details of these characters' lives, one can pick up the eternal themes of loneliness, jealousy, the desire for sexual fulfillment, for love, or simply for connection with others. Most powerfully, the ambivalent relationships between women, and between the women and the men who are present or absent in their lives, are so richly portrayed that their dynamic is as relevant today as it was in this remote Finnish village of an earlier time.

The Parson's Widow centers on the relationship between two women: Adele, the widow of a country parson, and Alma, her maid. Much of the book consists of conversations between the two women as they go over past events and argue about what happened, how it happened, and what it meant. In the course of these conversations, many dramatic events are touched on, sometimes in passing, sometimes in excruciatingly painful detail: a disastrous parsonage fire; sexual assaults; suicide attempts; drug and alcohol addiction; fights over inherited objects; threats to shoot family members; and moments when one character or another descends into madness. All this is potentially melodramatic material, yet Vartio's treatment of these events is far from sensational. The fact that most of the events come to the reader through the filters of the two women's accounts, which seldom completely agree, means that we are often not quite sure about what really did happen. Yet as the novel progresses, we come to see that the incidents themselves are less important than how Adele and Alma interpret them.

Here Vartio has put her finger on an old truth. Myths are created not only by communal, tribal, or national entities but also by and for individuals. Behind the constant arguments that fill the days and often the nights of the parson's widow and her servant, there is surely nostalgia and the wish to justify their earlier actions, but there is also a struggle for power. The competing stories are quite often a battle that asks the question: whose version of reality will win? Thus the tension lies not so much in the story itself but in what the particular story tells us about the status of Adele and Alma's relationship.

The Parson's Widow is not what is called, often disparagingly, a "problem novel." Vartio's characters are so rich in nuance, and there is so much intriguing ambiguity about what they are really thinking and feeling, as well as about the truth or untruth of the stories they tell and retell, that her characters emerge as multi-dimensional people, not as figures created simply to illustrate a problem or to espouse a political point of view. As we experience various aspects of Adele's and Alma's complex personalities, we gain more and more insight into the social, psychological, and even the spiritual situation of these women and the world they inhabit.

Vartio's narrative method does present challenges to the reader, but ultimately the task of dealing with them is rewarding. Despite their disagreements over details of past events, Adele and Alma do not provide each other with shocking or even surprising revelations in the stories they keep repeating. Most of the time, they simply focus on the accuracy of details as mundane as whether someone was wearing a plain or a flowered blouse. It might seem, then, that there is little or no suspense here, but as the two women go over these stories that are so familiar to them we become aware that our own perceptions are constantly changing.

In the early chapters, we see two women unpleasantly bickering over petty things like the way one should polish furniture or dust a stuffed bird, and they constantly blame each other for various transgressions. But as the novel progresses, we also learn about Adele's marriage to Birger, a parson who neglected his parishioners, had relationships with other women, and brutally shot birds after promising his pregnant wife that he would stop doing so. When the parsonage is destroyed by a terrible fire, a villager remarks that Birger was more concerned about saving his collection of birds than about rescuing his wife. We also find out that Adele had at one time contemplated suicide, and for that reason Alma had been brought in to live with her.

Even Adele's social status is ambiguous. As the wife of a country parson, she holds a much-respected position in the village, and her behavior and way of speaking toward her maid Alma follow the patterns of a socially superior employer toward a servant. Later, however, we discover that Birger's family had opposed their marriage because Adele had been employed as a postmistress, a position they considered lowly. When they met Adele for the first time, they refused to shake hands, and no one from the family attended their wedding.

Likewise, our first impression of Alma as a sullen, unsympathetic maid is mitigated, or at least altered, when we learn that she had been forced by members of her family to abandon plans to marry a man she loved. Later there is a devastating scene in which Alma and the widow's son Antti meet, apparently by chance when the widow is away, and they have a brutal, loveless, sexual encounter in a barn. Vartio skillfully renders the ambiguities of this episode which at first comes across as a rape, with Alma the victim, but which also portrays Alma as the initiator, awkwardly instructing Antti about the mechanics of sexual intercourse. Alma's threats to report the incident to his mother are met with laughter, and indeed when Adele returns home she not only understands the situation but implicitly encourages it.

Vartio's characters may indeed be locked in a claustrophobic world in which they obsess over past grievances, but while Adele and Alma already seem to know the basic content, and even the outcome, of the stories they tell, we readers are constantly learning more about these people and we can never remain comfortable in our assumptions.

Another reason for the continued popularity of *The Parson's Widow* no doubt lies in its use of humor. While a mere recital of the incidents in this novel might lead one to expect a grim work, heavy and brooding, Vartio's eye and ear register an antic absurdity even in the darkest moments. The depiction of the parsonage fire in Chapter Two reads more like farce than tragedy, as the men and women rush in and out of the building, ignoring the danger to their lives and crying out what they think must be saved: "'The birds, Adele,' the parson's voice shouted. 'The birds. Save the birds.' 'The linens,' shouted his wife." What makes the humor in *The Parson's Widow* so effective is that the humorous incidents are not inserted into the text as momentary relief but are integral to the darkest episodes.

With a poet's eye, Vartio establishes images of birds at the center of this novel, not as mere decoration but as images entwined with the actions and personalities of the characters. The parson had inherited a collection of stuffed birds from his Uncle Onni and then added to it by stuffing birds he himself had shot. As we see in descriptions of the parsonage fire, the parson rushed about trying to save the bird collection while others screamed questions about the church records, the baptismal font, a chalice, all of which he ignored. Even in his younger days he had shocked his congregation by preaching a sermon about his engagement to Adele, telling them that he had found a *rara avis* to share his life. This comparison takes a darker turn when he confronts Adele during an argument, asking whether he should now call her a *silly avis*. At one point he says that "God is in the small bird" and he calls her "godless."

After the parson's death, Adele inherits the birds and looks after them with obsessive detail, insisting that they be displayed as they are in nature. But like her husband, she often uses bird metaphors as weapons. When she and Alma are angry, they call each other "lapwing," "wagtail," "cuckoo," or some other kind of bird. At times these names go beyond metaphor, and the parson's widow actually sees Alma or someone else who has angered her taking the form of a bird. Yet through all this the birds retain a sacred quality for her. Referring to her collection, Adele tells Alma, "But all these are alive. Can't you see they've become immortal? The feathers are smooth, well-cared for, no moth holes, no stains. I will die, but the birds will live forever."

AUSTIN FLINT

The Parson's Widow

ONE

"Well, let's just not talk about it."

"That's not what I meant," said Alma, the maid.

"How could I have said something so silly?" the parson's widow said. "I'm not like that."

Alma was silent.

"That's just the way it is. If the sexton had only given the alarm right away, the parsonage wouldn't have burned down."

"But wasn't it the sexton who woke you up?"

"Yes, finally. But at first he didn't do a thing, not even when he saw the rectory was on fire," said the parson's widow.

"But it didn't burst out right away. The sexton thought the smoke was only a bit of fog," Alma said.

"Oh, was Alma herself there to see it?"

"You yourself said the sexton thought it was fog. How else would I know that?"

"Oh, my!"

"Those were your exact words, but it doesn't matter, far be it from me to insist."

"Let's not talk about it at all," the parson's widow said. "Let's just not say a thing."

But now that it had started they had to go on talking.

"People kept repeating the sexton's stories. That's what you heard too, Alma. I should know. The story was that he just happened to wake up a little before five, and what if he hadn't, well who would have been there to notice it? We all would have gone up in smoke with the parsonage if he hadn't woken up. He made sure to emphasize that. But why didn't he give the alarm right away? He could answer that one only by saying he had at first mistaken it for fog, since the parsonage had been built on such a swampy spot, too close to the shore. And how he supposedly hadn't been able to see it very well because the alder bushes had been allowed to grow so thick they even shaded the cabbage patch. That remark was aimed at us, you know. Five o'clock, a little before five, he kept repeating. I didn't hear that myself, I wouldn't have listened, but of course I've been told. Always this five o'clock, a little before five, as though he'd come to wake us just before the end of the world. I woke up a little before five, and what if I hadn't, what would have happened then? I woke up, went out, thought it was fog. That's what he kept saying. Thought the parson was burning trash. He'd seen Birger raking leaves the night before, Saturday night, so naturally he'd thought the smoke came from the piles of leaves. That was another bit of blame. Should have collected the leaves and let them rot into compost, and besides, Birger had no business raking leaves anyway. The leaves should have been left to rot, that's what the sexton really meant. But the parson was burning them at five o'clock on a Sunday morning. He didn't exactly say Birger did that, but what he meant was that he might as well have. I told Birger many times that he must be the only parson on this earth who'd put up with that kind of behavior from his sexton, but he only shrugged it off. Almost as if he thought the sexton had the right to behave and talk any way he wanted. What did that matter to me, it wasn't how I'd handle it."

"But it was the sexton who woke you up. And it's an awfully thick grove of alders."

"So Alma has been there. I haven't. Not since that day. I've walked past the place, but if they'd built the new parsonage in the same spot I wouldn't have moved in. I picked out the new site myself, but I didn't dictate anything, Birger was always the one who did that. But of course Alma's got the whole story from the sexton. No point in my saying anything."

"I don't know anything new. It's just that he was always talking about it."

"And Alma would listen."

"The way one listens to people. What's wrong with that?"

"Did he say anything special?"

"No. Just what we've been talking about right now, just like you, Missus. But he did say that if he had been any slower everything sure would have ended badly."

"I have no desire to take credit away from the sexton."

"He was an old man, too, by that time."

"Sure, sure, an old man whose heart was about to break as he raced to wake up everyone in the parsonage."

"The Missus shouldn't be so nasty."

"I'm not being nasty, but if people had talked about you as much as they've talked about me, then maybe Alma would know how to listen to gossip. I've had to learn that, all right."

"Well, he showed me right in that yard how he'd run straight to the parsonage. I think he did what anybody would have done, there in the middle of the night. I can't believe anyone else would have taken off as quickly as he did."

"Alma, I know how it was and I know what kind of talk there's been about it."

"The one thing he always blamed himself for was that as he was running through the cemetery he forgot about the little gate that would have led him right to the parsonage, and he wouldn't have had to climb, him being such an old man and all. That's what he said, nothing else. That if he'd somehow managed to move a little faster, the parsonage wouldn't have burned up."

"I don't think he could have stopped it."

"Well, who knows whether he could have, but as it was, he tried to get there by the straightest route."

"If, if. I was there."

"Or maybe if he'd managed to get down to the main road, gone along that, and then turned onto the road to the parsonage, that too would have been faster."

"Wouldn't have made any difference at all. We might have had time to save a few more birds if he'd done something as soon as he saw the flames and not just stood in his yard marveling at his notion that the parson was out burning dry leaves at five o'clock in the morning. They say he was hollering all the time, 'The parsonage is burning, the parsonage is burning,' but I wouldn't know. Nobody heard it. I was asleep. And what's the difference anyway, it wasn't his fire. The most important thing was for him to start making some noise. And Alma, you say he was blaming himself. That man has never blamed himself for anything. He might have criticized his choice of alternatives, like what road he should have taken when he ran to tell us the parsonage was on fire. But you know, he first thought the smoke was nothing but fog."

"That's what you said yourself."

"Alma, you wouldn't know. In the end, everyone blamed Birger. But let's not talk about it. Let it drop. You have your own views, and you can keep your own views, but it certainly is amusing how they agree with the sexton's stories in every respect."

"But the man's dead."

"I'm not speaking ill of him."

"And he never said a bad word about you."

"No, not a single bad word, yet there certainly was talk. And thinking. Just as one can hear in your talk, if one is used to listening not only to how people talk but to what they say. And I've sure learned to do that. And the sexton wasn't alone, many others thought the same way. Oh, yes, in your voice I hear the sexton's voice and his wife's voice too. I'm not speaking ill of the dead when I say that, Alma."

"I didn't say you were."

The parson's widow fell silent.

"It was a great mishap," Alma said.

"You call it a great mishap," the parson's widow said slowly, "but you don't understand that it was a terrible misfortune."

"Yes, that's right, a terrible misfortune."

"It was the great misfortune in Birger's life, and it wasn't only the fire. It was what people made of it."

Alma understood. She was silent. Then she went at it from a different angle.

"It's only that it was the middle of the night. Just think of it. Suppose this house caught fire some night. Not the easiest thing in the world to deal with. As the sexton said, he got scared by the sound of his own voice when he was already clear in the cemetery, screaming, 'Fire! Fire!' Heaven only knows, right in the middle of the night. High time to wake you up when flames were licking out of the windows. What could a person do?"

The parson's widow smiled.

"If it had only been a bit calmer, but the sexton made such a circus of it nobody could figure out what was going on. If he had calmly woken us up right at the start, but no, he was tearing around the house—and that sure took some time—he didn't have the sense to wake the maid or knock on our window. If Alma has ever been to see the charred ruins, she'll know it was a long house, even bigger than this one."

"Must have been a really big house."

"But he ran all around it. Heaven knows how many times. He kept pounding on the main door, and on the office door as well. What was the sense in that? 'A fire isn't the kind of thing you handle in an office' was what Birger said to me when he heard about that sexton's idiotic behavior. He certainly could have said that if he'd had a mind to. But he preferred not to. At first I didn't understand that the fire had destroyed a lot more than the parsonage. It was the great tragedy of Birger's life."

Alma knew what was coming next.

"Of course Alma's been there and seen the ruins. I haven't even been able to look that way after the fire."

"Went there once to pick raspberries."

"Well, what did you see?"

"Nothing much. They've cleared most of the stones out of there."

"Yes, they've taken the stones, the foundation's gone. They've used it to lengthen the cemetery wall."

"What you've still got there are those big trees, maples and the rest of them."

"It's all been destroyed."

"The new parsonage isn't as close to the lake."

"No, but before they could manage to get it built, that's what drained Birger's strength, and other things as well."

"How long did you get to live there, a couple of years?"

"Antti barely remembers we ever lived in the new parsonage, he can't recall anything in particular. Or his own father, for that matter. I've often wondered whether what people say is true—that some events can affect a child even before birth. Holger always laughs when I mention things like that. He doesn't want to talk about the fire. They don't want to see what it all meant. But I have time to think about things."

Alma poured the parson's widow a second cup of coffee.

"Birger died two years after the fire, when Antti was just a little over a year old. It wasn't as easy to build the new parsonage as they'd first told me it would be. Everybody said, come stay with us until it's finished, you'll get to move in soon enough. I didn't get to live there a full year with Birger, because that's when he died.

Then I lived there alone during my year of grace, and Holger and Teodolinda, who had just been married, began to prepare me for the fact that I'd have to move out of the parsonage when the grace period was over, as if I wouldn't have understood it on my own. Or maybe it looked as if I was bent on living there with Antti for the rest of my days, even though the fight for Birger's position was already going on. It was considered such a good job that there were plenty of applicants."

"It was lucky you had this house, so you had a place to go." That's what the parson's widow would always say at this point, but this time Alma got it in ahead of her.

"If it really was lucky," the parson's widow said. "They call it the sheriff's house, even though he's been dead for a long time. Birger bought it for his retirement years ago at a sheriff's auction. Then there was still some land that went with it, but that's been sold off, so there's no point in their being jealous of me for that. All I do is live here. Other people have their own lives. This is where I've stayed, and besides, where would I go? Of course, I'm an outsider in this family. But sometimes I have the feeling that the people I'm closer to are Birger's father, this sheriff, whom I know you've heard all kinds of things about, and Uncle Onni—I too call him Uncle Onni even though he's not really my uncle. I've never set eyes on him. He was the brother of Birger's father and an uncle to Birger, Elsa, and Teodolinda. He was older than Birger's father and lived in St. Petersburg most of his life.

"But here's where he died, and he was the one with the birds. Birger inherited his interest in ornithology from him. It was Uncle Onni who first got him interested, when Birger was still only a schoolboy. Onni must have been very old by then. He'd been a curator of birds at a museum in St. Petersburg. Naturally, Birger gathered birds for his own collection, and of course he wasn't so much a collector but a person who liked to study bird life. I've shown you, haven't I, how his name is still in books? He was a real scientist. But Birger also saved Uncle Onni's birds even though they were losing their feathers. Of all the birds I've got left, the only one from Uncle Onni's time is that owl. He had shot it, and of course he stuffed it too. It's a Lapland owl, so it's quite special that it came this far south. Before he died, Birger managed to get started on a new bird collection, not as good as the old one, but still, I remember how he seemed to calm down when he'd succeeded in getting some birds into display cabinets and behind glass doors again. Those cabinets were made for him right away."

It sounded like a rebuke, and the parson's widow didn't want to utter a single word of reproach.

And now, as it always happened when the parson's widow, whose Christian name was Adele, spoke so intimately with Alma, referring to the parson as Birger, to one of his sisters as Teodolinda instead of "the sister of the dear late parson" or "the pharmacist's wife," and to Elsa instead of "the dear late parson's other sister" or "the county doctor's wife," and all together called them "the late parson's sisters." You could hear in the widow's voice that although she had brought them close, right here in the kitchen, they were still unreachable, just as she herself was, even though she was sitting at the kitchen table drinking coffee. But little by little, though she didn't change her manner of speaking, it began to go more easily, and the distance between "the late vicar" and "Birger" slowly wore down.

"But let's not talk about these things. They're long and involved, much too involved," the parson's widow said. "Let's not talk, let's not talk," she repeated, and raised her hand as if to fend off further words, as if to repel someone who was demanding that they talk about them.

"The parson's widow is getting all excited for no reason, and won't be able to sleep," Alma said. "Let's not talk."

Two

The parson woke up, got out of bed, went over to the window, tugged the curtain to one side, saw a fist pounding on the windowpane, heard the pounding, saw the fist disappear; the pounding stopped and now someone was standing under the window, a couple of steps away from the wall. The parson looked down, saw the man standing there at the spot where the foundation was highest.

"Fire!" shouted the sexton.

Now the parson's wife appeared in the window, next to the parson; she too looked out the window and saw the man below. The parson started to open the window, pulling the curtain aside; in his long nightshirt, he looked out the window, leaning on the sill. He asked what was wrong.

"The parsonage is on fire! Get out!"

"What?" He didn't take in that the parsonage was burning, his own parsonage was on fire.

"The parsonage! The parsonage!"

"The parsonage? Is it the parsonage?" he repeated and disappeared from the window, leaving the sexton to wonder whether the parson had understood or simply gone back to bed. And so he started running again, shouting, "Fire, Fire!" in a voice out of breath, frantic, full of tears, fury, and reproach. He tore around the house, saw flames in the upstairs windows above the kitchen, fire that at first kept raising its head lazily, like a bored snake, drew back, and then, growing more and more angry, lashed ever higher, smoke billowing out of windows that had exploded from the heat. The sexton quickly walked around the corner and up the steps toward the main door. At that moment he saw the door swing open, and the parson and his wife stood on the chancery steps in their night clothes.

"There!" shouted the sexton. "There! Put out the fire! Put it out, ring the bells! Put out the fire!" And he raced off toward the church, toward where he could see the steeple, to wake up the verger and start the bells ringing. But the parson and his wife were running after him. "Birger! Birger!" she shouted at her husband, and the sexton turned and heard the parson shout, "I know, I know." And now the parson was heading back toward the chancery door. "He went in to telephone," she said, and the sexton stopped in his tracks. But right then the parson was back on the steps and came running toward where his wife and the sexton were standing. "The operator doesn't answer," he said. "No answer."

Then the sexton started running with the parson's shouts in his ears: "Got to ring the bells. No answer. Ring the bells."

The parson's wife, barefooted and in her nightgown, was on her way to the well; a pail had been left out on the kitchen steps, and with pail in hand she went to the well and now the bells were tolling over the misty village. She hoisted water from the well into the pail, lugged it to one side of the burning house, stopped. By now the housekeeper and a young servant girl had woken up. Tilda, the housekeeper, who slept in the room behind the kitchen, and the maid, who slept in the kitchen, had tried to get out through the kitchen but the entryway was on fire and they'd run through the pantry to the dining room, then to the chancery, and out the chancery door to safety.

"Tilda!" the parson's wife shouted. "Water, Tilda, water!" But old Tilda only kept bellowing, "My God, everything's burning! My clothes! My clothes!" And she tried to plunge through the entryway to the kitchen. "Water! Don't you understand?" called the verger and the three people who were carrying water. "Get your things!" the verger shouted, and he and his wife headed up the chancery steps.

"The birds, Adele!" the parson called. He ran to the chancery steps, shoving aside the verger, who stumbled out of the way, and the verger's wife stopped. Adele had heard her husband's shout and managed to get past the verger and his wife. "Adele!" the parson's voice called from the parlor. "Adele, the birds!" The parson had finally reached his study and was now coming out with his arms full of birds that he shoved into his wife's arms and then turned back to the study. "The church records!" the verger shouted. "For God's sake, sir, save the church records!" cried the sexton, who had returned by now. "You're out of your mind!" The sexton's words echoed in the empty chancery. "Where are the church records? Where are the keys?" But the parson was coming back in, rushing past him into the room that was already beginning to fill with smoke, stumbling on the hem of his nightshirt, over which he had tossed a black cloak; he was carrying his collection out of the chancery, birds and books, one of which fell as he was racing out, even though he'd tried to squeeze it tight between his elbow and ribs. "Adele, Adele!"

"Church records, keys, keys!" the parson's wife was calling. "Birger, keys. Where are the keys?" But the parson didn't hear, on his way out with his arms full of birds. "The Communion bread!" shouted the verger. "The chalice!" "Keys. Where are the keys, Birger?" And then the parson's wife remembered where the keys were. She ran to the bedroom and with trembling fingers reached into the pockets of her husband's pants and, keys grasped in her hand, rushed to the chancery. She passed them to the sexton, who started opening cabinets, shouting that the church records should be the first things carried to safety from the fire, far away from the yard—everything was burning. And the parson's wife took the bag with the chalice and Communion things and carried it out to the yard, set it down on a rock, came back in. In the doorway the verger's wife was panting, lugging a heavy armchair, and the verger himself was pulling at a plush sofa. "Take it farther away!" the verger shouted, and his wife, tottering under the weight of the chair, carried it off to the lilac bushes, returned to the parlor and began pulling down drapes and paintings until her arms were full. She saw the parson's wife standing motionless in the parlor, as still as if she didn't realize it was a fire, the room gray with smoke.

"The birds, Adele," the parson called. "The birds. Save the birds."

"The linens!" shouted his wife.

By now more people had come into the yard. Silently they rushed at each other in the doorways and on the steps, carrying away whatever they could get their hands on, senseless things. The gravedigger's wife was carrying off sofa cushions, one at a time. Her husband was yanking a rug from the floor, and the verger was dumping things out into the yard through the parlor window. The sexton was looking for the parson, running after him with empty hands, shouting over and over, "The church records! Official papers! Are they anyplace else in the house?" But the parson didn't understand, he was so busy carrying out his birds while the verger was in the chancery tugging at two locked doors for which he couldn't find keys. He pulled at some desk drawers and managed to get one open, yanking it so hard it clattered onto the floor; he looked down at his feet. The floor was littered with tiny fragments of eggshells. And he went away from the desk.

"The bed linens, the bed linens!" the parson's wife called—the verger's wife, the gravedigger's wife, and two other women plunged into the bedroom. They came down the chancery stairs with mattresses and pillows and blankets in their arms, and the parson's wife shouted, "The china service!" and ran to the china cabinet in the dining room. With dishes dropping from her hands and tinkling along the floor, she remembered the knives and forks, ran out to the yard with a soup tureen and a plate in one hand and a silver cake server in the other.

"Adele, the birds!" the parson called. At once his wife set down everything in her hands and headed back to the parlor, climbing onto a chair, she reached for the stuffed birds on top of the parlor cabinet. Smoke was pouring into the room, blackening the ceiling, and from under the kitchen window the verger's voice was crying, "Water! Water!"

"Adele, the birds! There are still some birds in the cabinet!"

"I understand, I understand," she called back. She went into the chancery, took the key from the top of the cabinet and opened the glass doors, told the verger to carry some birds while she herself grabbed an armful and headed out. "China!" a voice called from outside. "China!" shouted the parson's wife, setting down her armful and raced back toward the dining room with several women at her heels, emptied dishes from the lower shelves of the china cabinet onto the floor, and when the women had cleared the floor, went on working, scooping more things from cabinets and drawers: china, knives, forks, soup ladles. "China! Candlesticks!" the parson's wife shouted to the women picking objects from the floor. There was no other place to put anything. The table was gone; the verger and his wife had managed to drag it to the door of the chancery, where it was now stuck, stopping traffic.

"The other way!" the sexton shouted. "Everyone will be trapped in there with all that stuff blocking the way." And he gave the verger hell and started ordering him around, showing him how to tilt the table so it would fit through the doorway. He tugged it back in himself, grabbed one end, had the verger take the other, and with the verger's wife following them, all the time giving advice so that they wouldn't nick other things and the doorjambs, the men carried it through the parlor and out the front door.

"Farther, farther! Everything's burning!" the people outside were bellowing. The parson's wife kept on handing the women silver and china as fast as they came to get it; they carried it out and set it on the table. She herself had just filled her arms with silver when she remembered a silver candlestick that was standing on the window-sill. She put down her armload and went back to get it.

"Adele!" she heard the parson calling in a tone filled with command, reproach, and lament. For an instant she froze, holding a tall, five-forked candelabrum decorated with crystal pendants. She looked at her husband, who was passing through the room towards the door, his arms full with boxes of birds' eggs. She put down the candelabrum, looked about her, went into a small adjoining room and took a boreal owl from an open shelf and started carrying it outside, walking calmly past the people rushing this way and that, who said she couldn't stay here any longer and had to get out. She went down the stairs, holding the owl in front of her, walked towards the rock where others too had taken the birds. "The cellar! To the cellar!" the parson called; he was running past his wife and waving towards the cellar and its open door, but his wife set the owl down on the top of the rock. She looked at her husband, took in his voice, stopped, snorted.

The cry "Water, water!" was heard and the verger's son, panting, came running from the well carrying a small milking pail full of water which was splashing onto the road. "It's burning, it's burning!" the verger bellowed. "No people are coming, oh my God, no people coming!" Then other voices chimed in: "No, no people are coming, no people coming, it's burning, it's burning!" The parson's wife heard the voices coming from outside. She had followed her husband to the parlor, where the man was pacing back and forth. "My clothes!" shouted the housekeeper as she came into the parlor. She went to the dining room, made a few lunges towards the pantry door and finally managed to reach it and even open the door, but flames lashed out at her. With the door open, the fire gained strength; the pressure had already shattered the kitchen windows and now the flames came whipping into the dining room through the open doorway. "My clothes!" the housekeeper screamed again, now plunging towards the door, now pulling back, weeping and wringing her hands. Couldn't get to the kitchen. When the parson saw that, he went from the parlor to the dining room and tried to go save the clothes.

He had to withdraw, though, shielding his face with his arms, and the door stayed open. But the parson wouldn't give up; he rushed the door, and his wife, grasping the hem of his jacket, yelled, "Birger, no, no! You'll get burned! Don't go in!"

"You can't go in there! Don't act crazy!" the verger shouted, and together they pulled the parson back; the sexton, grasping him by an arm, led him out of the house through the parlor, away from the dining room. Standing on the steps, the parson seemed in his right mind again; he covered his face with his sooty hands, the hem of his nightshirt filthy. He hesitated on the steps for a moment, turned around, went over to stand beside the rock, and watched the women, like silent ants, moving dishes and furniture now that nothing more could be done, with the fire now licking into the dining room where the windows had broken. He saw the parsonage covered with smoke, burning before his eyes. And his wife came to stand beside him.

The last thing carried out of the burning house was the piano. The house kept burning.

The kitchen wall must have smoldered for a long time before you could see anything from outside, the firemen said. The well had gone dry, something wrong with the pump, they said. No point in doing anything but try to keep the fire from spreading to the outbuildings. The parson didn't answer; he saw the house burning, and now that nothing more could be done, he just looked on. As the sun rose, the roof had come crashing down, the log walls had burned up but had remained standing long before they crumbled, and while the firemen and the other people fighting the fire had been protecting the outbuildings, no one noticed that fire had spread to the tall spruce trees, those three spruces growing at the far end of the house, which were soon blazing like three torches. No one noticed them until the parson's wife cried, "The spruces! Look at the spruces!" But despite her command the fire brigade didn't move even the one small functioning pump over to the spruces.

"Wet alders won't burn, and the maples are so far away they won't burn either!" the sexton shouted. "Sparks are flying onto the roofs of the buildings! Water, water!"

The parson's wife sat on the rock, not crying, just staring straight ahead. One of the women had come by, draped a coat over her shoulders, then brought her shoes and told her to put them on. She put them on and sat down again, her black eyes riveted directly forward, and barely hearing what her husband was saying, she shifted a little to one side and answered, "No, thank you, I'm sitting here." The parson had just repeated the sexton's suggestion that she sit down in the armchair that had been brought out into the yard and was right nearby. The sexton's wife had first sat down in it, close to the parson's wife, intending to say something, but one glare from the sexton had lifted her out of the chair, and the sexton had offered it to the parson's wife because the rock was so cold.

The parson had stayed right next to her and there they had been, a strange sight, people said: both of them staring straight ahead at the burning building whose warmth cast a glow on their faces even this far out, looking without seeing each other, without so much as a glance to one side even when one of them said something to the other. The parson stood up. With the clerical cloak on his shoulders, that rescued cloak over his nightshirt, the parson started walking about the yard, looking for birds and boxes, arranging the birds and carrying them over toward where his wife was sitting. On the rock stood a boreal owl, and the parson was bringing others. His wife watched how he took the owl in his hand and studied its feathers, stroked its bill and sat down next to her with the owl in his hands.

"Don't cry, Adele. What are you thinking? Say something." The dog was whimpering, the parsonage dog. The sound brought the parson's wife out of her stupor and she began to cry.

"Don't cry. These are earthly things. We'll make a new home," the parson said. But she remembered: the photographs had burned; she should have remembered they were in a box in the cabinet, the photo albums. "Don't cry," the parson said. The verger's wife was picking up things, gathering them together and taking them to the sauna cabin. It was going to rain. "It's going to rain, but it did rain just a minute ago," the verger's wife was saying, "and that's all that's been saved."

A soup tureen sat next to the rock, along with useless random dishes, five plates, a long platter, a five-forked silver candelabrum, a dog skin, five sofa cushions, a rocking chair, and a rug. "There are a lot of things on the other side of the building," someone said, "all the stuff that was saved through the window, and here's the table and the piano." And the piano. But still it seemed that very little had been got out, and everybody kept going over the list of things that had been saved, and they always mentioned the piano last.

The verger had sat in the armchair, gloomily watching the smoldering ruins. The yard was now full of people, the whole village up and about.

"If this had happened in the daytime," someone began. "Didn't you hear anything?" asked the verger. "No, we were sound asleep." The verger was silent. "Where did it start?" someone asked.

"It wasn't my fault, the parson himself told me to," the house-keeper said. "The fireproof wall," said the verger, "it's been in rotten shape for a long time. It started in a crack in the attic." "Too early to tell the exact cause of the fire," the sexton said. "For sure it started in the kitchen end of the house. As you know, I was the one who gave the alarm. From my yard I could see the smoke rising from here." They talked. But they all knew what the parson had said, knew there'd been some explosive substance in the kitchen and that the parson had dabbled with some things that could explode if they got hot enough, and maybe he'd forgotten and left some bottle or other on the edge of the stove. He himself had told the verger about it, and the verger, knowing what he would do, wasn't even pretending to hear the explanation the parson's wife gave.

"But it isn't true," she said now, turning to her housekeeper. "It isn't true, Tilda."

The verger didn't want to hear anything more; he was already on his way, away from the women. He already knew.

Along the road, more people were streaming by, all coming to see the smoking parsonage. On the road behind the cemetery, some people were milling about while others turned off by the lane of birches and came up to say a few words to the victims of the disaster: the parson's wife, who kept smiling out of a strangely pale face, and the parson, who just sat on a wet rock in his wrinkled parson's cloak. Out of the corners of their eyes they saw the birds arranged on the rock and all around the rock. "Adele," the parson said for the second time, as if scolding her for having left them alone. But she didn't answer. And the parson began to speak in a high-pitched voice, as if he were preaching, saying that at least he thanked God that the birds, or at any rate some of the birds, had been saved. And though a great many irreplaceable ones had been destroyed, it would be possible, through exchanges and other acquisitions, to bring the collection back to its former state. Then, all of a sudden, he fell silent.

"At least it wasn't my fault," said Tilda, the housekeeper, who had come there.

"No, no," the parson said.

"I shut the dampers and saw to it that no fire was left in the stove, just as the parson told me to."

"Nobody's blaming Tilda," the parson said in that high-pitched voice. "Adele, what's wrong?"

But she didn't answer.

"Adele," he said, "get up or you'll catch cold. Get up."

The parson's wife didn't answer.

"Adele," the parson said. But his wife had sunk into deep silence and did not respond to the offer of the verger's wife, who suggested they come to the verger's house. "There's the side building," she finally said, pointing to the sauna cabin, as the verger's wife was explaining how they could first come to the verger's, listed where each one would sleep, it would be all right, there were plenty of bed linens, it would be possible to stay at their house until things got straightened out. "There's the side building," the parson's wife repeated. There was her home. "But Adele, one can't sleep in the sauna," said the parson. "Dear Adele, of course our home is open to you," said Elsa. "Of course you will come to our house." "No," the parson's wife said, "there's the sauna." "But it's not proper for you to stay in the sauna," said Elsa. The parson's wife didn't respond to her sister-in-law, who said to her husband, "Give Adele something." "I don't need anything, thank you very much, Elsa," the parson's wife said very calmly. "Holger, do give her something," Elsa said.

"So what was it," said Holger, "that caused this?"

"Birger, tell him," said the parson's wife.

"I know," the parson said.

"I don't know, but in the evening, in the kitchen, I don't want to put the blame on anyone," said Adele, the parson's wife.

"You know very well it wasn't Tilda's fault," the parson said. "It wasn't." And he explained how he had been handling some explosives, gunpowder, he'd been filling shotgun cartridges and they'd been left by mistake on the hearth, right next to the stove. "I see," said Herman, the county doctor. Holger didn't say anything, just gave Herman a glance and tried to signal him not to talk when everyone could hear him. The verger seemed to know already, a thin, bent man, Birger's enemy. Now he would get grist for his mill. "Be quiet," said Holger, the pharmacist. "Keep it to yourself, you're insane. Why do you insist on talking about it? And you aren't even telling the truth. No. No matter what you may do otherwise, you, an old hunter, would never make the mistake of leaving gunpowder on the hearth. You can get the women to shut up in some other way than by taking the blame on yourself."

"Well, don't you see?" said Elsa.

Now the verger had come forward, stopped a little bit away from them so he could ask where everything should be taken.

"So what have I done?" the parson asked.

"You're an honest man, Birger," the pharmacist said, "but there are times when honesty is just stupid."

"But that's how it is."

The birds were arranged in a single line, their bills pointing towards the burning ruins. The relatives looked at the odd group that seemed to be looking at its masters in silent contemplation. The verger glanced at the birds, then quickly averted his eyes and headed off. One after another, people began to leave, each one offering the victims of the fire a place to stay, and the parson's wife thanking each in turn. They left silently, looking back from the lane lined with birches, and when they had all gone the pharmacist took a bottle out of his pocket. "You need this now, Birger." But the parson shook his head. "Adele, you'll catch cold," the pharmacist said. Nobody listened to him, and he put the bottle back into his pocket, walked around the yard, looked at the burning and smoldering logs, went under the maples and took the bottle out of his pocket again. He stuffed it back in his pocket, stood right where the chancery window had been, looked up as if he could see the window that was now gone, pulled the bottle out of his pocket, took a swig from it, and went back to the others.

"Where are the church records?" asked the parson's wife. The verger had taken them to the sauna cabin. They had been saved. "Did the piano burn?" Elsa asked. "So it really did burn," she answered herself. "Did you save Father's picture?" Teodolinda's voice asked. "I don't know," the parson's voice answered. Teodolinda was walking around the yard. Things were standing propped against the fence. She saw her father's portrait propped upright next to the gate. They all walked around the yard, examining the things that had been saved; every so often, they glanced over at the rock where the birds stood as if on guard in a tightly packed line as though they were seeking security from each other, their bills jutting forward. Now they saw the parson go over to the birds, lifting them one by one, and the county doctor turned to his wife with a grimace. "I guess he would have let Adele burn up before those. That's the way it is," he said, furious at the man who was so carefully inspecting the birds, smoothing their feathers.

"Oh, dear God," he said. "Be quiet," his wife said. "Why do you talk like that? Adele will hear you. You'll catch cold, Adele. What in the name of heaven have you got there?"

"This?" said the parson's wife. "A soup tureen." And she stared at the object she was holding, set it down, studied it. "Don't be angry," she said after a moment. "What are you talking about?" But the parson's wife was deep in thought and got up to sift through the pile of things. "What are you looking for?" her sister-in-law asked. "I tried to save," the parson's wife said. "Of course, of course." "The shawl got burned," the parson's wife said. "What are you talking about?" "The shawl that belongs to you. I was trying to save the things that belong to all of you. That's what I tried to save. I thought whatever wasn't mine had to be rescued, but I didn't understand when the smoke came."

"Adele, you'll catch cold. Get up from there."

The parson's wife looked at them. They were all there, each one telling her something.

"Where's Birger?"

They didn't answer.

"Where's Birger?" The parson's wife got up from her rock.

"Calm down, he's all right."

"The man's out of his mind," she heard Herman say.

"We can't do a thing." That was Teodolinda's voice.

"Everything burned, didn't it?" asked Elsa's voice.

"Where are the doves?" asked a voice. Her husband, his face coated with soot, in his nightshirt, in his parson's cloak, was standing in front of her.

But she didn't answer.

"Come to our house," said Elsa. "I just have to make some arrangements first."

"Get up, Adele. You can't go on sitting there."

She felt them take hold of her on both sides and start to lead her away.

"Where's Birger?"

"I know," the parson's wife said after a while.

"You must think of yourself," said Holger. "You'll catch cold."

"Where are you taking me?"

"You need a roof over your head. Come, now."

But the parson's wife had stopped in her tracks, looking around as if she didn't understand who they were and what they wanted from her.

"Go on," said the verger. "The church records are safe in the sauna cabin. The sauna was saved."

"Where's Birger?"

They didn't answer. The parson's wife tore herself out of the arms of the people leading her away, and started running towards the smoldering ruins. They all thought she meant to plunge in to save something more, and they shouted after her, "Everything's burned up! You can't go in there!" But the parson's wife ran on and the relatives raced after her, catching up with her at the cellar door.

"You crazy fool!" said the county doctor. "Can't you think of your wife, in the shape she's in!" But the parson—"like Lazarus in his grave," the pharmacist said later—was examining the birds that had been taken to the cellar. He had counted them.

"Birger," said the parson's wife.

"Twenty-five," the parson said. "The doves are missing." And he burst into tears.

"Are you angry with me, Birger? I tried, I couldn't manage, should I have, this is what I've got in my hand, I didn't understand you wanted the doves, this is what I saved, I thought all of you had been baptized with water from it. The baptismal font, that's what I'll rescue, right next to the doves, this is what I saved, not the doves," the parson's wife said, and at that moment the font fell from her hands and broke into smithereens on the cellar steps. "The baptismal font, the parson's baptismal font. That was too bad," said the verger's wife, who was observing the scene from one side, her face and hands covered with soot. She saw the pharmacist take a bottle from his pocket. He offered it around and no one accepted so he took some himself, stuck the cork back into the bottle and said, "We have to go, it's going to rain. Try to understand, Adele, you must come. And you, Birger, leave them there."

"Who's going to watch over them?"

And then the doctor cursed, his face turned black with fury, as the verger's wife later told her husband, turned black when he said, "You're out of your mind. Leave them there and come, or stay there." He took the parson's wife by the arm and forced her up. But then something happened that people couldn't ever figure out, couldn't determine whether it was the truth or a lie, created out of the shocked mind of the parson's wife. She shouted, her face all twisted: "I, I was the one who broke it. I saved it but it broke. I broke it!" she cried, "I broke it on purpose. I let it fall from my hands, all of you were baptized in it; you, Birger; you, Elsa; you, Teodolinda. I broke it, it didn't just fall. It was no accident! I broke it, I broke it! Do you hear me!" But no one answered, no one said anything to her. They left, leading the parson's wife off between them, and as they drew further away and went out past the gate, the verger's wife turned and followed them with her eyes.

"Where are you going?" asked the people who were still on the road, and drew aside as the little group went past them.

THREE

"It's 'Jacob's Dream,' Alma."

How could she put it so that Alma's feelings wouldn't be hurt? Alma had ruined the surface of the painting. The parson's widow stood nervously in front of the window and tried to say what she'd had on her mind for several days but hadn't quite dared come out with. Whenever Alma left the house, the parson's widow would wander through the rooms and check on things. The painting wasn't the only object in danger; there were also the birds. Their feathers were all ruffled because Alma kept wiping them with a wet rag. How could she manage to put it?

"Alma."

Alma turned to look at her.

"It's 'Jacob's Dream.'"

"What?"

"That painting."

And she saw how Alma glanced at the painting and again started to wipe it with the rag.

"It's 'Jacob's Dream,' Alma."

Alma kept on rubbing.

"My husband painted it."

Alma didn't understand. She just didn't understand that you shouldn't rub a painting with a wet rag.

"Did you have paintings at home, Alma?"

"My brother bought one once and took it home."

"What kind of painting was it?"

"It was an eagle tearing a big book away from a woman."

"It was 'The Maid of Finland.'" So Alma had that sort of painting in her house. "How did your brother happen to think of buying a painting like that? Do you know what it stands for?"

The parson's widow noticed that Alma had just dipped her rag in water and was again attacking "Jacob's Dream."

"Alma, do you know why Jacob is lying on the ground?"

"No, I don't."

"Haven't you read the Bible? Haven't they taught you about it?"

The parson's widow went to get the Bible and then she read out loud to Alma about Jacob.

"But my husband said Jacob was suffering from sciatica, and that could well have been so."

"Is that why he painted this picture?"

"No, no. The parson was an artist. He painted a lot of pictures but then he destroyed them. I asked him to save this one for me. That's how I got it."

"Who is it, then?"

"This man? It's Jacob."

"How did the parson know what Jacob looked like?"

"He imagined it—maybe he painted a self-portrait. Do you understand, Alma? Jacob looks a bit like my husband. When I look at that picture I sometimes get the feeling he painted himself. He once said to me, 'Jacob had a dream. It's always fascinated me that he was so human. Jacob was cunning, sly.' 'Why do you say that?' I asked. It hurt me to hear him talk about Jacob that way. 'You don't understand,' he said. 'The people in the Bible were human beings. The more I study the Bible, the more I believe and understand it. Jacob had committed a crime. He had a great dream and in order to make it come true he used all the tricks he could. He wanted to be somebody and he cheated his relatives.' 'You see, Adele,' he said to me, 'sometimes I've had a dream and I understand Jacob completely. He's a child of God in all his weakness.' Alma, do you understand that this painting is dear to me?"

Alma didn't answer.

"How did you go about dusting at home, Alma?"

"I didn't do any dusting. We had only that one painting."

"Well, I mean . . . maybe you've never dusted an oil painting before. See, this is an oil painting and you shouldn't wash it."

But Alma didn't understand.

"How old were you, Alma, when that painting came into the house?"

"The parson's widow knows how old I am."

"Well, soon you'll be thirty. How long is it that you've been in my house?"

Alma turned, giving her a hostile look.

"I mean, I mean I'm only asking."

"Don't you want to keep me on any longer?"

Alma always misunderstood her. How could she say it? She made another try.

"That's 'Jacob's Dream,' Alma."

Alma gave the painting an admiring glance and then went back to wiping it.

"Well, Alma, what I mean to say is that you don't know how to handle paintings . . . or birds. I can understand that you don't know how to handle birds but I would have thought you'd know you mustn't wash paintings."

"But you yourself told me to do it."

"I said you should wipe them with a cloth, a dry cloth, but you've been wiping the birds with a wet rag."

Alma fell silent.

"Just look at the feathers of this owl! They're ruined! It's my dearest bird."

The parson's widow waited for Alma to say something.

"I've tried talking to you about it, Alma. But you haven't understood. Now it's too late. Would you take a look at these feathers?"

The parson's widow set the owl on the table in front of Alma and began smoothing the trussed-up ankle feathers. Alma looked, then turned her head aside and obviously did not understand. How could one put it, how could one explain to her that you mustn't wipe birds with a wet rag?

"Do you remember last Saturday? The day I was so nervous."

Alma said she remembered. "That was for the same reason— remember, Alma—when I was walking behind you and the whole time I tried to tell you but you didn't believe me."

"What was it you said?"

The parson's widow didn't answer. Then she asked, "How did you handle the bird you had at home?"

Alma hadn't handled it at all.

"But it was in your house when you were still at home, Alma. For many years. Wasn't it ever cleaned?"

"I don't know."

The parson's widow now wanted to know where they had kept the swan.

"In a corner of the parlor, under the big feathery asparagus plant."

"The big feathery asparagus plant," the parson's widow said with a sigh. "Whose was it? Was it Alma's?"

One of the neighbors had brought it, Alma couldn't remember exactly. But it was big; it grew in a barrel and needed lots of water. Once it had been about to die, in summer when it was hot and nobody had remembered to water it. People seldom went into the parlor, you slept out in the shed and only the guests were taken to the parlor and nobody went in there much. So the plant had been forgotten.

"Who's looking after it now?"

"I guess somebody is."

"But nobody knows how to take care of the swan." Alma didn't answer. "Did you say it was in the parlor under the asparagus plant?"

Alma shuddered: it was starting again. She was on her way to another room when the parson's widow came after her and repeated, "Just how was it? Did they keep the swan in the parlor under the asparagus plant?"

"That's where they kept it." Alma tried to think of something to do in the kitchen, but the widow pursued her, stood in front of her, regarding her with that terrible expression. That look in her eyes. Every time Alma saw it, it got under her skin, made her furious. And every time she saw it she wished she were somewhere else than in this house. Always lying. Once you blurted out a lie, you had to keep it up forever. What in the world had made her tell about it? The parson's widow had gone crazy after she'd heard it. That look in her eyes had terrified her and she didn't understand what had really happened when the widow suddenly bolted from her chair, dashed in front of her, stared silently, and then burst into tears. Had she blurted it out just to please, or to brag? Oh, why in heaven's name had she said it? "Where is it?" the parson's widow had asked. "Tell me, where?" "At our house," she had answered.

From that day on, it was the only thing the parson's widow ever thought about. She would trail her, incessantly asking, "Was it a trumpeter swan or an ordinary swan?" As if she'd have known. "Black bill. Yes. Yes, I guess." She couldn't remember, she had just said black. And that's how it had all started.

The widow's voice, now wistful, now exasperated, spoke to her in the kitchen, in the midst of peeling potatoes, in the midst of doing laundry, in the midst of just about anything. And when the pharmacist had come to pay a visit, the widow had run to the door, shouting to him about the swan. "You don't say so!" the pharmacist had exclaimed. And to please them both she had lied again: the bird had been in a corner of the parlor in their house, right next to the tub, and in the tub itself stood a big, feathery asparagus plant, which was called 'the dream.' "Listen, Holger, how beautiful." "Go ahead and tell it once more, Alma. Tell it again, Alma. Tell it again." How many times had she already told the story which was not worth telling, but the parson's widow made her tell it every time the pharmacist or other relatives came to call. "Tell them, Alma." At first it had felt good when the widow led her by the hand in front of the guests and said, "Look, she has seen a swan." She remembered how they had all looked at her, and soon she understood that they regarded her as they would a crazy woman.

And that's how the lying had begun. How could Alma have written to the relatives: she wants the bird because she is out of her mind. Who would have believed her? They'd have thought she herself had gone mad. "Have you written?" the parson's widow would ask. "I have." "What did they answer?" "I don't think they'll let go of it."

The widow had almost become sick when she heard that. And finally Alma had written: "Send that bird if you can. She'll pay for it for sure." There was no answer, and when she went home for a visit she discovered that the bird no longer existed. No one knew what had become of it. The parson's widow had raised her offer of payment, told her to write again. "They just aren't going to sell it," she had to say. The widow had only become more agitated. She ordered Alma to write that the bird could be sent to her on loan; she'd even pay a fee to cover the loan period. Alma lied that she'd written to her brother and gotten the answer that he wouldn't think of parting with the bird. The widow had finally become resigned, said she understood. And Alma thought she'd managed to put the whole matter to rest, but then it flared up again, like a disease.

The parson's widow was walking behind her and saying, "I can see it, Alma. I see it before my very eyes when you talked about that time. In a dim corner of the parlor, under the asparagus plant, oh my, how wonderful! Isn't it a pity your brother won't let go of it?" And now she had gotten it into her head that she at least had to get a look at it. "They couldn't have anything against my coming with you to see it, could they?" And Alma couldn't tell her there was no longer any bird, and she certainly didn't want to take the widow there with her—the relatives would find out what kind of job she was holding. But summer was almost here, and the parson's widow had said that when summer came, they should go see the bird. Alma had thought the widow would forget about it, but no. And now it had come about that the parson's widow had become so anxious that she talked about the bird all the time. She demanded an answer. Alma no longer dared say anything.

Alma could just see how the widow—if Alma were to take her to visit her family—would, barely after introductions, start asking about the bird. Of course, right at the parlor door she would look into that corner. And there would be no asparagus plant and no bird. Alma had prayed to God that the parson's widow, who was always changing her mind, would also change her mind about this and would forget it as she forgot other things, but God was deaf to her prayers. Every day the widow dropped hints, and if Alma was silent, started asking, "Was it so? You haven't been lying to me, have you?" Alma had felt like writing to her sister: "Go and see whether it's in a corner of the parlor, or did I just dream it isn't there and the feathery asparagus neither." Now that she had told about it, Alma herself sometimes believed the bird was still there, and it was all the same, but what in the world would she say if the parson's widow really insisted on going home with her?

Yesterday the pharmacist had been drunk when he came over for a visit, and Alma had eavesdropped on them.

The widow had said, "I'm going to take a trip with Alma. To see that swan, remember?" "So they won't give in and sell it?" "No, and

I do understand that. But I'll go see it. I can't go on living if I don't get to see it." The pharmacist had called Alma and they had gone into the dining room. "What the devil does your brother need that bird for? Wouldn't he sell it for a good price?" She hadn't answered; she didn't dare lie to the pharmacist. It seemed that he'd guessed how things really were. He had winked. People think the parson's widow is out of her mind, and yet each one had asked about the bird, and Alma always had to tell the same lie. Could she now say, without being called crazy herself, that there was no swan, not anymore? What in the world had made her say: it's at our house.

"How did it come to be in your house?"

The parson's widow was in the kitchen, standing right in front of her with that peculiar glare in her eyes. Alma couldn't fathom that expression; when she'd first noticed it she'd become scared, thinking she was being reproached for having done something improper, but it wasn't a question of that; that too she'd noticed on other occasions.

"Who shot it? How did it come to be in your house?"

Alma explained: she thought her brother had shot it and then taken it to be stuffed.

The parson's widow wanted to know the name of the taxidermist, but Alma didn't know it, didn't know another thing about the whole business. And now the widow had got it into her head that they had to travel together to see how the swan was being treated. How could Alma summon up the courage to tell her it didn't exist, that ages ago it had been taken up to the loft of the cow barn, where it had got riddled with worms. Good thing she hadn't told her that. But if the widow really made the effort to go with her, how could Alma explain there was no swan?

And so Alma decided to lie to her and say she had made up the whole story.

"How could you do that to me?" asked the parson's widow, and wept. "Yes," she cried, and went upstairs. She came back down.

"All this time I've been thinking about it, and now you tell me there's no bird, after all."

Should I tell her it certainly does exist but I just don't know anything more about it? Alma thought. And she said so.

"Have you written?"

"Yes. I wrote."

"What did they answer?"

"There's been no letter."

"Couldn't you write again? Or don't they want to? I do understand, but couldn't they just lend it to me for a while? Oh, I feel I would get so much better if I could only see it. Please write again, this instant!"

Alma couldn't tell her she was unable to write: "Send it here immediately or she'll go mad." Could Alma admit she was working at a place where her job consisted of looking after stuffed birds? That's what she'd been told when she came here, and she just hadn't grasped it at the time. Now she understood all too well. But never would she confess it to her relatives. No, she would never write the kind of letter that said they should send the swan right away, without a moment's delay. Because there was no bird. Her brother had said: "Those little brats ruined it." Took it to the loft of the cow barn; buried it somewhere there.

"Did you say under the feathery asparagus plant?" The parson's widow had come into the kitchen.

Alma started.

"That's where it was kept," she said, and headed off to another room.

But the widow came after her and said she'd had a dream about it, the swan in Alma's home, in the dimly lit parlor, wasn't that right?

"That's what Alma said, wasn't it? I've seen it right before my eyes, the swan's white neck in the dim corner of the parlor under the big asparagus plant, or 'the dream' as you called it. How beautiful! I've seen it right before my eyes." "Yes," Alma answered, "it was treated just the way the parson's widow said it should be. Dusted just so, just as the parson's widow said. No, no, not in the harsh sunlight. No." Alma was setting the birds on top of the cabinet and talking, standing sideways, but whichever way she turned, the widow was always in front of her, and Alma was afraid that the parson's widow would finally realize it was all a lie.

"Couldn't he let it out on loan?" the widow's voice pleaded.

FOUR

"It was Friday, not Saturday," the parson's widow continued after a moment's silence. "And besides, I've never heated a sauna myself even though you keep insisting I was right in the middle of doing just that."

Alma tugged open one half of the casement window. The sticky tape came loose and the wad of cotton used for soaking up condensation fell out into the yard just under the window. The wind picked it up and tossed it into a bush, where it caught and stayed, swaying in the wind.

"Fell out," said Alma. "I'll go get it."

"Let it be. The birds can use it for building their nests. In the old days, when the parson was alive, we never used the same cotton wads two years in a row. You're the one who thought that up."

"Well, got to save somewhere." And then Alma yanked open the other half of the casement. "Get away from here, there's a draft."

"You're sure in a bad mood," the parson's widow said. "Don't try to tell me you aren't."

"Have I said anything?"

"I can see it from the way you tug at those windows. So, you still insist I was wearing a flowered dress."

"I'm not going to say anything. I'll never say another word about it. But if you want to know, it really was flowered. I've asked the pharmacist's wife and she says that's how it was, but I'm not going to say anything more about it."

"I haven't worn a flowered dress since the days of my youth."

"Even now you're wearing something flowery."

"This is a blouse, not a dress. As you know, Teodolinda gave me this as a Christmas present and I can't hurt Teodolinda's feelings. Besides, this wouldn't fit you—you've put on weight."

"Well, I'm certainly not going to let this pass since it's started up a quarrel again. That dress had flowers on it, that's for sure, and it was frayed. You kept on wearing and wearing it . . ."

". . . until Elsa told you to tear it off me and then you took it home with you and used it as material when you were weaving rugs."

"You gave it to me yourself. Oh, dear, this is what my life is like."

Alma kept lifting birds, setting them on the windowsills to air out. Dangling the birds with their heads down, she ignored the sharp glances the parson's widow kept giving her and paid no attention to the ever-accelerating rocking of the chair.

"As usual, you've got it all wrong, but let it be. But do you still insist you weren't wearing a black skirt and that you had a red scarf over your head?"

Alma didn't answer.

"You were standing in front of me like a great red-headed woodpecker and I thought: what a beautiful woman. Listen: if you hadn't been wearing a red scarf on your head I probably wouldn't have taken you under my roof, or at least I would have given it a bit of thought, but well, you looked like a great redheaded woodpecker. Your hair was pitch black and shining with the sun on it and your scarf was exactly the shade of red of a red-headed woodpecker." The parson's wife gave a little laugh.

"That scarf too has been cut up as material for rug-weaving. When I went home for a visit I looked at the rugs Siiri had woven. 'There's my life on the floor, there it is,' I thought. 'They're walking all over my life.' It stabbed at my heart."

"Don't be bitter."

"Bitter . . . let her keep it. She's taken everything else as well."

"You should have held your own from the very beginning."

"If it happened today, I'd do exactly what I did then: leave empty-handed."

"The day was beautiful . . . Take that wagtail away from the owls. Haven't I told you that in nature, owls and wagtails are never in the same tree, and not the curlew, again you've set it next to the swallow. Put the small birds in a separate place, take them to the parlor windowsill and don't push them so close to each other, try to think how they are in nature, and besides, turn the owl's back to the sun, can't you even remember that owls move about in the dark . . . the day was beautiful and I looked at you and thought you were one of the people going to the pharmacy."

"You didn't think anything, you didn't even see me, I was standing in the yard and stayed there because the pharmacist's wife told me to wait. First she went to speak with you about me, only then did you peek out the door . . ."

". . . and looked strange, that's what you thought. Did you really think Teodolinda would hire you if I hadn't?"

"I'm sure she would have . . . and who in the world could possibly stay there? Certainly not me."

"Poor Holger. So kind and sweet. People just don't understand . . ."

After a while the parson's widow, looking at Alma with her head tilted to one side, said sharply, "What are you thinking, Alma?"

"I was just thinking that you and the pharmacist's wife look alike from behind."

"What about in front? I guess you thought differently when you got a look at my eyes. Yes, squinting and black. My husband said this slight, barely noticeable squint was enchanting. Antti inherited my eyes. Had to get him glasses, Herman took care of that. But did he take care of me? You know the answer to that."

"The county doctor's wife looks young for her age."

"But Alma, you're getting younger and younger all the time."

"Really?" said Alma after a while. "People do say so."

"You tend to believe everything people tell you. You've got a few wrinkles at the corners of your eyes. Maybe you haven't noticed. I took a close look when the sun was directly on your face. I got quite a start. Age is doing its work on you, too. And now your brother's wife is using your trousseau."

"That was no trousseau. I was only weaving and crocheting because it's what's done. Seemed they had a bedspread I had woven on the bed in the parlor. I looked at it, felt it with my fingers so she'd have to notice, and then Siiri says that her mother must have been the one who wove it. I didn't say a thing."

"You could have taken it away."

"When I left, I left for good."

"But you've regretted it, haven't you?"

"Should I have settled down as a maid to my brother's wife?"

"You always need to be in control, Alma. But anyway, put that grouse so that it looks straight towards the pharmacy, I've spoken to you about that, and open the window, the poor birds haven't had fresh air in ages, this slovenliness is bad for their feathers, dust is deadly poison to feathers, that's what my husband used to say when he was alive. And you simply refuse to understand that a bird, any bird, is always airing itself out. What's the matter—haven't you seen to it yet?"

"Who and what is it exactly that I control?"

"You control yourself. But didn't you have any suitors?"

"I didn't care."

"You once told me your sisters had said: take him, but you didn't. Why not? You said he was rich and you stole a glance at him when he was coming out of a tent at a fair, but then you got mad when your sisters said: take him, take him. Why didn't you? Didn't you care for him?"

"I don't know. You seem to have a good memory when you want to."

"You said the boy had red hair and that was what bothered you."

"Good memory you've got, and you still say the day was Friday. As if I wouldn't remember. It was a Friday night when I decided: now I'm getting out of here. I was threshing grain. Siiri came by to yell at me that the cow hadn't been milked properly and had an inflamed udder. She meant it was my fault. Whatever went wrong, Siiri would always come and yell something to my brother, and every time she put it on me. And when she came to the door of the hay barn, I listened. Never said a word. When she came around a second time, I jumped out of the barn. I remember it like the rock in front of me right here: I threw my threshing flail against that rock. I didn't say a word but headed up along the cow path. That was the last time I ever threshed grain. Nobody said a thing; they just looked as I went back and forth between house and storehouse, gathering up my clothes. I took whatever would fit into one box, nothing more, I said in the evening. My brother left the house, Siiri after him. Siiri came back to the house and went into the back room. My brother went over to the neighbor's, sat there drinking all night, got himself good and drunk. 'It was Hinttu Rasanen who did it,' Mother cried. She was in a bad way by then, paralyzed. I didn't say anything. I thought that no sound would come out of me but that I would get myself out. During the night, Siiri went to get my sister, Reetta. 'Alma's going to leave. Come set things right,' Siiri had cried to her. Reetta did come. 'So now it's you too,' I said to her. 'Weren't you the one who told me not to take him?' 'Me? Never,' Reetta said, and kept cracking her knuckles. She had that habit, she'd gotten it from our poor late mother."

"So you did regret not taking that boy."

"I don't know."

"Go on, tell me more. About how you quarreled. When the big fight broke out."

"We never quarreled at our house, never, not before they arranged to get Siiri together with that Martti. That's how it started."

"Begin at the beginning, close that door, sit down, let the birds take their time getting their fresh air, sit right here in front of me and talk."

Alma sat down.

"But you still could have stayed home and waited for young men to come calling."

"It wasn't just a question of that. 'Is this really my home?' I asked that night. 'Who's giving the orders around here?' Mother only went on crying and Reetta didn't know what to do besides wring her hands. Though later, the summer before last, when I went there for a visit, I asked my sister why she couldn't have kept me from going away then. Reetta insisted she did make a try but, according to her, there was nothing anybody could do with me. And then we drew up the final papers—a list of everything Mother had left us."

The parson's widow didn't even have to look up to know that at this point in the story Alma would start to cry, and that's just what she did; now she was weeping and sighing. And the parson's widow knew that when Alma would start up again her voice would soar to a higher pitch and she would sound as if she were in a trance.

"Yes, drew up the papers. And that was the end of the daughters' share."

"But you did get something."

"Five thousand. But what's that? Daughters thrown out of the house like so many sheep onto the road."

"But that's how it always is: the son inherits the farm."

"Mother, bless her soul, was already weak in the head when the papers were drawn up, and it wasn't any fault of my brothers, Martti and Frans, but it was all Siiri's doing. Siiri was always after Martti, egging him on from morning to night: draw up the papers, draw up the papers, she just couldn't live in the house one more day unless those papers were ready. Well, what can you do when, to put it bluntly, a man is as weak-kneed as my brother Martti? Well, he goes right ahead and has the papers drawn."

"Couldn't the will be broken?"

"I've told you, you know perfectly well. Reetta's husband, the one who then died, and then Reetta took another husband, so the first husband tried to prove that Mother had been feeble-minded, you know. I also showed those papers to the pharmacist, the papers with my name underneath, with a request to the court to reverse the decision, because poor dear Mother, rest her soul, was not in her right mind when she sold the farm to her son, but what good did that do?"

"So they couldn't break the will."

"What's going to break injustice in this world? It's truth that's going to be broken. I get a sharp pain in my heart when I remember the cover of the rocking chair."

The parson's widow could see it coming: now Alma would start to wipe under her nose with the side of her palm, always the palm of the left hand, and it happened that way again.

"And never mind anything else, but the black silk scarf that belonged to my mother, rest her soul, that too is still there. Let me have that, at least, I said to my brother the last time I was there. I don't know who it's been promised to, says my brother. Ask Siiri, he says. And when I do say to Siiri, 'wonder whose scarf that might be,' Siiri tells me to ask Martti. And so it's just as people say in those parts: what's in the wolf's mouth is in the wolf's ass too."

"And what about your younger sister?"

"She's got a nasty man for a husband. And that's my oldest sister's fault. She's the one who kept urging her, 'Take him, take him, go on, go on.' Just the way she did to me. But I said 'no.'"

"Where would you be if your brother hadn't taken that woman?"

"I don't know."

"And your sister's children?"

"Badly brought up. Disobedient. They talk back to their mother."

"Did you hear that with your own ears?"

"Hear it? Me? I sat on a bench in the kitchen and looked at that kind of life, the girl going off to a dance, just running out to an open-air dance, while the mother can't do anything to stop it. Their father tries to whip them but what's the point of whipping a girl that's almost full grown? I told my sister, you sure don't seem able to discipline your own kids, do you remember how you treated me? Didn't you forbid me to go to dances? 'Never' she said. As if it had been like that!"

"Well, did she really forbid you to go?"

"If she hadn't always told me not to, I wouldn't be here."

"Where, then? Would you be an Asikainen, or perhaps a Vihavainen?"

"You remember everything. I don't know."

"But I asked you to start from the beginning, and now you've mixed it all up. I said: start telling it from the beginning, from the very start, but now you've got it muddled."

"Whatever the beginning may be," Alma said. "It's getting windy, don't you see, and if I just sit here the wind will knock over the birds, and besides, wasn't I supposed to get this place cleaned up, you said so yourself. The relatives are coming for a visit."

"Polish the silver, and wipe the plates till they gleam," said the parson's widow after a moment's thought.

"Where are they?"

"In the dining room cabinet, of course."

"The spirits must be on the move again." Alma couldn't help saying that.

To her surprise, she noticed the parson's widow smiling, not angry at all.

FIVE

"You know, Missus, you were already well along in years."

The parson's widow fell silent and Alma realized how vain she could be about her age.

"You were well into your thirties when Antti was born."

"Alma, you just don't understand."

Maddening, the way she always said, "Alma, you just don't understand."

"A woman's no longer young at that age."

"But you're thirty."

"Twenty-nine."

"There you are, Alma. Each year is so precious it has to be measured out precisely. You too hold tightly onto your years, and still, you will talk to me like that." And the parson's widow went on, "You just don't understand. A child was on the way, you don't understand. I would go walking along the shore and I wanted only to die."

"What was it that was bothering you, Missus?"

"Yes, but I was still living in the parsonage then . . ."

"Who lived in this house before you?"

"Paananen, the shopkeeper. He's the one who ruined the garden. Oh, my goodness, do you think I'd have set out the plants in that kind of arrangement, right there under the window? The shopkeeper came to live here after Birger's mother died, but it certainly didn't take long before the spirit of the house got hold of him."

"You haven't shown those pictures."

"No, I haven't. I just can't. At first I didn't do anything but look at the pictures and cry. Then Antti was born, and when Birger died, my life was over; it ended on that very day, and I thought: I too am dead. Teodolinda and Elsa came to see me. I was alone, all alone. Teodolinda came over and said, 'You have to eat, Adele.' Elsa said, 'It's your duty.' And maybe I'd have given up the ghost if it hadn't been for them—better to have the worst family in the world than none at all—when one gets old, then one understands that."

"You had a good husband. People say that, deep down, the parson was a good man."

"Who's been talking to you about my husband?"

The parson's widow glared angrily at Alma.

"You're not trying to tell me that my own sisters-in-law speak critically to you about my husband, their own brother!"

"One hears all kinds of things."

The parson's widow was silent. Alma knew she was furious. Even the smallest hint that there had been some talk about them got her that way. With the tattered shawl having wrapped itself more tightly around her, and with her head turned towards the window as if she hadn't heard a thing, the parson's widow sat there as if deep in thought. To mollify her, Alma spoke again: "Shouldn't talk to people about them walking around here."

At once the widow's head snapped back and her eyes gleamed as always when they talked about this.

"But you've heard them yourself. Onni appeared to you, didn't he? And you still won't believe."

"I believe, all right, but anyway, one shouldn't talk. People wouldn't understand, and besides, I just don't talk about it to people, not even to my own family."

"Have you heard them now? Have they been moving about?"

"The last time I'm sure it was the cat. First I thought it was Paananen, when you said that's who it was, but frankly, the next morning I thought it was the cat. I can't believe every noise or I'll go mad."

"I can't swear it was Paananen. I only said I heard some sort of creeping steps that could have been Paananen's. He did do wrong and maybe he's trying to come back to set it right, but that other thing's sure."

"But you're not even sure how it happened."

"I'm not going to argue with you, and I won't force you to believe ... but would my own husband have lied to me? And besides, I was the one who opened the door when there was all that knocking. Who was it? I asked Birger after the woman had left."

"And what do you imagine they said to you?"

"I've told you, haven't I? They both laughed and said it was someone mad, quite insane. You know what happened. The prediction came true. And don't you remember what happened when you came to this house?"

"Yes, it's true. I came to ask why you were staying up at night. I heard you moving about downstairs, it was early morning, still dark. Don't you remember? You were sitting in the kitchen and your face was white. 'Why are you still awake, Alma? Can't you get to sleep?' 'Someone came through here,' you said."

"That's right. First I heard something like footsteps, and it was as if I'd woken up to the sound."

"You woke up to a water-logged man standing next to your bed and you asked, 'What do you want?' 'Paananen has sent the creditors,' he answered. First came the thought that everything was lost; it was just out of mercy that they'd left this house. And Herman will never forgive Elsa for not having anything. But the pharmacist. Though you say he's not a good man, he took Teodolinda although she came to him with empty hands, just the way Birger took me. I was a young clergyman's wife, despised by my husband's family. I don't deny I thought badly of my mother-in-law when I heard she'd died empty-handed. You know this house really belongs to Herman. He's the one who bought it at the bankruptcy auction."

Alma started: the widow's memory was playing tricks on her. Until now, she had talked about the house as her own.

"Sometimes at night I think I hear footsteps on the stairs and I think: Birger's mother. The day Birger brought me to this house, that woman came down the stairs, her steps ringing out from above, coming closer and closer. I stood waiting downstairs in the front hall, terrified, but she didn't say a thing. She looked straight at me when she came down the stairs. I held out my hand but she pretended not to see it, just sailed on past me into the dining room and shut the door behind her. That was the only time I visited this house while she was alive. Could I have guessed I'd end up living in this house, all alone, and that they would all go away? I think she may not have forgiven me even now, and it's as if I heard steps, as if she were descending the stairs, still looking at me. You don't understand, Alma. I'm innocent, but it's still as if I'd done something wrong, as if I were an intruder. Take a look at these rooms now. Are they meant for a person like me? There was an ornamental full-length mirror. I could see all of myself in it, and I thought: who is that person who is so afraid? I looked at my image and thought: who is it who is so afraid, and then I understood it was me. There were two mirrors in this parlor, and Paananen took both of them; four horses in the stables, and Paananen took them; cows, sheep, pigs, everything that was alive Paananen turned into cash. Teodolinda was still unmarried then, so Paananen didn't dare drive her out of her home. She was living here all alone in a tiny upstairs room. Paananen took the other rooms. We lived at the parsonage. Teodolinda would visit us but Elsa didn't like it. She said, 'Why do you go there? Mama wouldn't have approved.' Of *me*, she meant. Teodolinda was stiff and proud but I understood she held nothing against me. Paananen couldn't stand it; he moved away. Teodolinda never exchanged a word with

Paananen. Not even when Paananen's wife dug up the dahlia roots and took them away with her."

"But the dahlia roots belonged to the shopkeeper's wife."

"You don't understand, Alma. Could you have looked on silently while someone was digging up the dahlia roots from the flowerbed of your own home? 'You know you have a home with me, Birger,' Teodolinda said when the parsonage burned. She didn't say anything like that to me. And I didn't want to come. I was proud, very proud. 'I won't go, I haven't been asked,' I said to Birger. He made me come, and so I lived as a stranger in this very house, and Teodolinda too was a stranger. We each sat in our own rooms. 'How about something to eat?' said Birger. 'Ask your sister,' I said. 'Ask your wife,' Teodolinda said. Birger got thinner, I got thinner, Teodolinda got thinner. 'But we've got to eat,' Birger said, and then he wept. 'You're a bad wife.' 'Ask your sister,' I said."

"Who was the first to give in?"

"I was . . . That's what I thought at the time, but actually, both of us humbled ourselves. 'If I've wronged you in any way by coming into your home, I beg forgiveness,' I said to Teodolinda."

"How did you live? You had to eat something."

"Birger would cook some food and bring it upstairs to me. Teodolinda ate secretly in her own room. She wasn't as bad off as I was, you know. Behind our backs, she had made her connections with the pharmacy. 'I'm leaving now,' Teodolinda announced one morning. She had packed her bags. Birger burst into tears and asked, 'Dear sister, where are you going?' 'To Viipuri.' 'Don't leave. Let's all be reconciled. Please forgive us.' But she didn't go to Viipuri, she'd deceived us and gone to work in the pharmacy instead, and then Holger married her. That's what Holger's mother wanted."

The parson's widow went on talking but Alma was remembering another story, the one that people had told her. The parson's wife had been terribly selfish, the parson had come down with tuberculosis because his wife refused to cook for him. And the parson's wife had driven her sister-in-law out of her own home. It was the voice of the county doctor's wife that Alma was hearing: "She drove my sister out of her own home. It's all well and good for her to be sanctimonious now, she doesn't remember how my poor sister had to suffer. How could I forget how hungry Teodolinda was all the time! But she never complained. Is it a wonder that we daughters wanted at least a little something from our home, but Father was on Birger's side and left everything to him. Is it any wonder that of the tiny bit that was left after Paananen had been through it, we daughters wanted a memento or two? But that Adele—she took it, she ate it, she spent it all. Teodolinda didn't know how to look after her own interests. I wonder whether the parson's widow has even paid you any wages."

"I roamed through this empty house," the parson's widow was saying. "I thought: I won't touch anything, I won't move anything, this isn't mine. They had started building the new parsonage and people had begun to speak ill of the parson, as if he had deliberately set the parsonage on fire. There was talk of rockets, of gunpowder on top of the kitchen stove. An accident, that's what it was. I thought: I'll set everything in order as soon as I have a new home. Birger thought only of the birds. When the fire broke out, he shouted: 'Save the birds.' I ran right through the smoke, I carried out the birds, 'Jacob's Dream' with them, but the birds on top of the cabinet got burned. I saw them burning in the chancery, on top of the cabinet, the same cabinet where the Communion vessels were kept. Two doves and one smaller bird, I saw them burning. I had my arms full of birds, and Birger did too. 'Save the church records,' the verger shouted. Again Birger raced into the smoke and carried out birds while I stood at the door in the red-hot glow of the fire with my arms full of birds, and with people rushing by me, lugging pieces of furniture. The fire had broken out on the kitchen end of the house and we couldn't save anything from there, but we did manage to save things from the office wing. And in back of the office window there were three spruce trees and then I saw them burst into flame; it was too late, and the birds were all alone in the yard. But I carried them off to a hiding place, rushed to the cellar with them so people wouldn't see them. You know, people were kicking at them and asking, 'What are these? Where are the Communion vessels?' and when it was all over we went to the cellar together and there were the birds, blackened from the smoke but some of them completely unharmed. Birger inspected them right away and said, 'Thanks be to God.' 'Don't you thank God that I was saved?' I said, and burst into tears. 'You, you have legs,' he said. 'Could I have let these be sacrificed in the fire?' We went to Teodolinda's house with birds in our arms, birds in a wicker basket, birds' eggs in boxes, and do you know, that very same night, with Teodolinda's help, he set them in rows on top of cabinets and windowsills. 'Why aren't you doing anything?' he asked me. 'I just can't,' I said. And I couldn't. I could only cry, knowing he hadn't had a single thought about my life, but only of the birds. 'Thanks be to God,' he said. And then he added: 'You too could have saved them, if you'd only wanted to.' He was angry with me because he thought I didn't want to do it. 'You're godless,' he said, 'the two of you.' I didn't understand at the time, but his sister understood and together they cleaned the soot off the birds. 'If you hadn't insisted I save these, I'd have been able to save the spoons,' I said. 'Go to the cabinet, take as many silver spoons as you lost in the fire,' said Teodolinda. And then Birger preached, to a church filled with people. Everyone grew angry, and the next Sunday there wasn't anyone in church. He spoke of the birds, how through smoke and fire he had saved the birds. Not one word about the parish parsonage burning down. People became furious, filed a complaint with the bishop. Elsa and Herman came over and said, 'Out of your mind, that's what you are, out of your mind.' Birger lost his temper and threw them out. As she was leaving, Elsa shouted, 'That's a parson for you!' Teodolinda said, 'Control yourself, Elsa.' 'I won't control myself,' Elsa said, and began to cry. In the front hall, Herman was in a fury, wildly lashing the air with his cane. As you well know, there are eighty-three of them. Right after the fire, Birger started roving through the forests, and I had to stay up late to help him when he was stuffing the birds—you can't imagine—dead birds all over the hall table. I vomited. Antti was inside me, in my own eyes the birds' eyes were boiling when he dug them out of their sockets, and Teodolinda was helping him and forcing me to help too even though I vomited again. Night and day he didn't rest, went without eating night and day. Teodolinda took him some food on a tray and said, 'You have to eat, Birger.' The illness had started some time earlier, he'd been spitting blood for a good many years. His brother died of the same disease. He coughed and coughed; I would listen to it at night.

"The congregation filed a complaint to the bishop that Birger was neglecting his parish duties, but that wasn't true. How he preached! Oh, how he preached! He'd never delivered such fiery sermons before the fire, but people didn't understand he was preaching the purest word of God. With burning eyes he would preach on the tiny servants of our heavenly father who fly innocently through the pure air, not cooking, not spinning, not coveting; they fly singing to the glory of their Creator. 'What about hawks?' I said. 'What about birds of prey?' but he only went on preaching. The parishioners complained to the bishop that the pastor wouldn't come to bless the deceased, but that was only because he'd forgotten, it was only a matter of his forgetting. People are waiting, the sexton is waiting, the parson is out hunting. They came to tell. I'd rush to the cemetery to explain: please excuse him, wait, he's out hunting birds. 'Why on earth did you have to go and say that?' Teodolinda reproached me. We waited, watched through the window, but he didn't come home until evening, and that's how it all started, the persecution. Running and running, I stumbled over the gravestones, there in the cemetery with my head bare and no gloves though it was late winter. The funeral bells were tolling, and when I heard that, I remembered, as if a voice had announced: there's a funeral; Birger isn't there to read the burial service, to bless the body; he's gone out hunting. It was a disgrace. I understood right off that it was shameful. And that's how the persecution got started. People said their parson had refused to read the burial service; they spoke of the fire and how he hadn't wanted to save church records or Communion vessels, but only birds; they were carried off to safety before anything else. 'Save the birds!' Birger shouted to the verger and the sexton, but together with the gravedigger they were carrying the sofa, and again Birger called out, 'Birds, birds. Can't you hear?' But the verger had plunged into the smoke and was carrying out the dining table all by himself, and him an old man too, while others were carrying a bed and a washstand. 'Save the birds!' Birger shouted. 'Take some dishes from the cabinets, you lunatic!' the gravedigger yelled, addressing the parson too familiarly. But what Birger took from the cabinet was the box holding the birds' eggs. The verger and the gravedigger were the first ones to testify; they started the persecution, incited the other parishioners. The bishop came to make an inspection, but Birger was off in the forest. There he is now, in the heavenly forest where people's tongues can't do him any harm. There he is.

"That night was terrible. Teodolinda wouldn't comfort me, me, who after all was deeply in need of consolation; she comforted her brother. They totally forgot about me, banded together as if I didn't exist, and only because I failed to rescue the doves from the top of the cabinet. I was going to save them. I saw them but then I thought: the coffee pot. I tried to go into the kitchen but it was too full of smoke. 'The china service from the dining room cabinet,' I shouted, and some woman plunged into the dining room with me even though it was already full of smoke. We were about to suffocate, both of us. I was able to get the soup tureen in my hand, and she one plate, that was all; everything burned up, forks, knives, photographs of my parents, my girls-school picture that was hanging on the bedroom wall, everything, and still Birger and Teodolinda held a grudge against me. When we were digging through the ashes, metal wires and remnants of birds would turn up. And Birger wept. He kept picking them up and weeping. 'If the Communion vessels had burned, would you have mourned them?' I asked. 'Why?' he said. And I kept silent. The sort of small black bag that holds Communion vessels for the sick and the dying, when you had to go around the country giving Communion. I too carried that bag when we would go together to visit the sick and the dying. He was a conscientious clergyman, after all. Why couldn't people forgive him those birds? But no, the persecution flared up again. Yet the bishop understood. After Birger died, the bishop wrote me a letter. I've shown it to you, haven't I? The bishop was the only person who understood poor Birger. He wrote: 'Your husband was a real servant of God and now he is with his birds. God's birds now sing to him in heaven. People's hearts are ignorant and hard; it is not easy for a child of God to be in this world. I bless you so that you may be like a bird of the heavens, with a light heart . . .' That letter was such a wonderful comfort to me, and I wrote to the bishop that I hadn't understood my husband either, but called out 'the china service!' and managed to save only the baptismal font and it too broke into pieces, and my husband's sister Elsa never would forgive me for that because it was part of her poor late mother's service. But otherwise, Teodolinda was understanding. 'Don't you cry,' she said to us. 'Don't you cry either, Adele. You have a home here.' And at first all went well, but I don't know how . . . we couldn't look each other in the eye, not eat together. Pride had a hold on us, and then Teodolinda took Holger. Maybe it wasn't wise for us to live together. There might have been fewer sorrows if we hadn't.

"I wonder where I'd be now if the parsonage hadn't burned down," said Alma.

"Yes, where?" said the parson's widow.

Six

"A heart doesn't break that easily, Alma."

"Has the mistress a broken heart, then?"

"I? No. I've had heartaches, but no one has broken my heart."

She went over to the window, lifted a flowerpot, held it in her hands and turned to Alma.

"We'll take this to the grave."

"But I've told you time and time again you can't take flowers to the grave at this time of year. They'll freeze."

"You're so angry at me just because I called you a lapwing? Don't you understand that I speak in metaphors?"

Alma was polishing a candlestick.

The parson's widow reached up to the top of the bookcase to take hold of a wagtail, then sat down, placed the bird on the table in front of her and adjusted its position so that its bill pointed straight towards the window.

"You see, it should stand like this, just like in nature: curtains white as clouds, like the sky and air above. Poor little bird."

Alma didn't turn to look.

"Maybe my brains have turned into bird brains. Maybe you're right, Alma, maybe I am a wagtail. Well, how could I expect people to understand me?"

Alma kept on polishing the candlestick.

"When have you seen a wagtail running after a train?" the parson's widow asked sharply. "You pretend not to remember that time when we were coming back home from the city and you said to me, 'Don't run after a train like an old wagtail.' And anyway, it was your fault that we missed the train, but did I blame you?"

"My fault?" said Alma. "Who was it who dawdled in the park to look at birds instead of getting to the station on time?"

"Well, I think I have the right to observe the life of pigeons. You know pigeons don't do well in this miserable village. And besides, I was on my way to the doctor's. You don't think I'd trust Herman's diagnoses, I never have. And anyway, I said we could still get home on the evening train. I didn't force you to walk all the way home from the city, even though Birger, his uncle Onni, and the pharmacist have all bicycled that distance many times. What are you blaming me for now? You talk about your broken heart when you remember the miserable rocking-chair rug that you say your sister-in-law stole from you. Why don't you look after your own affairs? Now you just torment me every day with complaints about how your relatives robbed you."

"You wouldn't know anything about a broken heart when you look after your own heart like that. And get that creature off the table. Wasn't I supposed to do house-cleaning today? How can I wipe off the table if you keep it there?"

"Well, well. Now the truth comes out. You hate me because of the birds, just like everyone else. You hate the only defender of these innocent creatures. You're like all the rest of them. Because you don't consider me a proper parson's widow... as if I didn't know. It's pretty clear that you've gone around the village spreading stories about me. The hatred just oozes out of you ... don't contradict me. Because of the birds, that's why. Godless, I know. Do you want to hear the whole story of my suffering?"

Alma started flinging the birds down from the top of the bookcase so they could air out on the windowsill.

"It was a spring evening, not autumn as it is now, it was spring, and the road curved down to the shore through a birch grove. 'I beg you, don't shoot little birds.' Birger was standing on a rock with a gun in his hand, and this very same little bird on the shore, on a rock, on a rock by the shore, a wagtail, with its tail going up, down, up, and Birger standing there, rifle at the ready against his shoulder. I began clapping my hands to scare it away but the bird didn't hear, the shot rang out and Birger went running along the rocks and came back with this little bird dangling from his hand."

The parson's widow looked straight into the bird's glass eyes.

"I don't know whether you understand me. Who could I ask? I have nothing to ask, not of you, not of anyone. When I knew I was expecting a child, on the days when that became clear to me, I begged him: 'Don't shoot birds.' I couldn't bear to look at them, there was a churning in the pit of my stomach from morning to night, this very room, small birds in rows on the table, dead, stiff, and the smell in this room. I fled upstairs, the smell penetrated the walls when he prepared them. Birger promised that this small bird would be the last. But one spring night after another he walked the swamps and forests and lake shores, and I had to go with him, I had to pick up birds that plunged to the ground, from the grasses, from the edges of cliffs. I had to carry them on my side and feel the movement of the child against the dead birds. 'He's a master shot.' 'Who?' 'Your husband,' said the sheriff. 'He's a master shot. Just think how he can nail any bird with a single shot.' 'It's all right to shoot them, then? Is it legal?' I asked, trying in some way to stop it. 'Of course, of course,' the sheriff said. When the bishop came to visit, I again tried to put a stop to it. In Birger's earshot I asked the bishop whether it was permitted. 'Of course, of course,' the bishop said. 'The parson has remarkable skill. You know, I'm amazed he knows so unbelievably much about birds. Just be happy he's such a scientist and a clergyman at the same time.' 'How can you go to church and preach, "Look at the birds of the heavens?" 'Silly.' Silly. Silly. Always the same answer.

"I stopped asking. Towards evening the bishop and my husband went out to the shoals together and in the morning there were five new birds on the worktable, water birds, the ones that call out so plaintively on the open lake at night. When he came back home that night with the long-billed one in his hand—don't break it, Alma. A curlew's bill will break if you carry it like that. Carry it like this, like a babe in arms, this is how I've taught you. Put it on the other windowsill by itself, not next to the mallard, as far as I know they aren't close to each other in nature—well, when he returned home that night I stood waiting on the stairs and I'd had enough. 'What if you shot me?' I said. 'I'd like to see which hymn you'd have them sing after you prepared me. Take a look. Wouldn't it be fun to push a metal wire through these, take a look, I'll hold my arms like this and my legs like that. In what position would you set me? I've been thinking about it all night. Would you have me sitting, or standing on one foot, look, like this, or would you lift one arm in the air, or both arms, or an arm along the side, or both arms? I've been expecting you home all night, I've paced back and forth all night and looked at these birds and thought I'm nothing but another bird in your collection. What name would you give me, *rara avis*, or what? Would you put me up on the highest spot, on top of that case next to the owl, would you make glass eyes for me too, would I be a *rara avis*?' 'Silly, silly, that's what you would be. I'd put a *silly avis* label on your pedestal, don't you get any ideas of being a phoenix, you're just a nervous woman who can't take a normal attitude toward her pregnancy—try to learn from these country women.' And then I shouted the name of the girl they'd taken along with them to row the boat. He stared at me through his glasses for a long time and said: 'Go sleep in another room.' 'Forgive me!' I cried. I tried to wrap my arms around his neck, no, not these"—the parson's widow squeezed her arms, hooked her fingers around her left wrist—"not these, Alma, these arms are withered. Not these . . . I was young then and my arms were white and soft. I always wore long-sleeved dresses so I wouldn't get brown blotches on my arms. I feel I haven't had any arms since then, they stayed around his neck, torn off from me, stayed hanging around his neck forever when he pushed me off."

"Don't start that again, don't," Alma said. "You'll have another sleepless night if you start talking about that again. Go away and don't look at the birds anymore today."

But the parson's widow went on: "In the morning, while he was still sleeping, I came into this room and the curlew was on the desk. Long, pointed bill, the curlew tossed on the desk, its bill hanging over the edge as if it were taking a drink of water, the water of death. And you see, that's how it's been stuffed, in just that position, as if its bill were trying to reach the water of death forever."

"I'm not listening," said Alma. "No, I'm not going to get you any medicine, believe me . . ."

"But all these are alive. Can't you see they've become immortal? The feathers are smooth, well cared for, no moth holes, no stains. I will die, but the birds will live forever."

The parson's widow became silent, smiled at the wagtail, cocked her head and began chattering to the bird as if to a small child: "Look here, if you really are me. They say I am just like you. What if you do happen to be me? Then: I am alive. I exist, I talk even though I'm you. And look: you are not dead, not so long as I am talking to you, and when I'm dead, then you will be me even though I can't talk—but if another one comes along to whom they say, 'Missus, you're a wagtail,' then you'll carry on my life. When I'm gone, where will they put you, my mirror image? Alma doesn't care about you. She's fluffing up her feathers at me." The parson's widow took the wagtail in her hand, looked closely into the black glass eyes. "I see my own eyes in yours. Do you know, you slender little bird, that Alma is a wood grouse transformed into a woman? Can't you hear how she fluffs up her feathers, calls and cuckoos to me? Do you understand, just listen, soon she'll let loose her voice, rush back and forth, come in forwards and backwards. Did you hear? Just now she darted out of the room."

"Alma," the parson's widow called.

"Alma," the widow called again.

"You heard me all right!" she shouted. "But since you're a bird you don't answer. You go off and hide, stiffen up, and are on your guard."

At dinner, when Alma thought the parson's widow had already forgotten her topic of the morning, the widow set down her spoon so that it clinked against the rim of the plate. Alma was just about to get up from the table when the widow started: "Perhaps you'd show me how a wood grouse carries on in mating season."

"No."

"But if you'd just try. Remember what I've always said: your brother is a great artist, and although I understand that what you once performed for me was only a reflection, a mere suggestion of how your brother performs it, you still have to remember that I've never enjoyed a single theater performance as much as that one."

"No. Will you have some pudding or should it be cleared away?"

"I can't eat so much as a crumb when I think of it."

"Is it my fault you don't put on any weight? Yesterday you said that for the rest of your life you'd never get rice pudding again. Now you've got some right in front of you. Are we going to give it to the cat or whoever else will eat it?"

"You'll eat it," said the parson's widow with that particular smile.

"Now you're not going to get me to quarrel. I don't have the time. Soon it'll be tomorrow and first thing in the morning you'll say I'm causing you rheumatism if I happen to leave the door a crack open by mistake when I'm carrying rugs in and out. And still you'll say right off: oh my, the parlor rug hasn't been aired in months. When I aired it only a week ago."

"I'm not going to argue with you," the parson's widow said softly. "Look here, I got you to be exactly what I wanted. When you get angry your hair shines so bright that it sparkles, and when you put that lyre comb into the bun at the back of your head—by the way, when Elsa comes, be sure to take it out of your hair, it used to belong to Elsa's poor dead mother—you're the spitting image of a wood-grouse cock. In your bottom half you're a woman, all right, but in your upper part," and here the widow pointed to her own neck, "you're the very image of a wood-grouse cock."

"But I'm not going to go reeling about like some bird."

"And, Miss Luostarinen, what about your brother? Miss Alma Luostarinen, what about that brother of yours?"

"Shoots birds as he needs them."

"What about the swan?" the parson's widow said with malicious dignity. "What if I were to go speak to the sheriff? As far as I know, one isn't permitted to shoot a swan. And whose cow barn loft is it in now?"

"I never should have said a word about that stuffed bird," Alma said, and gathered the dishes onto a tray.

"Well, can you tell me now whether it was a trumpeter swan or a mute swan?" Alma took the plates to the kitchen, then came back to get the pudding dish.

"It was a sin, a sin. But perhaps God in heaven will sometime give your brother the soul of a swan, for he did repent, didn't he? Didn't you say so?"

"What are we going to do with the parson's widow," Alma sighed. "Your husband sure must have been a good man even though you're always finding fault with him."

"What have I found fault with him about?"

"Always talking about souls, supposed to be birds."

"Do you think all birds are good? Oh, my, when I listen at night, they scream out when they're coming. They scream."

"Now the parson's widow mustn't get started on that. Next thing you know it'll turn to blaspheming and you won't be able to sleep. The way it is, the widow mustn't get herself all worked up just before going to bed. If you get stirred up, then I'll get stirred up too, and then we'll go around the house all night, that's how it is, if you get all afraid then I'll start getting afraid as well. And even though I don't really believe, it still feels bad, it's like at home when my poor dear mother would get started. First thing in the morning it would begin, telling about a dream, and by the time it got to be night and dark, everybody'd be afraid; a person can't take it when somebody else is always telling their dreams, it gets one on edge."

"My husband wasn't . . ."

"Don't start in now, Missus."

"You know, sure, you know, but you don't know everything . . ."

"The widow mustn't start on that again. I won't listen."

"Shut the window. They're screeching, and I have a headache."

"That's what you get for always pondering over things. Didn't I say it would be better if they all were destroyed? Much, much better. Missus, in the springtime like this, you should get away, take a trip to where you can't hear them."

"Where would I go? Wherever I travel, birds will be flying over my head."

"But why does the parson's widow listen to that screeching? Go somewhere away from the shore; there'll be less of that gurgling. They're screaming like lost souls in hell . . ."

"Oh, Alma, that's just spring. Spring is cruel, isn't it?"

"It was spring when I left home. Then I had a home to leave. When I leave now, there isn't any place to go to, to come from, not a piece of the fatherland under my feet . . ."

"The fatherland is up in heaven."

"But the widow has a plot of land, doesn't she? Isn't this plot legally yours?"

"That's not the way I think. The ground on which I'm standing is always the fatherland even if I'm standing on a rock in the water."

"But Missus, aren't you bitter towards your sisters-in-law?"

"They think I am. Why in the world should I be? Of course I know they're coveting this plot because they want to turn it into money. They're waiting for me to die, they'd like to get their hands on my things. Oh my, oh my, the story you told this morning was very familiar to me, as if I'd been you, Alma, and cried for the land that had been taken away from me . . ."

"The thin one?"

"No, the fat one. They always hated me, always, my husband too. People did. Do you think one can't hate a clergyman or that clergymen don't hate each other? Oh dear, oh dear, I'll tell you everything. But some other time. I'll start from the very beginning, you've heard it all but I'll start from the beginning. Well, Alma, I was only a postmistress and he was from a fine family, a fine man. Walked past the post office, first he just walked and walked because he was a shy man. Then one day he opened the door and came in."

"Did you guess?"

"No, of course not. After all, he was such a fine man and I was only a postmistress. He was just coming back from hunting, holding a bird in his hand. 'Miss, would you like to go on a bird outing with me?' You see, Alma, how he was beating around the bush. In those days it was the fashion to go on outings, and he was carrying a herbarium can on a shoulder strap, and a pair of binoculars, and

I said, 'Thank you.' So I went out birding." The parson's widow sighed. "Sit down, Alma. Be my friend again, listen."

"And then?"

"Then? Then came the sisters-in-law, the one who's now fat, but who then was as slender as the one who used to be fat but is now thin—odd how everything in this world has to change . . . well, where was I? So they came. Not to the post office, no, not at all, but rowing in a boat to the rocky little island where we were on our outing. 'Who are they?' I asked even though I knew. 'My dear sisters,' he said and peered toward the boat through his binoculars and said: 'Teodolinda's rowing and Elsa's steering. Shall I shoot them?' He always had his gun with him. He lifted the gun and I let out a shriek and then he laughed and put the gun away, but it was loaded, I knew it. 'Why are they coming?' I asked. He shrugged—I remember that as if it were happening right before me. I was feeling chilled, but I had no idea what going out birding signified and I didn't understand it wasn't even proper to go out like that with a strange young man. I thought he was just asking me along to do the rowing for him, he was such a fine man and I nothing but a postmistress. Not even a full postmistress, just a girl in the post office, a trainee . . . Now where was I? Oh, yes, he came in and said to me: 'Miss, birds carry messages on their wings from one end of the earth to another. You too are a bird of the heavens, you have sent a message from this red wooden house.' I didn't understand. 'Well,' I said, and of course I should have grasped what he meant . . . and the sisters rowed, came ever closer, their mother had sent them with the message that their brother had to come back from the rocky little island."

"What did they do then?"

"Nothing at first, just kept on rowing around the island. The rock we were sitting on was very small and the boat kept circling;

the circle grew smaller and smaller until the side of the boat brushed the rock where we were sitting, and the one who was rowing, the one who's now thin but was then fat, lifted the oars. I remember how drops of water were dripping from the oar, I can see it as if it were right in front of my eyes, and at that moment, the very moment when the last drop dripped from the oar and I managed to turn my head towards their brother, and the one who then was thin but is now fat says from the stern of the boat: 'Birger, Mama tells you to come home now.' And then the one who was fat and is now thin says: 'Birger will row alone. Maybe it's safer for the postmistress to come in our boat.'"

"And then?"

"The gun was raised, a shot rang out. I screamed and covered my eyes. For a long time I kept my hands over my eyes and when I look, the thin one is rowing, the fat one is paddling and they are already far away. Their brother had pulled out his binoculars, and with an utterly calm expression was studying the opposite shore from where flocks of birds were on the wing, rising, and then he said: 'I think I hit one, let's row over there.' And I took hold of the oars and rowed, and in the water a bird was floating, dead, and that night I got to know the first bird of my life. It was a merganser."

"Then?"

"And when we got married, not a single one of the relatives was present. Soon after we were married, he said, 'Let's go out to the rocky little islands.' And the following Sunday he preached on the subject of birds, right there in the church; that sermon was burned, a beautiful sermon and it flew up into the air as flames. But the sermon he preached a short time before he proposed to me, that one I still have in my head and I understood he was preaching only to me that Sunday: 'A *rara avis* has been found,' he preached so that the rafters of the church echoed, 'you see the birds of the heavens looking for mates and I already know of a bird who has found a mate. God has put in human hearts the same longing which makes the migratory birds . . ."

"I won't say any more, Alma. Heathenism? You too have said it was heathenism . . ."

"Then why are you crying?"

"I didn't cry. I left the church right after the sermon. I left in the middle of the service, I went off to think. I had a long struggle for I didn't know whether I had the longing in my heart which he thought was there, and I wasn't sure whether he was speaking in parables, after all, because he was always talking about birds, and people said he was a heathen clergyman. Just think, they filed complaints and I often had to serve dinner to the bishop when he'd come on inspection visits, but Birger preached about birds as if to defy everyone, even though the bishop was listening, and he got the bishop under his spell. When evening came, the bishop went off to the rocky little islands with him. It was one spring, like this, when he went with the bishop. The bishop sat in the stern; he was fat and the bow rose high in the air. Birger was thin, always thin; he didn't grow thinner and fatter like his sisters . . ."

"Didn't he ever preach the pure word, then?"

"Oh, Alma, 'God is in the small bird,' he would say, that is, my husband, and the bishop said to him, to the parson, 'My brother, my eyes grow moist when I but think of your sermon. You are a pure soul, you go right ahead and preach about your birds, but now and then put in the Word for the simple souls too. Talk to the farmer about the growth of his fields. Don't talk of birds alone, but also say a word or two about agriculture.' Well, Alma, to this day no one has preached a purer doctrine."

Alma thought over whether to ask if what she had heard from people was true, that on Sunday mornings the parson would go to the sacristy straight from hunting, dangling birds by their feet;

before the church service, he would go hunting, and directly from there, gun resting on his shoulder, straight to the sacristy, and from there to the altar, mud still clinging to his shoes.

But the parson's widow went on: "Maybe, well . . . maybe he took me only because of my name. 'Adele, Adelaide, that's what I'll call you,' he said. 'It's like a bird call—Adelaide.' At times I've thought my suffering may have come from my name. If it had been Elsa, for example, my life would have been like Elsa's . . . but why did you start asking about things like that, I won't sleep a wink to-night and I'll get another of those headaches . . . and if you, Alma, aren't strong enough to bear my husband's spirit, go away, go some-where else . . ."

"But the parson's widow should go off and rest first."

"I don't want to . . . talk with me. Where do you think my spirit will be after I die? If I die before you, I'll move in with you. What do you say? I'll finally move out of this house. But what if Onni and Birger should follow?"

"I don't know, but why did you go down to the shore last night when it's so stirred up there? They scream like the children of the damned, shouldn't listen, it gets one all worked up. When summer comes we'll go to the woods, where the cuckoo will sing to you, that's quite different . . ."

"But you know. Why do you pretend even though you know what kind of a devil a cuckoo is?" the parson's widow said crossly.

"I know men are like that too."

"There, you see," said the widow, and at once relented. "It's those kinds of comparisons that I look for in birds. For some reason you always pull out the cuckoo as your trump card. You won't learn anything else, you just won't."

"A bird is a bird. Comes, goes, one big, another small. A grown-up human being wasn't created just to peer at birds."

"Soon the goldeneyes will be coming, got to go there very early in the morning, you'll go with me, won't you? You can wear my fur coat, but you do remember that one has to be perfectly quiet, they have sensitive feelings. Above all, birds' feelings have to be considered, oh dear, how long it took for me to learn that. Hour after hour I had to lie without even stirring. If I so much as sneezed he'd look at me as if he wanted to kill me. Do you think the bishop's council would have made him a parson if the gentlemen of the council had had to lie in the cold crevice of a rock, under his command on one of those bird outings? I had to suffer through it all. If they'd known what he really was. He preached, he was gifted, exemplary, say the sisters-in-law. What was it that changed him, they ask, and they look at me."

SEVEN

The thin sister-in-law was waiting on customers. As soon as that old woman left, the pharmacy would be empty and if no new customers happened to come in, as soon as that one left, Alma would get down to the business which the thin one, wouldn't you know, already seemed to anticipate. She had glanced toward the door once, not straight at Alma but at the carafe of water on the table next to Alma. The old woman was buying camphor. What else would ordinary people buy when they had heart trouble? Alma was looking at the thin sister-in-law, who was now pretending not to see her. She had to position herself right in front of the counter so the thin one wouldn't seize the chance to slip off to the back room. The matter to be dealt with was clear to both; each one knew what was in question. Would she be sent away empty-handed like last time? Then she'd have to wander over to the doctor's wife, who'd then telephone to this thin one. Should she threaten to leave? She knew how to deliver that threat, even without the advice of the parson's widow, but since she hadn't left then even though she'd threatened to, it wouldn't work any more. Must threaten less often. The thin one already had the look on her face that Alma called the "against-the-parson's-widow" look. That stuck-up, sour face couldn't muster many expressions, but this one was so clear that if Alma had just happened to come across the thin one on a road and had seen it, she would have known: she's thinking ill of the parson's widow.

"How do you do." Alma was now standing in front of the counter. Teodolinda nodded, pushed the drawer shut, and acted as if she were about to leave.

"The parson's widow needs some medicine."

"You know very well it's only five days since I last gave you some. I am responsible. I won't even discuss it. Haven't I said so?"

"She walks around all night long, crying . . ."

"There's nothing anyone can do about that."

"But you've given some before."

"That's exactly why."

"Well, who's going to take care of her if my health gives out?"

"So, do you take the medicine too?" Teodolinda asked, and all of a sudden turned her pointy nose toward Alma.

For a moment Alma said nothing. Then she burst into a long speech and Teodolinda tried to break in to say that the dose of medicine had been so large she'd suspected that two people were taking it, and anyway, she wouldn't find it a miracle if Alma had taken some herself to calm her nerves. She knew full well that it wasn't easy with the parson's widow, she herself had been forced to experience it when she had, on demand, spent the night at the widow's house.

"Does she wander about the rooms?"

"You know perfectly well what she does. As it is now, I simply can't put up with it. All last night I was up with her when she was cursing . . ."

"About Birger? I mean the parson, her husband . . ."

"If it had only been that."

"I see."

The sister-in-law had understood.

"So please give me some now. I'm an outsider, there's family around here. Why doesn't somebody else come watch her? You know perfectly well that I'm not family and don't have to put up with it. Nights on end I can't sleep a wink, you don't know . . ."

"I do know," said Teodolinda. "She has to be put in an institution. I've thought about this, and I've talked about it with my sister. To an institution—do you understand . . . ?"

"Why are you screaming at me about it? I haven't done anything to her."

"To an institution. It simply won't work if you can't cope with her. So—to an institution . . ."

"How do you think you're going to get her into an institution, her, a healthy person."

Teodolinda didn't answer but Alma knew she was waiting, could see the words on her lips: couldn't Alma testify with the relatives?

"People like that belong in an institution," Teodolinda said, and remained standing stiff as a ramrod behind the counter, looking out toward the road.

"Let me have some. If I go home without it, tonight will be even worse. She'll get started during the day, but if she knows there's something for the night she's calm and in a good mood all day. I can't think of anything else."

"Take her out walking. Wouldn't gardening do her good?"

Alma let her make these suggestions, which had been proposed many times before, in order to say, "The doctor won't give her any, there's no point in my going there. Last week she made me go ask, and since I knew there was no way he'd give in, I pretended to walk to the doctor's house but instead went into the woods behind the cemetery. I didn't even go in, just stood in the woods back of the house and felt ashamed when people happened to see me out of the window. I pretended to be picking mushrooms even though mushrooms don't grow there. You know, you're a relative, and she sure hasn't died of those medicines—she's just so calm when she knows there are some on hand."

"Doesn't she sleep at all?"

"Not a wink last night because the medicine had run out. She walked around and around, and I brought her back from the shore early in the morning. And she's so mean, asked why I was trailing her around, insisted she was going to die anyway. I said that a gutsy person like her wouldn't die, and told her just to come out of there."

Teodolinda listened and Alma knew very well that the thin one's expression meant it wasn't appropriate to talk about her mistress in such a familiar manner, but Alma wouldn't leave, wouldn't budge at all. She had stood right here giving these same speeches many times before, and always managed to get what she'd come for.

"Doesn't she ever think of going into an institution?"

Alma reminded her of what had happened when she'd been sent to take a water cure. Then she'd come back with rheumatism. Ought to remember that.

Teodolinda was silent for a moment.

"But if . . ."

"Yes, what?"

"I was just thinking that if all of us together talked to the doctor, then . . ."

Alma didn't answer. After a moment she said, "She knows it."

"Knows what?"

"She knows you're set on the institution."

"Did you really have to talk to her about it? Was it really necessary?"

"I haven't talked, if that's what you mean, but the way it stands is that a person doesn't even dare think something, because she'll know what's up right away. The other day, when I'd just finished thinking that from now on I'll no longer . . . let this be the last time, I won't go begging anymore, well wouldn't you know she'd come out with, 'You, Alma, were just thinking about me, I could see it. You thought you wouldn't go to the pharmacy anymore, didn't you?'"

Teodolinda listened, tried to swat a fly that had settled on the cash register.

"The problem is, how can I explain it to . . . if I give her the amount of medicine she wants, and the doctor has told me that I absolutely mustn't give it, he's strongly opposed to giving her any medicine at all. Who am I responsible to? I can't order packet after packet, and when nobody else around these parts . . . they'll think I'm the one."

"And besides, we haven't got any now . . ." Teodolinda tried to lie.

"Looks like a jar of it right there." Alma knew what was in each jar, all right. That was the very same jar she'd seen her take the medicine from, and one time the parson's widow had been after her just to go take it out of that jar if they wouldn't otherwise . . .

Teodolinda's face reddened with anger.

"She's your relative, not mine. I can get work somewhere else."

That was the threat that had done the trick so far; if the thin one didn't give in at that, the parson's widow would send Alma to the fat one to say the same thing, and the fat one, who couldn't even bear thinking she would have to get involved with caring for the widow, would call the thin one right away or go over to the pharmacy herself, as she'd done once. "Now, go," the parson's widow had said. "Elsa has gone and talked to her." And when Alma went, the medicine had already been prepared and the thin one said, "Just this once. Tell her this is the last time." That was long ago, long, long ago.

"Begging isn't my job," Alma had once said to the parson's widow. "Why don't you go yourself? I don't have the nerve to go begging." But the widow, ashamed to face her sisters-in-law, was never willing to go herself, no, a smile appeared on her lips, you didn't have to see anything else, all you had to see was that smile and you'd just know you'd have to go to the pharmacy again.

"Not especially, so long as she gets . . . when she gets the medicine she isn't at all restless. Yesterday she was helping me weed a flowerbed."

"And those outings?"

"Hasn't talked about them at all. And if she does say something, I'll just refuse to go."

"Maybe it would be a good idea for you to go. She might calm down then. What if she isn't getting outdoors enough?"

"Nothing helps with that."

"Oh, is that so? Well, that's the way it is, it's exactly what Elsa said. She knew, all right; Elsa tried to keep her company when it was really bad."

They had talked about all of this before. Alma knew she was winning.

And now Teodolinda was wrapping up the bottle, saying she didn't know how the widow could afford all this medicine.

"The parson's widow says that every pharmacy has got enough so that the higher authorities won't ask who has prescribed it."

"But I have to write out the prescription, and that's exactly what I'm tired of doing, having to come up with the names of non-existent people. I can't write her name on every single one of them. She has the idea that people don't know she's doing this, but the whole world knows. If she sends you, that's one thing, but when she used to send strange children to ask for her! Should never have given any in the first place, but you know what started it all. At that time she really did need the medicine."

Alma knew. Each one of the sisters-in-law had told her separately how they'd taken turns running medicines to her. The parson's widow had been endlessly going around and around in circles, screaming, and had calmed down only after getting a strong dose of medicine, and finally it had become a habit. If she didn't get it, she'd start going in circles again and trotting out her earlier fits. The relatives would give in, and could think of no way out but to place her in an institution.

"See to it that she doesn't take too much."

"I will."

"And try to get her outside."

"I sure have been trying to."

With the package in hand, Alma left the pharmacy and Teodolinda remained behind the counter, as if wondering how she had once again, despite her refusals . . . "Was she here running an errand for Adele?" Holger asked.

Teodolinda didn't answer. Her husband asked why she'd given in, when they'd already decided to put a stop to it. Wouldn't it be possible to arrange for institutional care bit by bit?

"It's difficult."

"Won't she consent to it?"

"Who?"

"Alma."

"I don't know, I haven't spoken to her. I did mention a water cure but she doesn't seem to think much of that either. After all, she's got a job there. Where else would she have it so good? Adele's totally under her thumb."

Holger was looking at Alma, who was still in view on the birch lane and was just turning onto the main road.

"You didn't give her any, did you?"

"What?"

"Money."

"No."

"Was that what she asked for?"

"Yes."

"She looks more like a man than a woman. Yes, yes, there's more man in that woman than there was in your brother Birger. I wonder whether there was any man in him at all. There may be a pretty simple reason for Adele's insomnia, yes, yes, she's not decrepit yet, and was left a widow . . . wait, how old was she then?" The pharmacist counted: "Less than forty."

"Thirty-six," said Teodolinda.

"And now she's about to turn fifty."

"Add it up," said Holger. "And how old is this man-woman?"

"Who?"

"Alma, that's who."

"I guess she's over thirty."

"She looks like she's been eating well," Holger said. "I wonder where Adele gets the money to pay her wages."

"That's just it. Adele hardly pays anything."

"Out of kind-heartedness, is that what it is?"

Teodolinda snickered and said "Kind-heartedness! She's got it good, gets to be the boss. That's why she stays there. Well, Adele has her pension. I guess they get by, but sometimes I really do wonder what they manage to live on."

"Getting richer and richer, I'll bet. Alma has planted a vegetable garden and keeps a cow and a pig. She wanted to take in summer guests but Adele got all upset, I hear she can't take it. Did you know Alma has made over the carriage shed into a pigsty? Plans to keep ten pigs there. That's a man for Adele," Holger added. "As for Birger, someone even had to write his sermons for him. Birger was a gifted boy when he was young. I don't understand what went wrong with him. Was it Adele's influence?"

"Adele? Your brother was a fool, a sillier fool than Adele. If you don't remember, I'll tell you."

Teodolinda was silent.

"It's not that I cared for Adele. She wasn't an appropriate wife for Birger at all. Wonder what on earth made him take her."

"You mean, take her as a cross for us to bear."

"You could say that. He himself dies off, leaves us a widow and a bird collection as a cross to bear."

"Well, you sure haven't had to put yourself out. I guess I'm the one who's related. Anyway, I don't know why I should be the one responsible for looking after her. She's not a blood relation."

"Your brother's widow. It's out of pride that you look after her, the pride that possesses all of you. You're very impractical people. If I were you, I'd let her stew in her own juice and lead her life any way she wants to. She'd be perfectly capable of helping herself . . ."

"Adele?" asked Teodolinda. As if her husband didn't know how many times Adele had been left to look after herself and what it had come to. The best possible solution was to have that man-woman stay with Adele.

"Who was it, then, who asked her back last time?"

"I did. Do you think for one minute that Adele would manage to bring herself to do anything? All Adele knows is how to weep and beg, and then I have to take action."

"Why don't you do what I tell you? Why?" Holger had moved over to take a cigarette from the table in the back parlor and was now talking with a cigarette in his mouth. "Why wasn't it done? It shouldn't be difficult to convince that man-woman to testify in court that Adele needed institutional care."

"And you'd leave her there for the rest of her days?"

"Who said anything about that? They would weed those habits out of her . . ."

"You know perfectly well that no one gets out of there. And besides, who's going to pay for it? She isn't considered indigent. And your pride wouldn't let you acknowledge that she's indigent, isn't that right?"

"Well, she's got her house, and she'd get some money from that."

"It would have to be sold first. Do you think Adele would agree to it?"

"Oh, that's right."

"Helander the storekeeper would be ready to . . ."

"And what would he do with it?"

"Move his store here, right by the road. He'd have a house all ready."

"And would Adele stay as his tenant?"

"Could rent something for her someplace else."

"Can't go very far, after all. Your practical suggestions are pretty simple. You know, she's got a son too," Teodolinda said.

"The boy will grow up and leave home."

"But what would the boy say? Adele is his mother, after all, and when you come down to it the matter isn't so simple."

The pharmacist was eyeing the Latin labels on the sides of the crocks. The sun was dappling the porcelain, a lone tree branch cast a shadow on the side of the camphor jar as if it were a living thing, a round one that kept turning its head.

"I once asked Adele for the boreal owl, but would she give it to me? No, she certainly wouldn't. I would have brought it here to keep the other one company."

"What if you'd ask, say that you won't give her anything more until she gives up that owl?"

"No way to do that, no question about it. If she were to start that, before long all of Adele's birds would find their way here to the pharmacy. That man-woman would be standing with a bird in hand at the pharmacy door. Don't you think the man-woman wouldn't like to get rid of the birds, she hates them more than anyone."

"You've been at the bottle again, go away." Teodolinda coldly shoved aside her husband's hands. "Do you give some to the man-woman, or . . . doesn't she come by to ask for some? You know Adele sometimes takes a nip."

"I don't think she's exactly a drunk." Holger burst out laughing. "Don't say such crazy things. It makes me laugh to think that Adele . . ."

"Do you think I haven't known it for a long time? She calls it medicine, and even when Birger was still alive she asked me for medicine, and besides, you've taken some to her yourself, don't pretend you haven't—do you suppose I wouldn't know?—and once the man-woman told you to get out. It certainly wasn't very pleasant when she came to tell me about it and again I had to give her some new medicine. I think that Alma takes some too. Bromides for Adele; *spiritus* for her."

But it made Holger laugh even more. He simply couldn't control himself as he imagined his wife's pious sister-in-law with her whiskered maid. That the two of them, the one pious and the other virtuous . . . Holger knew it, virtuous. Alma didn't even want to be touched. "That woman's really got something, 'some real pizzazz,'" he said aloud.

Teodolinda glanced at her husband and she knew. She couldn't care less, for a long time she couldn't have cared less about things like that—and besides, she didn't care about Alma. She was sure about Alma; her dour, mannish face floated up before her eyes just as it had turned away a while back at the pharmacy door. Adele always gave Alma a reward after these trips, a silver spoon. Alma had already stored away two dozen silver spoons. "What am I going to do with them?" Alma had asked, but she took them greedily anyway. She kept collecting Adele's things in boxes and chests in her room.

"Adele's going to give her another silver spoon, you'd better believe it," Holger said. "One time when I was joking around I took a bottle over there: why the hell don't you give me a spoon too? They both acted all dignified as if they had no idea what I meant. I took the bottle away. Damn it, I've got to get at these dignified ones somehow, I thought, I'm going to have my fun out of it and since it isn't good enough for you, I'll take it away, and I said straight out that I'll take it away since it isn't good enough, and the women only sat there in the same position. You'd have thought they didn't even realize they had a visitor . . . silly, silly, that's what they are. Sometimes I go there just for the fun of it. It makes me laugh when they look at each other as if they were having a secret session on how to get rid of this one, well, let's see, Adele gathers the last shreds of her gentility and addresses me by name and tries to hold a conversation . . ."

The wife looked at her husband so coldly and for such a long time that his speech dried up.

EIGHT

"Yes," said the fat one, "I understand."

Elsa had already made up her mind not to ask Alma to sit down in the kitchen as she'd done last time. She wished Alma would be on her way as soon as possible.

"Have you spoken to the people at the pharmacy?"

"It's no use. They tell me they don't know what to do. And me, I'm not even a member of the family. What can I do about it when it starts up again?"

"For heaven's sake keep your voice down so the children don't hear." Elsa shut both doors that had been standing open. She went over and stood on the threshold to the parlor, and after waiting there a moment and gazing about her with an air of indifference to show it was time for Alma to leave, she started dusting the leaves of the India rubber plant.

But now Alma in turn stepped over to the threshold of the parlor. She followed the fat one's movements as she was dusting the piano, the gleaming curves of the easy chairs, and noted that the rubber plants, which used to be on opposite sides of the window, had been moved so that they stood side by side in back of the piano. The drapes had been changed too. In summer there had been lace curtains, but now they were kind of velvety; she'd never seen the likes of that fabric anywhere. The floor was gleaming. The sound of children's voices came from the dining room. The fat one disappeared quickly into the dining room, and Alma heard her speaking in a commanding tone. The children's voices stopped. They'd been ordered out of the dining room.

"Has the pharmacist been by?"

Elsa was shaking out small lace doilies, organizing objects on top of the bookcase. Alma was studying a picture of a warship until she became aware that the fat one had noticed her looking at it.

"It's none of my business."

"It's just too bad the whole village knows it," said Elsa.

"I haven't been talking," Alma answered quickly.

"Is that so? You told *me*, at least. Maybe you've told others too."

Alma didn't answer.

She'd gotten into the habit of searching, with her eyes, for those objects the parson's widow had said had been stolen from her, and as Elsa kept opening the cabinet in which the silver was kept behind glass, she tried to guess which ones of those . . .

"Well, she's got her silver, all right," Elsa burst out in a scornful, bitter voice. She stood with her back to Alma as if waiting for something.

"I don't know."

"Well, isn't it there any more?" Elsa had turned to face her. "Where has she hidden it all? I've asked you about it time and time again. You can't really imagine that I believe you don't know. Has it been sold?"

"I don't know."

"I only remember that Adele gave you a cake server as a Christmas present."

"I sure didn't steal it."

"No, no, of course you didn't. Anyway, most of the silver that stayed with Adele after the parson's death doesn't really belong to her. It was agreed that we sisters would get our share. It had all been agreed upon. Birger was honest. When Mama died, I asked Birger whether that wouldn't be the time to see what was whose. He promised. Year after year he promised."

Elsa became silent, then continued. "There's no point talking to you about these matters. They're not the business of any outsider, just as you said a moment ago. But I too have had many sleepless nights. I guess it's a guilty conscience that keeps Adele awake. For me, it's the injustice. Oh, well, it's my own fault. I should have demanded at the start that everything be divided. Birger had no right to keep everything that was left in the estate after Mama died. And if my sister had wanted, she could have filed suit against Adele. Teodolinda didn't even get her own things, her own personal belongings mind you, away from Adele. I asked her, doesn't it break your heart to see Adele wearing the shawl that Mama, bless her soul, crocheted, the very shawl that was promised to you. She only answered, 'Why?' Supposedly, she had promised it to Adele. And whatever I asked, the answer was always the same: 'I've promised it to Adele.' I've never denied that the piano was bought specifically for Teodolinda. She showed clear musical talent from the time she was a little girl. My father and mother were cultivated, fair-minded people. Could they possibly have foreseen how life would change after they died? Our home was always sparkling clean. Mama certainly knew and understood how her only son's home ought to look. Even when they were in the parsonage, it was the same story. Never in her life has Adele known how to put a single thing in its place, though she was always coming around to complain about cleaning from morning to night. At first I tried to help her, to teach her a little, but instead of being grateful she jumped on me."

Elsa stopped talking.

"It was the same story with me," Alma said.

"I know."

After a while, Elsa asked Alma to sit down. She pointed towards an easy chair. Gingerly, Alma sat down on the edge of the chair. Elsa settled herself on the sofa, between two pillows. Alma wondered which of them had been stolen from the parson's widow. She had talked about a blue-and-yellow one with cross-stitches. Both of these were cross-stitched and were more or less the same color, but this one looked a bit more frayed.

Elsa broke the silence. "And what about the boy? His mother has spoiled him rotten."

"I don't know," said Alma.

"My husband isn't home now."

What do you need your husband for in this matter, Alma thought, remembering full well the doctor's glances when he'd happened to be at home whenever Alma, pressed by the parson's widow, had stopped by to borrow some money from the fat one.

"Did Adele really say so again?"

"She sure did."

"It's true that sometimes, simply to avoid an argument, you understand, I've condescended to write out a prescription for Adele without telling my husband. I've had to forge his signature then. Teodolinda and I have agreed about that. We have little in common these days except these crimes Adele forces us to commit. My husband has flatly refused to write a single prescription for her, but Adele's a clever one, always has been. She just doesn't give up. She even went so far as to send some of the village children to the pharmacy, and if they didn't succeed in getting anything there, she told them to come to me. And when I'd done it once, I had to do it again. That's how it got started. If not me, she'd call Teodolinda. If not Teodolinda, she'd go weeping to the pharmacist. Holger . . . oh well, what's the point of hiding it? You know his habits. I would say to Adele, 'Don't talk on the telephone. Come over here and talk about it yourself.' That only made it worse. She would come here and not leave until she got what she wanted. And if she didn't, she'd talk on the phone on purpose, would keep calling and calling so that either Teodolinda or I had to run over and grab the telephone out of her hand, to break off the call so the operator wouldn't hear. Of course they heard anyway. Teodolinda and I had an agreement on that. Whenever it was Teodolinda's turn, either Holger or some-one who happened to be in the yard would run over here from the pharmacy. We had agreed that if Teodolinda couldn't come over herself, she would tell the messenger to say, 'The pharmacist's wife asked you to stop over for coffee.' I would then say to the messenger, 'The doctor's wife has given an invitation for coffee.' What shows we had to put on! Once, when we had visitors, one of the little boys from the village comes running straight into the parlor to bring the word. 'What?' asked Herman. 'Where are you going now?' Had to lie that Teodolinda was sick. 'But I just saw her walking in the yard.' 'Aren't you going to let me see my sister?' My husband began to have his suspicions. But there was no other way. Adele lived on the telephone. She talked for so long that one always had to promise in the end. She'd cry, say she was dying. We would run, as Holger used to say, like pawns on a chess board, along the edges of that square field, which doesn't even belong to us but to Paananen, as you know, and when Paananen, a far-sighted man, moved into town and leased the fields and the renter planted grain there, our running left paths along the edges of the field. Teodolinda walks on the left side, when you're looking at it from here, I on the right side by the edge of the woods so that people wouldn't see. Teodolinda doesn't give a hoot, never has, about what people will say."

Elsa became silent. Her face and neck became red, flushed. She dug a handkerchief from the folds of her puffed sleeve, dried her eyes.

"It's the same with me," Alma said. "Do you think I don't under-stand? It's through the woods that I come here, through the woods to the pharmacy. I've often been ashamed when someone's seen me climbing over the cemetery fence. Once I fell into a nettle bush but the parson's widow only laughed. But I can't go in and out of the pharmacy without someone seeing me. I've got to go through the yard before I can get to it."

"What about using the kitchen stairs?"

"The pharmacist's wife told me not to."

"That's what my sister is like, and if I try to talk some sense into her she just says, if she answers at all, that Adele is her brother's wife. Of course, she's my brother's widow too, I've tried to explain. 'If you don't want to,' she answers, 'I'll forge Herman's name.' I have to give in. And it's impossible to write every prescription to Adele's name. Each one of us, including you, even the washerwoman who never in her living day has put a single drop of medicine into her mouth and is proud of it, even she has gotten her name on a prescription more than a couple of times. This endless lying, all for Adele. Can you doubt I'm on the verge of losing my mind . . . ?"

"The same with me."

"Where's the silver?" Elsa looked sharply at Alma. "Has it . . . ?"

"It has."

"Been sold?"

"Been hidden away."

"Why?"

"I don't know."

"Is she afraid of thieves?"

"I have no idea."

"Where is it?"

"Under the birds' eggs."

"Did she show you?"

"Put them there herself. I started cleaning one day. The parson's widow walking right behind me. Of course, she's always walking around and talking. Sometimes it makes me mad because I can never do anything in peace. If I go out, she comes after me and talks; if I'm washing dishes she comes and stands behind me and talks. One day I got mad and said, is any cleaning going to be done now or not? The widow went upstairs, got mad but didn't say a thing. I started in. I thought, now I'm going to do that thorough, that really thorough cleaning, the one the parson's widow is forever talking about but never lets get done. Well, you know . . ."

Elsa nodded.

"I thought, now I'm really going to do it. I thought, first the bureau drawers. I'll empty out every one of them and see what's stinking in there."

Elsa nodded.

"It was the same thing when Birger was alive. Poor Birger. Mama was tidy, our house was always sparkling clean. Birger's life wasn't easy. One time I went to the parsonage. I wouldn't have gone but Teodolinda asked me to come, on account of people. On account of people, yes, it's always on account of people that she wants it, never when I want it, never, nothing. I went. I looked around. I could understand that the whole downstairs was a mess. Birger had come in from hunting and was skinning his birds. I went upstairs, to the 'neater' part of the house as they call it. I took a look around, and then stared right at Teodolinda and asked whether she knew why a line had been strung across the parlor, from one door to another. Teodolinda pretended not to see me. 'Why is that line there?' I asked Adele. She was only a little over thirty then. Any other woman, and a clergyman's wife at that, would have been ashamed, but guess what Adele answered? 'Birger put it there so that clothes wouldn't be all over the floor. Birger's so tidy that he won't, even by accident, step on bed-linens, or even on my scarf.' 'Why don't you hang your scarf on the line, then?' I asked, and picked up Birger's clerical cloak from the floor, do you understand? Adele had tossed her husband's coat onto the floor just like that. 'And this doesn't belong on the line. Its place is on a coat-hanger, neatly, in the office.' I couldn't control myself. Teodolinda gave me a furious look. 'That's right,' I said, 'you go right ahead and look.' 'Control yourself,' Teodolinda said. 'I won't,' I told her. 'What if the bishop happened to come by, and this coat was lying on the floor?' And when the bishop really did come, I took off for the parsonage before you could even blink. Another woman would have been grateful for the help, but Adele only got angry. I didn't care. I had to save Birger's reputation. Without saying a word I took down the line. Without a word I did a big cleaning. I baked, took my maid with me, and I absolutely refused to leave until all the guests had gone. But what did Adele go and do? Lock herself in. The bishop asked, 'Where is your wife?' and Birger had to lie that Adele was sick. But the minute the guests had left, Adele got better right away. And that wasn't the only time it happened, until Herman finally forbade it and said that my place was in my own home and not as head cook of the parsonage. And do you know what Adele gave me as a Christmas present? A bird's egg."

"Same here, and her torn apron."

"And Teodolinda, my only close blood relation still alive, not counting my own three children, insisting that Adele isn't a penny-pincher." Elsa let out a sound that began as a laugh and ended as a bitter snort.

"You've had quite a time of it."

"And what did she do when the parsonage burned? I'll admit it was a shocking incident, but that's just why. One would have thought she would have grown a bit more humble, but no. She drove my only sister out of her own home. What my poor sister had to suffer because of her sister-in-law! And it wasn't enough for Adele to keep Teodolinda half-starved, but her own husband too. People do talk, and it's no lie that the parson simply starved to death. If he had had a different sort of wife, his health wouldn't have broken so quickly. Strong and ample nourishment, a good, balanced diet could have saved him. And rest, rest, Herman says. But Adele didn't quarrel only with Teodolinda; she tortured her husband day and night. Teodolinda didn't say anything. She suffered, suffered in silence, that's the way she's always been. Teodolinda has never confessed to me that she knew everything ahead of time. She knew all right, had heard it with her own ears that what was left of the estate and which was supposed to be divided between us two sisters . . . just then, when Teodolinda was living with Birger and Adele, that's when it must have happened. I'm sure that Adele forced Birger, brother to the two of us, Teodolinda's and my only brother, forced him shamelessly to falsify our father and mother's last will. Adele had the papers drawn up at that time. That's what those perpetual nightly fights were about, the fights that started rumors flying through all the parishes. Adele wasn't one to keep her voice down, not she, and Teodolinda didn't say 'control yourself' as she'd often say to me. I remember very well how cleverly Adele managed it: by pretending to be devoted to the birds, she trapped poor Birger in her snares, and then Teodolinda, who was devoted to Birger. He was dear to me too, but his devotion to birds I did consider a sickness. Because Birger was physically weak, we sisters had been taught to be nice to him ever since we were children, and of course he was a gifted boy, but then Adele came along. It was as if they egged each other on into this insanity about birds. Adele did it in a calculated manner. Even if Birger's devotion to birds was sick, it still was, as Herman says, scientific, but what, then, was Adele's?"

Elsa fell silent.

"Well," she said after taking a good many deep breaths when her long speech was over, "well, what happened? Did she let you do the cleaning?"

"Hummm," Alma began. "Did she ever! Every single day for years. People have always talked about it. When the pharmacist's wife hired me, when she led me over to have the parson's widow take a look at me, she talked to me just as we were standing at the gate, about to go in the door, and suddenly said in a low voice, 'You will do a big, thorough cleaning as the very first thing, won't you?' The next day I tried, I started in on the kitchen . . . and I said that however back-woodsy our own place was, and even though my poor departed mother didn't exactly keep things as neat as a pin, we still didn't have the kind of mess the parson's widow had. I took a pail and a basket and started gathering stuff up from the floor. There was a pile of all kinds of junk in the corner: bits of grass, birds' wings, pebbles, and whatever else I took for rubbish, and suddenly the parson's widow asks, 'What are you trying to do?' 'Take out this trash.' Did I get to take it out? Well, you know." The fat one nodded.

"I've done the cleaning by brute force, I've done it in secret. Every time. But the windows are open even in winter. I close the windows by force. And always get scolded for it."

Elsa nodded.

"And she scolds you most of all."

"That doesn't surprise me."

The fat one did seem to have got her feelings hurt, though. Alma changed her tone.

"Not directly, of course, but I guess I understand."

"What about the silver?"

Elsa had asked about that a couple of times now.

"That's what I came over to talk about. Because if it comes up, and I wouldn't bet against it, she might even say thieves have run off with it. That's the kind of look she has now. She's got something on her mind again."

"Has the pharmacist's wife been over to the house?"

"No, not for a long time. The pharmacist stopped by on Saturday."

"Did you hear what they were talking about?"

"The pharmacist? You know, he's always drunk."

"Well, he does take care of the pharmacy."

Elsa gazed past Alma.

"Did Adele make tea for Holger?"

"She always serves the pharmacist tea."

"Did she have the silver laid out on the table?"

"Oh, sure. She always has the silver service brought in when the pharmacist stops by. But you just said something about the silver."

"Well, that was on Monday when I tried to clean again. I got up before four o'clock in the morning. I thought she'll still be asleep, it's in the morning that she sleeps if she sleeps at all. I went into the parlor very quietly, to the cabinet where the birds' eggs . . . well, there are some in every single cabinet, but the one right in the middle, that shelf smells the worst. Now I'm going to take a look, I thought. You can pry it open if you push in the point of a knife and raise the lock with it. Once, when it was really smelly I used the same trick, and there was a piece of cheese, the very same cheese that a farmer's wife had once brought in and which had then vanished. The parson's widow and I had been looking for it, and I'd thought the dog had gotten into the kitchen, the pharmacist's hound dog that always jumps right into the parson's widow's lap, but well, it doesn't carry any contagious diseases and she's not afraid of it even if it's run straight in from the outhouse, but with people, no matter how clean they are, she's always imagining she'll catch some disease from them . . . anyway, it was the cheese that turned up that time. I took it out. The parson's widow didn't notice a thing. I guess she'd hidden it away so that I wouldn't get my share of it, and then forgotten it, I don't know. Now and then I get something anyway, and that time I cleaned it out. And again the cabinet began stinking. I didn't say a thing, just kept on sniffing. And guess what I found?"

"Another piece of cheese."

"Half the chunk of pork that the pharmacist's wife had sent along with the pharmacist as a birthday present for the parson's widow. Unsalted meat. Just guess what a stench that made after it had been rotting there for a couple of weeks. And now guess some more."

"Dirty clothes. At least, that's what it's been until now."

Alma didn't say anything for a while, only looked.

"The silver . . . ?"

"The silver."

"The spoons? The spoons Mama got as a wedding present, the ones I haven't seen for seven years?"

"All of them."

"All the spoons. Was it eight? Yes, there were eight of them . . ."

"All of them. All the silver in the house: the service, the candlesticks, spoons, everything that's got even a tiny bit of silver, the paper-cutting knife she keeps between the pages of her prayer book, that, too."

"Did you see for sure?"

"Yes, I did. There, mixed in with the birds' eggs, first she'd hidden the pork, and she must have put the silver there the night before because I heard her making some kind of commotion all night long, and I thought, my God, what is it now, usually she stays upstairs even when she's awake."

"What did you do?"

"I took the rotting stuff out of there. It was so rotten you couldn't have boiled it into soap anymore. She'd tried salting it, but you can imagine what her salting would amount to . . ." Elsa nodded.

"Now you know. So if the question comes up, that's where it all is."

"Have you told anybody?"

"Who would I tell? The pharmacist's wife won't condescend to listen to anything about the parson's widow, and the pharmacist, he only laughs. I've got to be responsible for everything."

"So she sent you to ask for some medicine?"

"That's right. It started back the day before yesterday. She stayed awake all night and all day, trailing after me the whole time. I thought, all right, walk, you'll get some fresh air, you'll sleep. On purpose I walked over to the sauna cabin and to the shed where the fish nets are kept, did a little cleaning around there. All the time she was walking around and whining. Once I even pretended to go get some. I'll go right away, I said, and set out walking. I guessed she'd look out the window, so I walked along the road as far as you could see from the window. Then I jumped over the fence next to the woods and walked in the woods for a little while, worked my way back along the road and said that the doctor's wife wasn't home. 'Go to the pharmacy,' she said. 'But you yourself said it was the doctor's turn to give some,' I said."

"You mean money."

Alma nodded.

"Medicine and money, prescriptions and money," Elsa repeated several times over. "But to be fair," she went on, "I'm not the only one to suffer from all this. Teodolinda has, too. The pharmacy folks have the idea that it's my responsibility to give more often than they do. And at least Teodolinda has a husband who understands the matter, but my husband has principles."

"I guess the pharmacist's wife doesn't care whether the money goes to Lappeenranta or to the parson's widow."

"Have you been getting your pay?" Elsa asked, but something in her voice put Alma on guard.

"Well, what about my pay? Do you think she leaves my money alone? If she does pay me my wages, and she pays whenever there's money, she gets all high and mighty and says, 'There it is,' like she'd be tossing a scrap of bread to a dog, but only a few days go by before she's ready to borrow from me. 'Where have you been squandering your money?' she asks if I tell her I don't have any. When I first came, the pharmacist gave me some advice right away. He told me to put my pay in the bank as soon as I got it. I wondered about that. I wondered a lot. Now nothing surprises me. Not even when I found all the silver."

"So where does the money go?"

"Where?" Alma smirked.

"When her pension money comes, couldn't you take it away from her and give it out to her in small amounts?" Alma asked.

Elsa sighed. "That's been tried. Everything's been tried. Nobody can control Adele."

"And she doesn't even read the books that come in, she only orders them. The tables are flooded with books and pictures of birds, and all the time she's teaching me. 'See what this bird is,' and oh, my God, if I don't learn. Not to mention those papers, the whole mess of newspapers. 'If you'd only let those older papers be carted away.' 'No.'"

"I know," said Elsa. "I remember it as if it were yesterday. I was just about to throw out a rusty old can. She grabs hold of my hand, and I thought she was having a heart attack. 'What are you doing?' I said, and I got scared. 'Give it to me.' 'What are you going to do with it?' 'Look at it.' After that incident I spoke up and said to Teodolinda . . .at that time Adele was barely a fiancée, if that, and if Teodolinda had firmly taken my side, Adele would never have had the chance to develop into even a momentary fiancée for poor Birger . . . I said to Teodolinda that this marriage had to be stopped. But what did Teodolinda go and do? She even embraced, stiffly, to be sure, that young woman whom Birger brought to meet

Mama. But Mama just looked, didn't extend her hand. Where was Adele's pride then? Wasn't her behavior calculated from the very beginning? Before they were married, she cooed to Birger like a dove, a real vulture—but there's no point talking about it. I've gone over these things a hundred times, and not even Teodolinda, however well I know she understands all this, has ever confessed that moment when Adele asked to keep that rusty can for herself, supposedly to look at the picture on its label, that very moment when we sisters should have mounted a fight together. Mama fell ill from sorrow. Then came Paananen, came Adele. All at the same time. Poor dear Mama."

"Let me have some," Alma sighed. "If I go back empty-handed the same thing will start all over again."

"Does she really not sleep at all?"

"Not a wink for at least two nights. Me, I'm going crazy too, because she doesn't let me sleep either. If you only knew . . ."

"You're not the only one. Everybody who spends as much as one day under the same roof with Adele wants to get away from there in a hurry. Have you tried to talk?"

"She guesses."

"Have you said, then . . . ?"

"I don't even have to think, I don't dare think. She can even read my thoughts. She stops in the middle of a room, cocks her head as if she's listening, as to some non-existent telephone receiver. Yesterday she said, 'Now the doctor's wife is telling her husband bad things about me.'"

"What then?"

"She laughed to herself."

Elsa was silent for a moment.

"What time was it?"

"Around five in the afternoon."

"Herman wasn't even home then."

"How much is she asking for?" Elsa asked after a while.

"Didn't say how much. The books are in the mail. They've got to be paid for."

"I'll call the pharmacy."

NINE

"So you walked along the road together?"

"Road?" said Alma. "What's wrong with walking along the road?"

"Did you meet anybody?"

"There's always people walking along the road."

The parson's widow took a drinking glass out of a cabinet, looked at it against the light.

"The lilacs are blooming," Alma said.

"So they are. You stopped in front of the little bush together, Holger carrying the fishing poles and you the birch-bark creel."

"Why has the parson's widow started doing the dishes?"

She was allowed to be in her own kitchen, doing her own dishes, wasn't she?

"Did you meet Elsa?"

"No."

By now Alma could guess the meaning of all the dishes piled on table and floor.

"You're looking at me," said the parson's widow. "Why shouldn't I be allowed to wash dishes in my own kitchen?"

"Caught some fish."

"Where's the pharmacist? I just happened to see out the window that you were petting a cat together. Puss, puss, you said, and both of your hands were on the cat's back at the same time, and the cat was curled up on a rock. You know very well that I can't abide cats, and you know why. It's the doctor's cat. Why does Elsa let her cat come into my yard?"

"Cats always run around in the springtime."

"Did the pharmacist give the cat a fish?" The parson's widow kept polishing the drinking glass and again examined it against the light.

"One, a small one."

Alma tied an apron around her waist.

"You don't have to work today, you must be tired."

"Then I'll go clean the fish."

The parson's widow looked out into the yard.

"So you're going because the pharmacist still seems to be out there near the lilac bush."

"The pharmacist is playing with the cat. If a cat or dog comes along, he always plays with it."

"So you were taking the bream nets out of the lake." The parson's widow was trying to reach up to take some dishes from the topmost shelf.

Since Alma didn't answer, the widow repeated her words, adding, "This is the fourth time. I only wonder why the pharmacist is still hanging around near the lilac bush."

"I guess he's watching the cat eat all the fish."

"You just said he gave the doctor's cat only one fish. And besides, I happened to look out the window when you were both standing near the lilac bush and I saw you tossing one fish after another to the doctor's cat. I also happened to see the new postmistress walking along the road, probably on her way to the store. I guess you didn't notice her, but she certainly noticed you. You see, she stopped at the gate and looked into my yard. All right, Mrs. Broms, parson's widow, keep on taking dishes from the cabinet, I thought. For once, wash your dishes yourself so that once in your life you can drink from a clean glass. I'd also intended to go fetch water from the well because as far as I know, that water has been standing there in the tub for over two days, with no cover on it, but because the postmistress was right at the gate at that very moment, of course I couldn't. You'll take a towel into your hand, I said to myself, you'll dry and polish the drinking glasses first, then the china."

"I'll go clean the fish, then."

"To the well? Is that where you're headed?" The parson's widow was smiling that peculiar smile of hers. "The cat has a fish in its mouth," she said, looking out the window. "The pharmacist seems to be sitting on the well cover. The doctor's cat is eating, crunching away right next to my well. And you know there's a chaffinch's nest in that birch whose branches curve so beautifully over the well."

"The pharmacist asked me to go row for him."

Alma was looking around her. Table and chairs and floors, all full of dishes. The widow had also carried into the kitchen the china and silver that was kept in the dining room cabinet. The coffee pots, pans, and cooking pots were all out.

"I wonder when this coffee pot was last polished. When my husband was alive, I had my coffee served from a gleaming copper pot every morning. When I was looking after my household myself, the kettles weren't blackened with soot, and while I may have spoken ill of my late mother-in-law, I certainly held to her tradition and never let my pots and pans get all blackened. I wonder who could have set this poor little kettle over an open flame. The parson's widow was speaking in a wistful tone, and was attempting to scour the sooty bottom of the kettle with a wet rag.

"We haven't got any Sampo powder. You yourself said not to polish it."

"And what about this?" The widow took a wet rag from the wood-box next to the stove. "This smells bad," she said, and tossed it back into the wood-box.

"I see the pharmacist is coming in. Oh, dear, when my husband was alive, people certainly didn't set fishing poles leaning against a ladder. They hung them on nails on the wall of the house so children wouldn't hurt themselves on the hooks. They were hung up high enough and no one brought a smelly fish creel into the house. Fish used to be cleaned down by the lake."

The pharmacist's steps resounded in the vestibule. The door opened.

"Good day, Adele. You were sleeping when we left."

"Good day. Beautiful weather, isn't it?"

The parson's widow took a gravy boat out of the cabinet, set it onto the floor.

"Fish were biting well. We got seven good-sized perch."

"So I see."

The parson's widow kept moving dishes from one place to another. She kept her back to the pharmacist and was busy stacking dishes. First the soup bowls, then the dinner plates. She kept muttering under her breath.

"Well, now some coffee would really hit the spot," Holger said behind her back.

"Alma, would you be so kind as to make some coffee for the pharmacist."

Silence followed. The widow was arranging dishes, quietly humming a hymn and taking great care not to turn towards the bench near the door where the pharmacist was sitting next to the blue tub.

"But dear Adele, do you have a headache?"

"Oh, my friend, whatever makes you think that? These crystal plates belong in the dining room cabinet, not in the kitchen cupboard," the parson's widow said in the tone of a shopkeeper doing inventory, as the pharmacist said later, when he was describing the scene to his wife, who listened to him in silence, as always.

The parson's widow started walking back toward the dining room door, carrying a stack of crystal plates in both hands.

"Wait, I'll open the door," Holger said.

"Thank you, I can get the door open myself," said the parson's widow, and set the pile of plates down on the floor even though the pharmacist was already holding the door open. The widow closed the door, opened it again, picked up the stack of plates she had set on the floor and carried the plates to the dining room cabinet and returned to the kitchen.

"What's the matter with you?"

"I'm only doing a bit of cleaning. It's a lot of fun to clean. Oh, dear, one does forget what one owns, so it's fun to take a look at them. I'm sure you know how much Birger loved order."

"Is that so?"

Silence came over them.

"I'm also going to clean the dining room cabinet," said the parson's widow. One could hear her taking dishes out of the cabinet.

"I think I'll go clean the fish," Alma said.

The widow was listening. Alma's footsteps sounded in the yard, and the creel was set down on a rock next to the well cover. The pharmacist came to the steps and said it was best to give all the little fish to the cat. Alma's voice answered that the little fish shouldn't go to the cat, she herself could use them to make chowder. "Please, take those bigger perch home and fry them," said Alma. "No," said Holger, "I'll take only three. My wife doesn't care for fish." "But I'll clean them," said Alma. "I'll get them all cleaned up." The parson's widow slammed shut the cabinet door, and at that very moment she was exhausted. She felt like crying as she looked at all the things from the cabinets that she had spread out onto the floor. Lace for sheets, started years ago; no one would ever finish crocheting it. "I pay the wages," she said aloud, "but I have to clean my cabinets myself."

The pharmacist was standing in the vestibule, and overheard.

"What's bothering you?"

"Isn't she making coffee for you? What in the world is she doing?"

"Oh, never mind the coffee. I think you've got a headache, you're so pale."

"Not at all. I'd make the coffee myself, but as you can see, I've got to do this cleaning."

"Can't she take care of all of that?" asked the pharmacist, eyeing the things all spread around.

"She—as far as I know, she's cleaning fish, preparing food for flies, as you can see. Year after year I've taught her that fish are not to be cleaned near the well or on the steps, and you're an educated person, Holger, do you understand, the kitchen steps are still full of fish scales from her cleaning fish on the steps the day before yesterday. And now she goes and cleans them on the well cover. You can hear, can't you, how she's going scritch-scratch at them with a dull knife? Do you hear?"

As Holger listened, you could actually hear Alma scritch-scratching scales off the perch.

"Anyway, it's not worth getting all excited about. Tell her to clean away the scales, that'll get rid of them."

"Don't you worry about me. Why don't you go to her, that one, the one who's cleaning the perch you caught when you were out angling together. What she told me was that you'd gone to take the bream nets out of the lake. I didn't know anything about angling. You certainly didn't ask me to go along."

"But you were asleep, you know, and if I remember correctly, you don't like angling."

"Look here, this is how she treats Birger's mother's china service, whatever is left of it. Look. She's put these two delicate plates on top of each other without the lace doily that's always been between them. I've told her that old pieces of china mustn't be stacked on top of each another, but individually, with a cloth between . . ."

"Oh my, that's a beautiful plate."

Holger had come from the door to the dining room and picked up a plate that had been set down on the floor.

"Do you like it? Please take it to Teodolinda."

"No, no, I couldn't do that," Holger said, and set the plate on the table.

The parson's widow took the plate from the table, handed it to him, and said, "Be so good as to take it to Teodolinda. It belongs to her, I understand that now." And she turned a deaf ear to the pharmacist's protests.

"Take it," she said, smiling. "Teodolinda will know how to handle it. You see, Holger, for a long time now I've understood what all of you want from me. These things. And you're right, I can't protect them. They may break or get lost so long as they're with me. Yes, take it to Teodolinda. This is my wish, and I think it would also be Birger's wish."

After saying that, the parson's widow started upstairs without looking behind her, even though Holger called, "Adelaide, but my dear Adelaide, what do you mean?" After she had climbed the stairs and just as she was opening the door to her room, she turned and said, "By all means, ask her to make some coffee for you. As you could see, she doesn't obey my orders, and therefore you will perhaps also understand why I want to give that plate to Teodolinda. Well, I don't have a home. I haven't had one for many, many years."

Lying in her bed and wrapped in blankets, the parson's widow could hear the pharmacist's footsteps downstairs. They went out, hesitated on the steps. She heard Alma come—with the creel in her hand, of course, she could imagine—from the well to the kitchen. "Good-bye." That was Holger's voice. "Aren't you going to wait for coffee?" That was Alma's voice. "No, thank you, not this time." That was Holger's voice. The parson's widow grunted and smiled to herself. And Holger was already going along the road. You could hear his footsteps around the corner of the house. The parson's widow got up, quietly snuck to the window: Holger was going, not once looking back, walking faster than usual. The parson's widow settled back in bed. Alma's footsteps resounded from the kitchen and dining room. Looking for me, the widow thought. When I go down, the dishes will have been put back into the cabinet. I'll take them out again and start to clean. For three hours she lay without stirring. She knew that the house was full of bad spirits. Downstairs in the kitchen, Alma was moving about and the bad spirit in Alma was singing. She could hear it, a wicked humming that wanted to incite her to greater wickedness. When three hours had passed, she said aloud, "Now I will go downstairs and tell her, I heard the bad spirit in your voice." But the kitchen was empty, dishes scattered about the floor and on the table. In the dining room, cabinet doors stood open and things were on the floor, and on the table stood the plate. Holger had decided not to take it. And when she saw all that, the parson's widow burst into tears. The kettle was on the stove, full of hot water. No, I will not take the water she has boiled, the widow said to herself. She took another kettle, picked up a bucket, fetched water from the well, and without turning her head, noticed Alma in the vegetable garden.

The kettle was so small that water boiled in it wouldn't be enough for washing all the dishes that were spread about. Still weeping, the parson's widow took from the fire the kettle Alma had filled, carried it to the steps, rinsed them with boiling water, returned to the kitchen and put the empty kettle back on the stove. But one bucketful of water wouldn't be enough for washing everything. Tears were flowing from her eyes when she had to go once again to draw a bucketful of water from the well; she was tired, so very tired, and all the dishes were still unwashed.

In the meantime, Alma had come in from the vegetable garden, stopped next to the stove, and was just looking on as the widow was lifting dishes off the floor and stacking them on the table to be washed.

"Shouldn't we get something to eat?" asked Alma.

"Whose food? Yours or mine?"

The parson's widow was washing dishes and the hot water was burning her hands, but she wouldn't turn around to ladle cold water from the bucket to mix with the hot because Alma was standing behind her.

"Is that so?" Alma said a second time. "When a person's possessed by the devil, another human being can't be of any help." And the kitchen door slammed shut behind her.

"So I have to wash these dishes myself, all these dishes," the widow was saying to herself, and she could feel how a plate which she was in the middle of washing with a scrubbing brush, was yanked out of her hand while she was shoved away from the table.

"You consider it your right to take my china away from me, you consider it your right to break the china service of my late husband's mother, don't you? Give that plate back to me at once."

But Alma started washing dishes. The parson's widow looked on, trembling from head to toe. She could see Alma's broad, fleshy back, wet armpits; she looked at Alma's open-necked summer dress and was disgusted by her disheveled, indecent appearance.

"You're going too far," the widow said. "The least you could do would be to cover your arms, cover up your armpit hair."

But Alma went on washing the dishes and singing.

"So you were taking the bream nets out of the lake—I'd rather use another word to describe what you'd have wanted to be doing."

"When the devil gets into a person, human help has no power," said Alma, and continued singing.

"From this day on, you will not touch my things."

"Well, if that's the way it is, I won't."

Alma left the dishes and went out. You could see her walking through the yard. Feet pounding the ground like sledgehammers, the widow thought as she watched that disgusting mannish walk.

"Feet thumping on the ground," the parson's widow was saying to the pile of dishes. She took a plate in her hand and spoke directly to it: "And Holger goes out on fishing trips with that animal." She put the plate down, went into the dining room and took a plate off the table, the one Holger apparently hadn't wanted. And she pretended she could hear voices: "Adele offered me that plate again." "You didn't take it, did you?" "Me, I would have been out of my mind to take the plate she offered in a fit of anger."

"They have all forsaken me," she said to the plate. "Holger made a point of not taking you because he knows why I'd like to give you to Teodolinda. They've all decided together that none of them will take you so you can torment me for the rest of my life, because you're from their grandmother's china service. 'Give it to Elsa,' says Teodolinda. 'Give it to Teodolinda,' says Elsa. They're just waiting for me to break you so they can say: now she broke a plate from our grandmother's china service. They remember what I said: 'Take it away so it doesn't break while I have it in my possession.'"

The parson's widow cradled the plate in her arms and sat down on the sofa opposite the boreal owl. "A gentle landscape in you," she said to the plate. "Flowers, trees, bushes, a man and a woman, a young man and a woman in each other's arms amidst the flowers, the woman's leg just the way Elsa's leg was when she was sitting on the veranda looking at me, who was emerging from this house with her brother on the day her mother wouldn't deign to greet me. Red, blue, faded, worn gentle colors. Why are you colors in this plate? Why would I hate you? Is everything that has happened in this house the fault of you plates?" She sat with the plate pressed close to her breast. The clock was ticking on the wall. "It isn't you I hate," she said to the plate. "I hate people who want to take all beautiful things away from me. I love objects."

There was the sound of a door. Alma had come in.

She heard the sound of dishes being washed in the kitchen. After listening to Alma moving about for an hour or so, the widow got up and went to the kitchen door.

"Go over to the pharmacy. Take this plate to the pharmacist's wife and say that if she won't take it I'll smash it tonight. It's better to take it out of here before it gets broken. She'll understand. Please go and take it there."

"It's been taken there before. You know they won't accept it."

"Tell her that she will understand my intention."

Alma took the plate. The parson's widow looked at Alma's rough hands that gripped the plate and started to carry it off.

"Take the tureen as well, it's from the same china service. But wash it first."

"Do I have to carry these uncovered again so that everyone can see?"

"Is that what you're thinking of? You don't have to think."

"I'm only thinking because I'll have to carry them back from there again. I guess there's time for all this carrying and hauling, though."

Alma came back from the door to pick up the tureen.

"Why so humble all of a sudden?"

Alma pretended not to hear.

"You don't have to serve me. Put the dishes back on the table."

"Are these going to be carried away or brought back? That's what I want to know. The cabbages ought to be thinned out and the thrushes are stirring up the flowerbed."

"You're deliberately mistaking starlings for thrushes—you don't have to serve me. Right at this moment you're freed from being in my service, if that's what you want."

Alma put the dishes back on the table and went out.

In the early evening the parson's widow telephoned the pharmacy. "Teodolinda, is that you?" "Hello, how are you?" "Very well, thank you. Could you come over right away? I have something I need to talk over with you." "I can't right now. I'm all alone. Holger isn't home and I have to stay at the pharmacy." "Where's Holger?" "I don't know. Maybe he's gone for a walk, or he could be out fishing." "Oh, I see. I too have been home alone, ever since morning." "What did you want to talk about?"

The widow was silent until Teodolinda repeated, "What did you want to talk about?" "I'd like to discuss an important matter with you." "Couldn't you do it tomorrow? What if I came over tomorrow?" "I can't promise I'll be home alone tomorrow. Now I am and it's only now that I can be sure that's how it'll be. Goodbye, Teodolinda."

Even though the parson's widow knew Teodolinda wouldn't come over that night, she still waited. "Adele, what's the matter with you now?" she said, looking at the tureen and the plate, and then she answered, "Please sit down, Teodolinda. I am just fine." "But I know something has happened again, since you offered the plate to Holger. Tell me, Adele." The widow rolled her head and answered aloud, "Nothing, Teodolinda. You do know that I would so much like to give you these dishes. They're yours, after all, as you once said. Why don't you take them?" And the answer came: "No, Adele, I once asked you for one plate, just as a memento. As you know, I thought no one could do anything with three plates and a tureen, I mean from the point of view of eating. I thought you would give one plate to Elsa, another to me, and you'd be left with one plate and the tureen, but you wouldn't consent to that. No, Adele, this matter has already been dealt with. No, Adele."

While the parson's widow was talking aloud to herself, Alma had quietly come into the kitchen and listened behind the dining room door. At once she headed off to tell the doctor's wife.

"It's started again."

"What? Speak softly," the fat sister-in-law said, so that her husband, who was sitting in the study, wouldn't hear.

"Speaking to me very formally, that's how it starts. I went off fishing with the pharmacist and when I get back home, the parson's widow began speaking formally. I could predict it would start up again."

"Was it wise to go out with the pharmacist?"

"Had to get some food. She herself said yesterday that she wished she could get some fresh fish before the end of her days. The widow hasn't got fish traps or nets and she won't go angling with me."

"And then?"

"Talks to herself."

"About who now?"

"The pharmacist's wife and the china service."

"Has she had it taken over to the pharmacy?"

"First told me to take it there, then told me not to. As you know, I've taken it there before and brought it here, too."

"You and I both know I've said, if either one of us, my sister or I, were to take it, she would come get it back."

"That's clear. As you know, I've gone to fetch it from both places."

"I'll call the pharmacy. You can head over there now."

Ten

When the boy was there, Alma felt that she had always been some
kind of victim, and that's the way it had to be. The other one did
what he did because he was a man and knew what he was doing
and what he wanted to do, and it was his fault. Alma had been a
girl, she'd set out to be a girl, or maybe she was like a young cow
that turns its head away, eyes rolling. But here was a boy, and now
Alma woke as if emerging from a memory. She became conscious;
she snarled and took hold of the boy, who was trying to break
loose. And all the time Alma was aware of the surface of the water
beyond the shed where the fish nets were stored; she was conscious
that there was a road leading to the shore, to that very shed. Alma
took hold of the boy, showed, taught, without a word, as if she
were scolding, expected that the boy would now be a man who
knew how, and she, Alma, would be a girl, a woman, thirty-three,
to whom this was happening, and that the man was doing it. But
the boy was not a man. There remained the feeling of her being the
mother who was doing the teaching, and of the man who knew
how it was done also teaching, who knew what the man-woman
in her wanted and how the other felt.

"Wait."

And Alma saw herself standing there next to both of them,
standing, but it wasn't her alone; it was in one instant a man, a man
and a woman at the same time, on edge, and the boy, a whomp of a
ruttish bull-calf but not yet a bull, a puppy dog that was giving it a

try, looking after its own thing. And unsatisfied, furious, Alma rose from the nets. She sensed the sudden darkness, saw the red glow of the sunset through wide cracks between the wall boards of the shed, and saw the fishnets on the walls of the shed stirring, heard the wind start up, breathing through cracks in the boards. A rustling sound when she got up, straightened herself. Her hair had come loose, and she was fumbling for a comb, asked the boy if he had one, and Antti searched his trouser pockets for a comb and handed it to Alma. The double-doors to the night-shed were closed, the boy had shut them. Alma turned, combed her hair, sighed, and now the boy was standing behind her at the door of the night-shed.

"The fog is lifting," Alma said, combing her hair with her back to the boy, her face toward the wall as if a mirror had been there.

"So it is."

Alma turned around, pulled long black strands of hair out of the comb, thrust it back to the boy and went out of the shed. "Where are you taking it?"

The boy had followed her onto the wooden dock. "The fog is lifting," Alma said, and started dragging a washtub along the dock. "Inside, into the shed. Help me." Alma bent over with her back to the boy, tugged at the tub which was teetering, about to tip over on the slippery planks.

"Take hold of it. Lift it," she said. The boy grasped the other handle of the tub and they carried it into the shed.

The wind was whipping through the nets, and the netting awls were swinging quietly to and fro.

"Come fishing with me. I'll do the rowing," the boy said, looking her straight in the eye. "Go fishing with you? No."

"But you go fishing with Uncle Holger."

"Who told you that? I went out once."

"Once," Antti said, with the smile of the parson's widow on his face, a diabolical, all-knowing smile, baring teeth behind his lips, thick red lips like a girl's, and Alma went around to the other side of the tub, knowing full well why the boy was laughing. "What is it you want from me? What?" she asked the boy as he was looking at her, for the boy, the boy's eyes, the parson's widow, the parson's widow's eyes, were glinting from the other side of the tub in the dusky shed, and the boy came, taller than Alma, a lanky boy with the parson's widow's eyes and the lips of a girl, so close to her that Alma retreated into a corner, the wall behind her, and underneath, a heap of rotting nets.

"Let's sit down," said the boy.

"There's not going to be any of that stuff here."

"Why won't you go out fishing with me? We could go angling off the island."

"The fish aren't biting now," Alma said.

"All right, let's go angling," she heard her voice say; it came from far away, as if someone else had been speaking through her mouth and she herself were there, a third person listening to the meaning of the words.

"What did you do with Uncle Holger when you went angling? Mother said you'd gone out angling with him."

Alma didn't look at the boy. "What about it?" she answered. "What do you mean?" she asked the boy, knowing perfectly well what he wanted to say, but her common sense refused to answer, refused to explain to the boy that it wasn't what he'd really meant, or what those eyes and that smile meant. Hadn't the boy stood in the vegetable garden looking at Alma from across the fence, and when she had moved to the other side of the cabbage patch, her face towards him, taking care not to squat with her back to him, the boy had turned towards her like the sun.

"What do you want with me?"

Alma had always tried to dodge him, but wherever she went the boy would come after her.

"Leave me alone," Alma said.

The boy smirked, just like his mother.

"Go collect your insects, mind your own business. Leave me alone."

But suddenly Alma realized the boy was mocking her, making fun of her by grabbing her, touching her, impudently standing there with no intention, no aim. Everything went black before Alma's eyes, and she grabbed the boy. He yielded but Alma could feel he didn't want to; he struggled to get away, away, now that she was the one who wanted to. And she wouldn't let him escape. Door closed, latch on. Alma followed the boy when he came near. A moment ago Alma's hands had shoved him off, but not now. And the boy started to act blindly, went to it against his will. But Alma waited, and like a lithe animal the boy clung to Alma's body, hands on her back, on her hips, as if there were a countless number of hands, like an arm wrenched from a leg, and again down the back, further down, a hand clutching hands, the hand tearing clothes, not just one hand but many, which Alma couldn't control.

"I'll kick," Alma said, and tried to kick out but the boy let go with his hands, moved to one side, and as she was panting and trying to get to the door to undo the latch, the panting and the boy's head and wet mouth on her neck, the boy on his knees at her neck, pushing her back with his hands, holding her by the throat—like the devil, she thought afterwards—had taken her breath away, held her by the throat so roughly that not a single sound could come out of it, like someone drowning, and her hands pushing the boy off, holding onto him until she let herself down on the nets, and the boy, the boy's hands on her legs, hips, in her blouse, a hand, hands, a thousand hands under her skirts, not grasping that it was the boy who had knocked her down.

A boy like a calf that greedily shoves its muzzle into a pail, the bull calf she had watered when she was a girl at home, at the gate when it would poke its head into the pail so that she had to yank the pail away, muzzle still in the pail, the full length of its head reaching after the pail, and the boy, the parson's widow's son, a boy, nobody's son but a bull that was now poking, as in its sleep, shoving, poking at her belly, holding her by the feet, jerking, not knowing how to do anything in particular. And as soon as the woman in her understood that, she said, "Right in there." And Alma took hold of the boy as if she were undressing a child, pushed her hand between the boy's legs, as if fed up, and said, "In there." Alma waited, and she felt good, she felt the boy's weight; he was panting, flopped, as if dead. "Your mother's coming."

It was a lie, she had just popped out with it.

The boy. Not a boy, a bull. Alma's mind had got stuck onto this image of the bull and had been lost in it until, realizing what was happening, she'd recovered her voice: "I'll tell your mother." A hissing sound, her own, she who had given in, had let the hands come, fumble, she, fleshy knees, the boy all skin and bones, hissing voice, her own, and the other, not grasping. Between the boards of the shed glowed the red rainy sunset, someone was rowing on the lake, the steady sound of the oars, a bird was flying across the lake, it was calling, and her fury, it rose, and silently, as the boy was lying on his side on the nets with his eyes closed, lost in what had been done, she struck, blood was flowing out of the boy's mouth, she struck again, and the boy still there, on his back, the boy's face in the dusk, eyes fixed in a stare, giving no resistance as if expecting that she would hit out again as blood was trickling out of a corner of his mouth, from the base of his nose down onto his neck, and suddenly, footsteps—footsteps coming from behind the shed. The parson's widow, she knew it right away, was standing still in the dusk outside, ahead of her the wide expanse of lake, fog, an island in the fog, the pharmacist's boat moored to the dock, nets drying, a bird and a bird call that seemed to come from far away but the bird was making sounds nearby, on the roof of the shed, in a tree, in a birch, in an aspen; she thought of trees and a birch and an aspen and knew it was the plaintive cry of the parson's widow sounding in the birdcall, a bird chirping alone and innocent, like the parson's widow. They were sitting in the dark, both pondering who they were and what had happened to them.

"Where will I go?" Alma asked. "Where will I go?" she repeated to herself. "Where?" And all at once, feelings of being homeless, an orphan, poured into her mind like rain, stifling all sounds, clouding her eyes, and she remembered a day from her childhood: she was coming in from the drying barn, brown ferns at the edge of the forest, rain, rain, she got up on a rock and looked around her and she felt that she didn't know where she came from, who she was, as if there were no father, no mother, no one in the whole world. The world was fog, dusk, the gray of houses, autumn, the gray of rocks, gray of the drying barn, silence, no one, no knowledge of anyone, no one, nothing, lost, all alone in the world. The boy stirred. Alma heard the boy's voice and saw him go to the door, undo the latch, go out, away, along the shore, his footsteps crackling on twigs. Alma sat there for a long time, the half-rotted nets beneath her; she heard the sound of the wind and the heavy rushing of the lake, heard the rustle of the nets, faint rustling from the roof, and thought: the pharmacist's boat, and then, where will I go, where?

The wash she had come to rinse had been sitting on the step in front of the shed; it had started raining softly, then harder. From the door of the shed she had watched the raindrops breaking the surface of the water. The rain had grown stronger, the patter against the roof of the shed, and she had sat down on the nets to be out of the rain, monotonous patter, and all of a sudden the wind rose and the boy was at the door of the shed. Alma had no idea when the rain had stopped. The boy had grabbed hold of her; that's how it must have been, she thought, without saying a word, and how long it must have gone on! The rain had ended, they had carried the tub inside, the soaking-wet wash in from the rain. And then she had wanted the boy to be a man. Now the boy was going away. From the doorway of the shed, Alma could see the headland on the opposite shore of the lake where the farm's three heifers stood still at water's edge. Soon they'll be taking them in; autumn's on its way. The rain, she thought, soon it will rain again. And she straightened the rotting nets that no one had touched for years, exactly as they'd been, and she went out of the shed.

Darkness had fallen by then, the fire had died under the pot; she'd been going to stoke the fire but it had gone out.

It had grown dark, but she was still sitting on the step of the shed. When the parson's widow came, she got up and looked her straight in the eye.

"Why are you sitting here? Are you sick? Come into the house."

They walked up the hill single-file, neither one saying a word. Alma heard the parson's widow walking through the rooms but she didn't come into the kitchen.

In the morning, the widow came into the kitchen and said that Antti had gone to the village.

"Did you see Antti go?"

"Said he was going fishing."

"Did he take the boat?"

"I don't know. I guess so." But it had all started as far back as last winter, the night the boy had followed her into her room, had begun long ago, when they were left home alone while the parson's widow was visiting the pharmacist's. The boy had come into the kitchen late at night, had sat at the kitchen table, staring at her, not saying a thing, and many nights when Alma would go to her room she had started undressing so that he would leave, and the boy had come in there. "Your mother's going to come," Alma had said. "No, she won't come. She's at Aunt Linda's." Alma had turned towards the wall and shoved the boy away. "Well, you can stay if you stop that silly business." These exchanges had gone back and forth without any talk of what they were really about, until Alma, perhaps tired of it, or who knows for what reason, had let the boy get next to her on the narrow bed, just like when he'd been a little boy. Then he had gone back to school in the city, and she felt relieved; she'd been ashamed of her thoughts and afraid the parson's widow would find out; she'd been afraid of talking in her sleep; that had become a real nightmare, that the widow would discover what was going on. At night the parson's widow roamed from room to room.

The next day the boy came home. Alma, the boy, and the parson's widow: no one said a thing. The boy didn't leave his room, didn't come into the kitchen; he sat in his attic room from morning to night. The days were rainy, and he came downstairs only to eat, got up from the table before the widow was done. Came and went like a thin ghost. Alma could hear the widow urging Antti to eat more now that school would soon be starting again. The boy wouldn't answer. Alma was listening to the boy's footsteps in the attic, right above the ceiling of her room; she'd listen to the boy going to bed at night. Alma was watchful, kept an eye on the widow's expressions, but she could find nothing in her face that would let on that the widow knew.

"Alma, make some coffee, and just have it yourself. I don't want any today," the parson's widow said. But she'd sometimes said that before.

"Why should I do it only for myself?" Alma asked.

But one morning, when Alma was still in her nightclothes, Antti came to the door of her room, and just as he'd done in the shed, he wrapped himself tightly to Alma's body; like a puppy he clung senselessly to Alma's lower body, to her waist. His hands, the parson's widow's small hands, drove into Alma's large, fleshy body as if one animal were wrestling with a much larger one, long arms and spindly legs wound around Alma. And Alma listened, remembered that the widow was out, wouldn't get back till afternoon. "I'm going over to visit Linda. I'll spend the night there," the widow had said. And hadn't she, Alma, hadn't she known this when she'd heard the parson's widow would be going, hadn't she planned for this without thinking so much as a single thought but still knowing exactly how it would turn out? And hadn't the parson's widow known, or planned for it, or allowed it to happen, that which had to happen? Alma understood that was why the widow had gone, and hadn't the boy also known right away? And hadn't she wanted the boy to come, lain awake listening to the boy's movements from above, footsteps on the stairs and in the kitchen. She felt as if she'd wanted to take revenge against the boy for something, anything. That he'd left her alone in the shed with the drying nets and gone on his way like a puppy.

Alma struck. Her hand rose and hit the boy right in the mouth and out of the boy's mouth a sound curled out, unraveled, a scarcely audible whisper, a curse. "Fucking whore! As if I wouldn't know. Uncle comes here too, the drunk!"

"I'll tell your mother." And Alma was shaking all over. "I'll tell your mother," she repeated.

"And who'll believe you? You do this all the time. I'm underage. Who'll believe you? Mother? She still thinks I'm a little boy. Who's going to believe you? You're the one who seduced me, I didn't even know how. Now I do know, so let's try again. Let's do it again," Antti said and laughed, this time like his Uncle Holger. "You take me for a kid, and I was one, too, but not anymore. Come on. You're crazy."

And Alma, at a loss, trembling in her night clothes, armpit hair dripping wet over the edges of her nightgown, grabbed the boy and shoved him towards the door, but he clung to the door jambs, said that Mother wasn't home, they'd have plenty of time, Mother had gone to Uncle Holger, and then Alma struck him a second time, with the strength of her whole arm, and her fury; she struck him on the nose, blood started to flow, and Alma said, "I'll tell your mother."

"No one's going to believe you, but they'll believe me when I tell them you forced your way into my room."

"Come on. Come on in for another one. I'll hit you! I'll hit! I'll hit!" Alma shouted. She was banging the boy's head against the wall, and the boy, smiling a satisfied, demonic smile, looking at Alma curiously, saying, "You're crazy. First you . . ." Alma struck the boy one more time, driving her palm straight into his mouth. She took him by the shoulders and shoved him out the door.

She heard the boy's mocking voice coming from the other rooms, saying, first you do it yourself and then you turn all virtuous.

Alma started gathering her things, forgetting she had not yet gotten dressed. She would go find the parson's widow and tell her it was all over. Gathering her belongings, she opened the closet door. In the middle of the floor sat a round veneer traveling case. She had already tried to close it but the strap had snapped, and when she took up the strap to tie the broken ends in a knot, she found it already so knotted that it wouldn't go around the case, and she started crying and crying, face down on the floor. When she heard the widow's footsteps in the front hall, she cried even harder and was lying there, still crying when the parson's widow opened the door. The widow didn't say a word. She had seen the traveling case, seen Alma, and asked in a quiet, indifferent voice, "Where's Antti?"

Alma stopped crying. She got up, and after taking a few steps, she took her veneer case by the strap and tried to tie it.

"I know everything. It wasn't your fault, Alma."

Did the parson's widow mean that she, Alma, had gotten undressed so that she'd be all ready when the boy came?

Alma's hands stopped. She stared at the clothes in the veneer case. "This is nothing new for me," said the parson's widow.

You could hear the boy whistling in the attic. Now footsteps, a chair being moved.

"It was Antti, wasn't it?"

Alma didn't answer.

"I won't ask. Let's not talk about it, but there's no reason for you to go anywhere, Alma. Antti will be leaving. You know school will be starting soon."

Alma waited.

"It'll be just the two of us here, Alma. Alma, it wasn't your fault."

What should she say? The parson's widow was waiting for an explanation. Alma was thinking. And now Alma looked at the parson's widow, the boy's eyes, devil's eyes; they were aimed at Alma's half-naked body, arms, armpit hair, and she had the feeling that the widow was the devil, and that her eyes were looking for nakedness in her, just as, a moment before, the boy's eyes had done, coldly curious, scornful, knowing, and at once Alma reached for the nearest piece of clothing and covered her body with it. She remembered that the widow had never seen her naked. They went to the sauna at different times, and the widow carefully covered every part of her body, which—that much Alma had noticed—was the withered body of an old woman. And now Alma knew that it wasn't only pious modesty but woman's shame, and just a moment ago the parson's widow, eyes focused, had carefully examined her arms, her half-bare breasts, as she sat on the edge of her bed, her neck, her hair, which, black with sweat, was hanging down her back. With her back to the widow, Alma arranged her hair, tied it up quickly, and still with her back to the parson's widow, as a feeling of superiority began filling her limbs, she now turned toward the widow; with her hair in a bun, she regarded the thin, flat-chested figure who, half leaning against the wall with her feet crossed, was examining her with those black, squinting eyes, the boy's eyes, and the smile, the boy's smile, made Alma say, as if someone else had spoken through her mouth, used her tongue, three words that first came clear from her mouth: "I won't stay." And then: "I won't stay among devils."

"Devils," said the parson's widow, and smiled.

Alma looked away.

"Don't talk about devils, because you don't know they're speaking through your own mouth. You're not free of temptations. How would my son be? It's the devil at work in you, Alma. If you'd only get married, but no one will have you, isn't that right?" And the parson's widow turned away, went to the door. "Unpack your things, go to the kitchen, and make some coffee." The widow turned away, and was gone. Doors were opening and closing. The parson's widow went upstairs and spoke with her son, and Alma could hear them laugh. Alma pulled the veneer case over in front of her, opened the lid, took out her clothes and put them back in the closet, got dressed and went into the kitchen. The house was quiet. Alma made coffee, walked silently through the rooms, took the coffee to the widow and said at the door, "What have I done for you to say that?"

As the widow didn't answer right away, Alma asked, "I'd like to know, what have I done?"

"It was good that you hit Antti, I'm not angry at you for that. You're not the first one, I've hit him too. Antti is my son, and I take the bad with the good. You don't understand these things, Alma. Now go on out."

Alma set the tray on the table in front of the parson's widow and left the room. The widow crossed her hands, prayed. She prayed for a long time and asked God's forgiveness for having been mean to Alma, for having hurt someone who does not understand things. I understand everything now, and that's why I hurt her. I could tell what she was thinking as she was looking at me, putting up her hair, and that's why I hurt her. Forgive me, God, the parson's widow was praying. She prayed for a long time, then went downstairs, straight to the kitchen, and said to Alma, who was scrubbing the kitchen floor, "You could get married, but maybe you don't want to. You want to be in charge, and that's your fate."

Alma didn't respond.

"But I guess that you too have had some suitors. Have you had any? Tell me."

"You're a pious one," Alma said in a thick voice.

"Don't you think that I too am a woman?"

"Well, you've been married."

"That didn't make me a woman."

Alma was drying the floor and didn't know what to say, how to go on.

"Antti said he'd had a fall," the parson's widow said after a while. "His mouth is all swollen up."

And after a moment: "He knows that I know. And you don't say anything."

"What would I say?"

Alma was silent.

"You threatened to tell me, didn't you?"

And after a moment: "You don't have to remember it, doesn't mean a thing. I have nothing against you."

Alma couldn't get out what she'd first intended to say, that it wasn't her fault. The widow's eyes were staring, and Alma knew there was no point trying to explain how the boy, not just this once but whenever his mother was gone and even when his mother was at home, would go after her in the halls, certain that Alma wouldn't let out so much as a peep.

"If that only was the last time," Alma said. "What do I do if it's not?"

"You'll smack him. And besides, he'll be going off to school. There'll be just the two of us here."

The widow's voice was so calm that Alma wondered whether she understood what they had even been talking about.

"I do understand, Alma," that voice said.

Alma wanted to hate this voice, the parson's widow. But what was there to hate about her?

ELEVEN

It was deep into the night when Alma had woken up to a noise. She could hear something stirring around in the clothes closet. Rats, but how could there be so many, there hadn't been a sign of rats for ages. She had listened, the noise came from the clothes closet, from the clothes closet right next to the vestibule door. Something was there, moving among the clothes. If she had gone to wake the parson's widow, the widow would have said calmly, "It's Onni, or maybe Birger, go back to bed." That's what happened when the cat had been walking along the eaves of the house, and although Alma could swear it was the cat making the noise, the parson's widow said, laughing, "Maybe it was Onni, he liked cats." Alma had got up, put on her clothes, and crept on tiptoe towards the widow's room. "You have no reason to be afraid, but I'm coming—don't worry, don't cry. See, I am not afraid," and together they went towards the clothes closet, the parson's widow ahead, fearless, in her night-gown, Alma after her. Now you could hear something resembling a human being uttering sounds. Someone was weeping in there. Alma had fled, gone off to her room and locked the door. She had listened: you could hear the weeping clearly now, the sound of a weeping man and the soothing voice of the parson's widow, and then a voice that belonged to the pharmacist. And the parson's widow: "Sit down, Holger. Why did you, you shouldn't have."

And the widow's knock on the door, the parson's widow pale, asking for hot water. And when Alma took the water into the parlor, she saw the pharmacist on the sofa, blood congealed on his wrist, and the widow quickly took the basin of water, set it down on the floor next to the sofa, got down on her knees and took the pharmacist's bloodied hands into her own, while the pharmacist sobbed like a little child. "Alma, you go to bed," said the parson's widow. But how could she have slept? She had listened in secret. "Now why did you do that?" And the pharmacist: "I showed her I am a man. I did it myself. She shut me in, you know, you must know what my place is in that house, down in the cellar. She put me in the cellar, and that's where I was." "But why do you drink so much, Holger? Oh, sure, I know, but don't you understand you can't do something like this, it's a sin." "I know for certain that's what she wants, she wants me to die, you all wish I would die, well, don't say anything. If you hadn't . . . if you had come to me I would never have done anything like this, you know what she is . . . yes, you know even though she's your husband's sister." "How did you do it? With a razor?" "No, there was a piece of glass there. Maybe from a jar of jam. I sat there and looked at it glistening, I saw when she opened the trap door, I looked at it and took it in my hand and said, 'Just put an end to it, put an end to everything. When you slash with this, you'll be rid of me, it'll be over and done with. Finished, finished. Do it, I give you my word, you may go ahead and do it.' But she just stood there with a candle in her hand, you know how she stands when she's looking at me, but do you know how she looks at me when I'm in the cellar? Never mind, I sleep in the cellar, I go there on my own, she doesn't have to take me. I go myself, I say 'I'm going to the cellar since that's what you want,' and I went, I slept, and then I wake up to her standing by the trap door and looking at me. You know, I've taken it all these years. 'Here,' I say and stare at the piece of glass, 'the bottom of a jam jar but it'll do, it'll do the job if you just go ahead and slash,' and I stretch out my arms. But she just looks like death, like a ghost. 'Why don't you do it yourself since that's what you want,' she says to me, 'the ancient Romans did it themselves,' and she leaves, it's dark. Dark." "Calm down," said the parson's widow. "So I have it in my hand, what is this, I think, it's the bottom of a jam jar, so it's glass. And I keep feeling it, it's sharp, and I am a man, I think, and the ancient Romans did it themselves. Teodolinda wants to get rid of me, and so she wants me to do it myself, has always wanted that . . . don't interrupt, it's perfectly true, just think, she's mocking me, the man hasn't got the courage, I'm not brave like the Romans, you know, Adele, they would go . . . when they did it themselves, they would go sit in warm water and make the cut and the blood would flow slowly, slowly, painless . . . painless. But I haven't got any water, what if it hurts, I think, and there she is, mocking the whole time, you don't know, Adele, or I guess you do know. But now it'll be finished . . . 'Here is a man!' I shouted so she would hear, here's a man, and I pressed the glass against my wrist, blood was flowing out of it, it was running here, under the sleeve, and I shouted, 'Now you'll be rid of me, I'm dying now, come see the blood flow.' I tried to raise the trap door, I thought I would show her, but she had locked the door, didn't even want to see although I had dared to do it." The parson's widow asked whether Teodolinda hadn't opened the door. "Didn't you say you were bleeding?" But the pharmacist just went on talking. "Come see," he commanded, "come on." He spoke as if his wife were in the room, shouting, "Teodolinda, come look." "Don't get all excited," said the parson's widow. "Tell me what, what you're thinking. Am I going to die?" "You're not going to die," said the widow, "it's a little surface scratch. I've bandaged you up and you're not bleeding anymore. Calm down." But the pharmacist only said, "When I was a young man I was handsome and my horse didn't stand in front of houses like the ones where your son's bicycle is parked . . ." "Calm down," said the parson's widow. "Is it deep?" "No, it's not, only a surface scratch, and I'll give you one piece of advice: don't show it to Teodolinda." The pharmacist had burst into tears and Alma had understood he was crying over his failure of courage.

And now he was coming along the road, his hand healed; of course, it was, after all, a year ago now—no, even more. Alma had once dared to laugh about it: "When I was a young man I was handsome," but the parson's widow had fallen silent and got her feelings hurt and said the pharmacist had indeed been a handsome man.

The pharmacist was walking along the road, and the women glanced at each other and pulled back from the window. "You'll let him in, of course," the widow said before Alma had the chance to ask whether they would let the pharmacist in or turn all the locks and sit there while the pharmacist tried to get in through the door to the kitchen and then again through the front door, banging, knocking, calling them both by name, calling Alma an old maid, a female bear, calling the parson's widow in turn Adelaide and dear sister-in-law and muttering, "Where have those crazy women gone," and then, as they kept peeking through the curtains, the pharmacist heading off with his back straight, looking like that so the village people couldn't say he was drinking, no, when a man had an erect posture no one had any business saying anything.

"Let him in."

The parson's widow had settled herself in a corner of the sofa, ready to receive him. Alma didn't go to open the door. The pharmacist's coming at such a late hour would mean she'd have to sit up late. It was just past seven o'clock and they wouldn't be able to get him out of the house until the early hours of the morning. Now there was a knock on the door. The widow nodded. Alma didn't open the door for him, she thought the man would know the way in. And there he was.

"I thought I'd drop in because we haven't had a chat for quite a while."

"Please sit down."

"Adele, you're always so good to me. Haven't I always said I should have married you? How are your little birds?"

The pharmacist looked at Alma and Alma blushed. The parson's widow liked that kind of talk, Alma was sure of that. She liked it too that the pharmacist came here with a bottle. "Well, you too have a seat. You have such red cheeks, sit down, red-headed woodpecker—does she always get so furiously angry?" The pharmacist's voice carried to the kitchen where Alma was.

"So how are your little birds?" And right away: "Do you know whose house that is?"

"Yours, of course."

"That one with the yellow doors. Do you know, say—do you remember when I painted them myself?"

"You, you painted."

The yellow color had faded, and the pharmacy was certainly in need of painting, but it hadn't been done.

Holger was going through the motions of adjusting his tie although he wasn't wearing one. Now he was patting his pockets as if feeling for his papers and wallet, even though—as everyone knew—Teodolinda took away his papers and wallet whenever he started off on a drinking binge. From his breast pocket he pulled out a bottle without a tremor of the hand, poured *spiritus fortus* into the hot water, put the bottle back in his pocket, scooped a flat green flask from his left breast pocket, cognac, poured it into a shot glass, took a sip, grabbed hold of the coffee cup and emptied it all at once. That's what he always did, and then, as always, all dignified, he turned to the widow.

"And how are your little birds?"

Alma heard the same sounds, they came like the striking of a clock, two glasses, the pharmacist insisted it had to be two glasses.

The parson's widow coughed, a clink, silence, and now Alma knew: the widow is carefully lifting a glass to her lips and pretending to taste it—and then it came:

"Don't deceive me, Adelaide, you're not even tasting it, you're only faking it, oh, it's just as well you don't, this isn't, this isn't really proper for you. But just tell me why Teodolinda runs my pharmacy."

"Teodolinda is your wife, when all's said and done."

"Don't try to be so clever. You know what I mean. I've said to Teodolinda: all this, any moment now, will be taken away from you, go stand on your own plot of land. That shuts her up. Doesn't speak for weeks. Tell me, Adele, is it any kind of marriage when she doesn't speak to me for weeks? 'Has my shirt been washed? I'm going to the city to take care of business.' No answer, not a sound out of her mouth when I ask whether the shirt's been washed. I washed it myself, your red-headed woodpecker can iron it."

"Alma," the widow called toward the kitchen, "bring the pharmacist's shirt."

"I'll pay you."

"No need for that."

"Money's always money. Here, I hid it in my pocket, they steal it, here it is."

"Alma will take it," the parson's widow said.

And Alma took the money and thought just what she always did when the pharmacist brought his shirt over: since this money is going out in any case, it's all the same whether it goes to me or to the women in the city.

"How is Teodolinda?" the widow asked the pharmacist, who seemed about to fall asleep in his chair.

"Medicine in the bottle, like this." He gestured with his hands.

"Give me a bottle, I say, I'm going to visit Adele. She does give, she does it for you, you know."

And once again the green flask emerged from the left breast pocket and appeared on the table.

"Please have some." The pharmacist extended the glass towards the widow and Alma hastened to pour hot water into the coffee cup.

The pharmacist pulled the other bottle from his right breast pocket.

"I wish you wouldn't take any more," the widow said.

"What? I'm as clear as fresh spring water. I'm heading for the city to take care of business, see, you have to take care of business, you do, it's only that you Broms family heirs don't understand it. Don't look at me like that, you know what I mean . . . a hundred hectares, listen, almost a hundred hectares slipped away from me because of you. Teodolinda doesn't lie, no, she's a good wife, my wife, you understand! Teodolinda said it was you, Adelaide, who did it, egged Birger on to take a loan from Paananen, putting up the land as security. You ate up the inheritance of your husband's sisters, of my wife. Well, so be it."

The parson's widow was silent.

"But who owns the pharmacy? Tell me," he said.

"You, you, my dear friend."

Alma stood in the kitchen, listening. She would have wanted to see the look of the widow's face at the moment the pharmacist brought up the business about the inheritance, but now that had gone by and they were talking about something else. Hardly ever did the pharmacist blame the parson's widow for that. Would talk about it when he was drunk. And now the widow coughed, and a bit of silence, and glug, glug, the sound of a bottle, and a clink, and then silence, and the pharmacist's voice: "Don't cheat, you didn't even take a taste, you're coughing for no reason, you're pretending —well, I won't make you—but how are your little birds! Why are you laughing at me?! Who planted the lilacs, who?"

"You."

"So I have done some work, haven't I? Tell me."

"You have, of course you have."

"But go ask Teodolinda! Haven't I stood in her damned pharmacy all these years! Is that any kind of life! I ask you, Adele. What? You can't answer . . . What kind of pharmacy person is Teodolinda anyway! Everything has come to her from me. She doesn't have the right to, no legal right . . . did you hear what I'm telling you, but she puts medicines into their bottles anyway. She's learned, I've taught her. One day the authorities will come and take all this away from you, I said, you don't have the right, it isn't legal, show me your pharmacist's license. What are you, anyway, you thin raven's fledgling that I took in, a pauper, your father a worthless sheriff . . . you graduated from some girls' school and your sister couldn't even get through that, you belong in the kitchen, get in there, away from my apothecary counter, the customers don't trust you . . . That's how it was, Adele, they were poor and to some extent it's your fault, just remember what a luxurious style of life you forced poor Birger to keep up, remember, to Vienna on borrowed money . . . Well, you're not of that family, you know who I mean, these sisters, one of whom is my wife, but I can't stand the other one, never have, I've told them not to visit but she just barges in, well, let her come, can't separate sister from sister, can one now? You're not going to take offense if I tell it to you straight: you had a strange husband. You've suffered, just as I have. Sometimes I thought, but take note, only sometimes, very rarely indeed: why God in his great wisdom didn't lead me to marry you, why did Teodolinda cross my path? To tell the truth, though, you're probably not all there. You laugh, I understand, but you're not always fair to Teodolinda. But realize this: If I took you to court the judge would say, you, Mrs. Broms, the parson's widow, have swindled the estate. Well, let it go. Your brother was crazy, I say, whenever the Broms daughters blame you.

Don't you blame Adelaide, I say, if the man didn't have the wits to control his wife it's not the wife's fault if the man lived beyond his means."

"Let's talk about something else," said the parson's widow, heaving a deliberate deep sigh and rubbing her temples, for she knew that Holger would then say:

"Man is above his wife, isn't he . . . for God's sake get rid of that owl."

"I won't give away my birds."

"Look here," said Holger, and with his back straight walked over towards the desk. "Watch me put these eye-glasses on its head. Look, there's Birger. Alma."

Alma headed for the parlor to do what was expected of her: she took the owl off the desk and carried it to the kitchen, hid it in the china cupboard so what had once happened wouldn't happen again: the pharmacist had gotten it into his head to play with the owl, had put a lit cigar into its beak. Five feathers next to the beak had been singed. The parson's widow had wept, wept and run at him, but the pharmacist had plucked some tips of feathers from the owl's belly side and glued them so skillfully next to the beak in place of the singed feathers that you couldn't notice the accident.

"Alma."

"You vestal virgin, come here," said the pharmacist's voice.

Alma came.

"Sit down. I have something to say to both of you."

The women waited, Alma with her hands in her lap, her face sullen. She felt sleepy, exhausted.

"You don't behave correctly or reasonably towards me," Holger said after a while, and regarded them both sternly. "Don't contradict me," he said. "Last Saturday, yes, you were home, you didn't open up when I knocked. There they sit, I thought, they let me knock.

What, am I a beggar? Anyway, it made me laugh. Listen, it made me laugh. Hydrangeas on the windowsill, there they sit as in a ship's cabin, the old hags, curtains drawn tight across the window. Well, let them sit, I thought, they'll let me in when they get around to it."

"But Holger, we didn't hear."

"You're lying," Holger said with all dignity. "No," said the widow. "You're lying."

"No, no."

"But I came, and I will come," Holger went on. "I am a man, and I am not good enough for you. Tell me, do any other gentleman callers come around? No. There's enough man in me for both of you."

And he laughed, pleased, took the green flask and poured.

"Have some, Alma," the widow said, "it's not a sin, have a little, for medicine."

"Yes, I bring you medicine, but you don't let me in when I knock, do you? Look at my head, Adele. Remember, curly blond."

And he laid his bald head in the widow's lap.

"Don't cry, Holger."

"You're so damned old," Holger said, and stared at each one of them in turn as if seeing them for the first time.

"But Holger, Alma's only thirty-four."

"Old, old, don't contradict me."

That's when Alma got up and walked out.

It was seven o'clock. It was morning and Alma was angry.

Seven turned to eight and the voice of the parson's widow came from the parlor:

"Are you going to the city now?"

"To the city . . . no. I came to see you."

The pharmacist was restless, went outside, went into the kitchen.

It was ten o'clock. Alma called the pharmacy and said into the telephone:

"He's here, don't worry, he'll be coming home. The car just left. He's sobering up, I took away all the bottles when he was sleeping."

Alma was lying. The bottles had been emptied during the night.

TWELVE

"So, how did it go again?"

The parson's widow laid her knitting onto the table and got herself ready to listen to Alma's story, which this time had started with the words: "How would I have guessed it that morning when I left home for the harbor?"

"Well, how would I have guessed?" Alma sighed.

"Why do you sigh? You used to say it was divine guidance."

"I don't know. Or maybe it is. You know, I could have ended up just about anywhere."

"So you left home early in the morning," the parson's widow said to get the story going.

"Early." Alma's voice carried a hint of disdain. "Well, that's early for some. For people who stay in bed 'til ten, even seven o'clock is early."

"Well, let it be. Leave me out of it, forget about me and just talk about yourself."

"The Mikanders were sitting in the parlor, eating, and through the window you could hear the clinking of dishes. The window was ajar, or maybe I should say it was open . . ."

"Don't worry about that, just go on."

"'Who is it that's there?' the shopkeeper asked a second time, and the maid said once again: 'Some girl.' 'What girl?' said a woman's voice, the shopkeeper's wife; it was, though I didn't know it at the time. But no one came out to see, though I'd been sitting there for over an hour, by my reckoning, right there on the steps of the house, looking at the walls. Walls blue, like cornflowers, window boxes yellow, a horse going up the street and people going by but I was just sitting there . . ."

"You're forgetting about the cat, you used to say there was a cat on the steps and it made you mad that the cat was so fat and looked so well fed when you yourself didn't have a piece of bread to your name, and you started to feel all weepy when you looked at the cat."

"I guess there was a cat, so it was, but then out came the missus herself, although I didn't know then it was the missus herself, came all the way to the stairs, looked me up and down and didn't say a thing. Do they take me for a beggar, I thought, but I wouldn't budge because I'd made up my mind to go from house to house and keep asking till I got a job."

"So you just sat there and thought that's what city people are like, they come and look at you and go away, but go on," said the parson's widow. "Let the scrubbing be, don't scrub anymore, that floor is already clean, sit down and take those socks, start darning them and tell me, it'll soothe my nerves."

Alma sat down and put a pile of socks that needed darning on the table in front of her.

"'Where, can't see anybody here,' that's how it was," said Alma after a moment's thought. "Yes, that's how it was: someone opened a window, but on the other side of the steps, not the one right above where I was sitting on the steps. 'Where, can't see anybody here.' And when I heard that, I got all startled and stood up. And then the shopkeeper himself came out to the steps, but I didn't understand at the time that he was the shopkeeper himself, and said, 'There's no one here, where?'—you see, I was sitting on a rock, that's how it was, I had moved from the steps over to the rock. Well, and that man asked me whose daughter I was. I told him whose and said where I was from. 'What do you want?' he said."

"And you: 'Do you need someone to help out here?' you said."

"'Do you need a maid here?'" I said."

"'Don't need one.'"

"And you just go on sitting there."

"I sit. And the sun is shining, it was hot, although it was already autumn. I sit, I thought, and all of a sudden I made up my mind that I'm not going anywhere, I'll just go on sitting. Then they send the maid to tell me, although I didn't know then that it was only a maid, 'Well, what are you sitting there for? Go away, are you out of your mind to just go on sitting there? Not supposed to sit in people's yards.' 'Can't one even ask if they know of some gentlefolks who could use some help?' The maid went back inside and I could hear talk through the window, somebody looked out the window and pulled it shut."

"But you just sat there."

"I went on sitting even though the maid came to shut the kitchen door. I just sat there on purpose, because I thought they really did think I was a thief."

"And then came the shopkeeper himself," the parson's widow quickly put in. She didn't want Alma to leave out this part of the story: to her it was exactly this part that was so exciting. Would Alma say the sentences that belonged right here, just as she had learned to say them earlier, although it had taken quite a few reminders.

"And then came the shopkeeper himself," said the parson's widow, and looked at Alma.

"A bearded man with a skullcap on his head," prompted the widow.

"Yes, although I didn't know it then. 'Cat got your tongue, you don't say anything? What are you looking for, girl?' 'Good day,' I said, and got up from the rock."

"'Are you selling something, we don't buy anything,' said the shopkeeper when he saw your veneer case."

"'Need a person to work here?' I said to that, that's right. And he started laughing. He just stands there and looks at me. I guessed. I thought, I sure know what you've got in mind, old man, but you just guess."

The widow put her palm in front of her mouth, giggled.

"Well, the old man told me to come in and I went in after him. A dim hallway, smell of leather, door open to the store, lines of shoes on the shelves, oh, how I liked that smell, like the smell of a new life, and I thought that as soon as I got some money I'd buy me a pair of black shoes, patent leather. 'Come here.' I followed him into the parlor. Big India-rubber trees, white lace curtains, red velvet furniture, just about the same as yours . . ."

"Not India-rubber trees, palm trees," interrupted the parson's widow.

"I got them mixed up, because we had one like that at home, or maybe it's not like it, it's 'the dream,' but in a tub anyway, and a potted palm looks more like a 'dream' than like an India-rubber tree . . ."

"You mean like an asparagus . . ."

"Well, whatever it was . . . I'll sure get them mixed up when you go at me over each word . . ."

"Well, go on."

"They were sitting on the red sofa in the parlor, one of them wearing a black dress, the other a light brown . . ."

"Yes, Teodolinda always wears black, it started when her father died. Oh my, Alma, that was one of the causes of Holger's suffering.

'Buy yourself something colorful,' he'd say. Doesn't say it anymore, Teodolinda simply won't do it. And then it started up again . . . well, why go into all that?"

"What? What started with what?"

"Well, I guess I can tell you if you don't blab about it to people," the parson's widow said after considering a moment. "When they got married, Teodolinda said: 'I think I need a new winter coat.' 'Again?' Holger said. He said it by mistake, he's sworn many, oh how many times that it just popped out. And I do believe Holger. But after that, Teodolinda has never said she needed anything. Holger has to force her to buy clothes. Oh, you don't know what a cross Holger has to bear, too. Go on."

"They were sitting on the sofa, and the tall and thin one takes a good careful look at me. I wondered why she was looking and what was in me to look at, she takes her glasses off and the shopkeeper is saying, 'Ask, go ahead and ask.' But the thin one just keeps on looking. 'If you need one, you could ask,' the shopkeeper says again and clears his throat. 'Said she's a good worker,' says the shopkeeper again, but sure didn't dare look at me the way he did in the yard. 'Are you honest?' asks the shopkeeper all of a sudden."

"And what did you say to that?"

"I've told you. 'I don't brag, but since you ask, I'll say: yes, I am.' 'I see, I see,' says the shopkeeper and gives the thin one a nod to go ahead and ask."

"Just like Teodolinda, she always takes a long time to think, too long," the parson's widow sighed. "And then?"

"'Let's sit down at the table,' says the shopkeeper's wife, although I didn't know at the time . . ."

"Go on."

"And nothing more. They sat down at the table, started eating."

"And you're standing in the doorway."

"Yes, I stood there. I'm not going to be in a hurry either, since they haven't sent me out, I'll wait and see whether anything is going to come of this."

"'I see, I see,' said Mikander," the parson's widow put in again to help things along.

"That's what he said all the time, he's got that kind of habit."

"Yes, yes," sighed the widow. "I remember: 'I see, I see,' and then he'd rubbed his hands and moved to the city, grew rich, started a shoe store. A strange habit, it's odd what strange habits people have . . ."

"Well now, let me go on. I remember it like yesterday. It was the smell of the food. They ate and the maid kept carrying dishes to the table, roast of veal, pudding, and with the veal roast they had carrots, and when I saw the carrots on the platter I felt so hungry it made me cry. Not a crumb had I eaten since I'd left home, I did have some money but I didn't have the heart to part with it, I thought you never know what you'll need money for, I didn't dare waste a penny, and not even a piece of bread with me . . ."

"Mikander asked, 'Are you hungry?'"

"So he did. But it took me so long that they'd finished eating, and the maid was carrying the dishes away. 'Are you hungry?' the shopkeeper asks me so abruptly that I started. 'Well, answer me straight.' 'Well now, since you ask, I'll tell you straight: yes, I am.' 'You can eat in the kitchen,' says the shopkeeper. The women don't say a word."

"But you just stood there."

"I stood there. How did I know where I was supposed to go? 'Go to the kitchen, don't you understand?' says the shopkeeper after a moment. I started off and the maid pretended not to see me. Shoved a plate in front of me. 'Sure seems hungry,' the maid says. 'Never seen food at home?'"

"You didn't answer."

"No. I ate. I thought I wouldn't spoil things by arguing."

"Were your feelings hurt?"

"Well, I'd seen maids before, and that's what I was going to say."

"You didn't say it."

"No. And food has never tasted so good as that veal roast. 'Is that the shopkeeper himself?' I asked. 'Who?' said the maid. As if she hadn't understood."

"As if she hadn't understood, that's right. And I thought: you there, just you wait. 'That man,' I said. 'Don't you know the master,' and 'you, you young girl, why are you asking about things like that?' That maid had to be over forty. 'Are they going to take me on?' The maid doesn't answer, all she's doing is rattling dishes. 'You go in and ask if they'll take me on, or whatever they say, you go listen behind the door,' I said. 'Who in the world are you to suggest things like that, to go listening behind people's doors,' and the maid turns all red, she was so mad."

"And so you went yourself . . ."

"So I did, but the maid, she got to yelling at me just like a raven. 'The least you can do is take a towel in your hand, dry the dishes.' And nothing was good enough for her. 'This glass is wet, for God's sake, can't you even dry dishes,' she said when I was putting a glass into the cabinet. 'The glass is wet, give it here,' and she grabs the towel away from me, out of my hand . . .'"

"She was jealous of you, that's all," said the parson's widow, and gave a nudge as if to signal: go on.

"Jealous, that's for sure. And right then the door opens and the thin one is standing there. 'Would you please come here?' she says. And that's how it all started." Alma sighed.

"But she did promise you wages right away, didn't she?" the parson's widow put in quickly so Alma would get on with the story.

Alma was silent.

"Teodolinda promised."

"I don't know."

"Now you're mixing things up on purpose," the widow began, agitated. "Teodolinda promised, it was the shopkeeper who winked at Teodolinda as a sign that one shouldn't promise any wages right away, that she'd be happy enough just to get a roof over her head, you, you see, that's what you said, and I say, have always said, that was a brazen thing for Mikander to do. And haven't I explained to you over and over that it wasn't because of the shopkeeper himself. It was because of his wife . . ."

"I don't know."

"But for goodness' sake, don't stop the story at this point, don't always stop here, you have a distinct inclination to disobey the words in the prayer, Our Father, 'Forgive us our trespasses as we forgive those who trespass against us.' I've told you that, haven't I?"

"I wonder if I'm the only one," said Alma so bitterly that the parson's widow was taken aback for a moment.

"Well, let's not bother ourselves about all that. So, you're sitting opposite Teodolinda and thinking that she's me. Go on."

"How could I have known which one of you was which . . . ?"

"I've never asked that of you, you get irritated much too easily, and you grasp at trifles, of course I know how reticent Teodolinda is. Do you think I didn't suffer from that very characteristic of hers which she directed at you, a young person who couldn't make head or tail of anything, no, maybe I should say, a poor orphan . . ."

"All right." Alma's voice grew vehement. "An orphan, I'll say. The first time in my life away from home, it wasn't easy. That sort of person right in front of me on the train seat . . ."

"Like a chicken hawk, you were going to say."

"If I said that, I learned it from you, you're the one who blasts the pharmacist's wife as a chicken hawk."

"Now you're mistaken. Once I compared her to an eagle, never to a chicken hawk, I certainly have a high enough regard for my husband's sister not to mix up such very different birds, even though they do belong to the same family, not to compare her to a chicken hawk. Maybe to some other kind of hawk, but not to a chicken. Anyway, go on. So, you're sitting opposite each other in the train. And you think she's me, the strange parson's widow whose bird collection you have been hired to care for." The widow's voice was full of laughter, sarcasm, and bitterness. "Go on."

"There wasn't any talk about birds. I have told you that, haven't I?"

"I know Teodolinda has always been so considerate, and do you think she was thinking of me." Now the widow's voice had grown even more clearly scornful. "No, it was the birds she was thinking of, just like her brother, the parson. The birds are an inheritance from the sheriff's family, and sometimes, I'll tell you, bitterness gnaws at my heart when they go ahead and die without giving any thought to it, first Onni and then Birger, and leave all the birds for me to look after, you know, I've told you that's the reason for my insomnia. Many a time I fall asleep, then wake up in a cold sweat and as if a trumpet had blared in my ear, 'moth and dust will corrupt,' and I jump up, walk around, lift the owl off the shelf, check the feathers . . . but go on, or don't you want to talk with me any more although you know a calm discussion is the only thing that assures me of even a wink of sleep . . ."

"The trip was already half over before the thin one spoke to me, asked my name, although she'd already heard it."

"That's just like Teodolinda, she doesn't know about anything else. All dignified, like her mother back in her time, 'va heter ni,' 'what's your name,' and then she's silent."

"Single file along the lane of birches, and then we were in front of the house, lilac bushes, red blossoms in the flower bed."

"But not dahlias. As you always say, Teodolinda hasn't been able to stand dahlias ever since Paananen's wife dug up the dahlias when she left this house."

"Geraniums, I've already given in to that—well, all right, we were coming along, single file, and on the wall of the house it says Apothecary and the thin one goes up the stairs, acts as if I don't exist. I stay out in the yard, sit down on the well cover, I think I'll just wait here. I thought she was going on an errand to the pharmacy and would be right back. 'Why did you stay back there?' she says, stands at the door and asks why I stayed back there."

"And you don't say anything."

"What could I have said? 'Come in,' she says.' "Come in, *please,*'" the parson's widow corrected. "Go on." "Why did you just stay sitting out there?" Alma said pointedly. "You're forgetting. While Teodolinda might say, 'Why did you stay back there?' she still wouldn't forget to say 'please' when she asked you to come in. The sheriff's daughters were well brought up, whatever may be said about their mother, she did teach her daughters good manners. But go on."

"I went . . ."

" . . . and you were about to stumble over a broken board in one of the steps. That's the way Holger's always been. Can't put anything back in its place, can't fix anything when it breaks, Teodolinda has always been responsible for everything in that house. That's because of Holger's mother, she spoiled Holger to bits, as I've told you, he was his mother's only—oh my, it's all a result of that, why then blame poor Holger. Go on."

"From what point? If I do go on, you'll say right off: now you're remembering it wrong."

"So you went and the smell of the pharmacy was like the smell of new life to your senses."

"I've never said anything like that."

"You did, too, once. Go on. Tell about when you saw the pharmacist."

"How could I know then who it was? The front hall was like the sacristy of a church, big and dark, and the thin one goes on ahead, up the stairs . . ."

"Little by little, you could leave out those adjectives when you speak about the pharmacist's wife and the county doctor's wife, especially since their roles have been reversed. As I've told you: the one who was thin is now fat and the one who was fat is now thin."

"That's not the way it is. The pharmacist's wife is just as thin as she was then, you've said so yourself. The county doctor's wife has turned from thin to fat in front of my eyes."

"You're right, excuse me, go on."

"'Come in!' she shouts from the stairs. 'Why did you stay there . . . ?'"

"Poor Teodolinda hasn't ever learned to speak Finnish properly, but that's her mother's fault. The mother was Ostrobothnian Swedish, spoke Finnish all right, but didn't really want to, and it's Holger's fault too. He condescended to speak Swedish with Teodolinda, and because Teodolinda generally speaks so little anyway, she hasn't had much practice, but go on. So you were in the front hall of the pharmacy."

"'She waits there!' she shouts. I wait."

"And you felt strange."

"I don't know."

"But you still insist there were birds in the hallway?"

"Pictures of birds. And a picture of a fox."

"No, there wasn't, there was only one picture, the same one that's always been there. A fox with a bird in its mouth, a partridge, a gray partridge, but the coloring's all wrong. Go on."

"The door opens . . ."

"And you stand there in the light like a dazed owl."

"That's not what I've said, I said the sun was shining through the doorway so that I couldn't make out whether it was a man or a woman, because I couldn't even understand . . ." "Because you didn't understand that he was speaking Swedish. "'*Va i helvete*,' how like Holger. 'Who are you?' Go on."

"'I came with the parson's widow,' I said. 'So where is she now?' 'Went that way.'"

"And you point up the stairs."

"Yes. 'She said you should wait.'"

"'*E de sant?*' . . . 'Went that way?' And Holger points upstairs."

"That's right."

"And Holger wonders aloud: '*Va in helvete*? Why did she go there?'"

"That's right. 'I don't know,' I say."

"And Holger swears, he always swears when he's in a good mood, never when he's in a bad one, that's strange too, it's usually the other way around. But Holger has always been unusual. Go on."

"So he asks: 'But who are you, anyway?' I said my name. 'And you came with Adele, I mean, with the parson's widow.' 'Yes,' I say. 'Where the hell from?' 'From the city,' I say. 'By train.' 'But why did she leave you out there, why did she go there?' And the pharmacist looks up the stairs."

"That's because I hadn't visited them for some time, and when I did I never went upstairs directly from the hall without being invited to do so. That is, after all, where their bedroom is."

"You were on bad terms then," said Alma. "Minor disagreements with Teodolinda, though it wasn't really Teodolinda's fault but Elsa's, as always. But you know, don't you, I have told you: when I start hating someone I hate everybody, even the innocent ones, when it comes to the sheriff's descendants. But go on."

"He swore in Swedish, later I learned that swearing is what it was, and he started up the stairs and you could hear it all the way down when they were talking, 'Where, where is Adele, where in the world is she.' 'Who?' says the pharmacist's wife. And they both come to the head of the stairs and the pharmacist's wife says 'she's at home, of course, why are you talking such nonsense,' or something like that. 'But this one here says Adele went up the stairs,' says the pharmacist and points to me. 'Where did the parson's widow go?' asks the pharmacist's wife. And I can't come out and say you are her, that I'd just asked, 'aren't you the parson's widow.' 'What?' says the pharmacist and begins to laugh, they speak Swedish with each other and the pharmacist swears, I understand that only later. 'Do you, girl, think she's the parson's widow?' says the pharmacist. 'My dear girl, she's Teodolinda, my missus, my own wife.' And he laughs. But the pharmacist's wife didn't like that. She said in a dark voice that there was nothing to laugh about, the girl has made a mistake."

"So like Teodolinda, she's never been able to laugh. Poor Holger, as sunny as a child, all kind-hearted and jolly, and if he hadn't married Teodolinda . . . but go on."

"The pharmacist says: 'Now you'll be taken to the parson's widow.'"

"'Now you'll be taken to the parson's widow.' Just like Holger. Go on."

"That was it. I don't remember."

"You're thinking of something," said the parson's widow after a moment. "What are you thinking? Tell me."

"So it was a Saturday when I came."

"You still insist it was Saturday."

"But my God, Missus, I've always said it was Saturday." "Do not take in vain . . . but go on. Do you still insist I was heating the sauna?"

"Yes, you were, and you were wearing a flowered dress."

"Never. Never once since my husband's death have I put on colorful clothes. Don't shake your head, I haven't. First you think Teodolinda is me . . ."

"I wasn't very far off, you look the same."

"But how could you know what I look like when you hadn't

seen me, and do you still insist that Teodolinda's dress had velvet buttons?"

"Yes."

"Teodolinda once had a dress like that when she was young, but she would never have gone to the city and let herself be seen by the Mikanders in such a threadbare dress. The Mikanders are relatives of the sheriff, cousins to Teodolinda, Elsa, and Birger. Never, Teodolinda . . . and do you still deny you were wearing a red, not a white, scarf on your head?"

"Yes."

"That scarf was red." Alma grew angry.

"Tell me, what did you think when you saw me?" the parson's widow continued in a soft, coaxing voice. "When you stood there on the steps with a bucket in your hand?"

"I wasn't standing on the steps but I was inside, in the room. Maybe I looked out into the yard through the curtains when I heard footsteps, as is my custom."

"But how could I have seen you if you hadn't been on the steps?"

The parson's widow controlled herself and started on a new topic.

"Have I changed a lot since those times?"

"No, you're the same as you were then."

"You're lying. I don't know why, but go on. How about Teodolinda?"

"Not a bit."

"And Holger?"

"He's a bit fatter, and lost some hair from the top of his head."

"But do you still insist there were many pictures of birds in the front hall of the pharmacy?"

"Yes, there were."

"I can tell you're mixing things up on purpose," the parson's widow said bitterly. "It's always been just that one picture, although

the coloring of the partridge is all wrong, and Teodolinda, an ornithologist's sister, certainly knows that, but she still hasn't demanded
that the picture be taken off the wall and destroyed, as Birger, in his
day, advised her to do. Teodolinda lets it be, that's the way Holger
wants it. That's how it was when Holger's father was alive and that's
how it will be. Teodolinda understands and I don't blame her for it."

A silence followed. Knitting needles were clicking in Alma's
hands.

"Tell me, which one of us do you think is the strangest? So it's
me." The parson's widow answered her question herself.

"So you were walking here behind Teodolinda and you thought
this house was quite a wreck."

"No, it wasn't then."

"No, not yet. Now the roof leaks, and the pharmacy's roof, too.
They both leak."

"People do wonder about it."

"Have you heard something?" the widow asked vehemently.
"People think the medicines are going to get wet. They're dry. They
all say it's my fault," the widow said after a while. "They're asking for it again." Alma was silent. "Someone walking on the road?"
They listened.

"Who would be coming here?" Alma wondered.

"I'm expecting Elsa. She comes to see me only when it's a question of that. Herman sends Elsa to convince me."

"Why would you be forced to sell your house out from under
you?"

"Is that how you see it?"

"Why would you let yourself be driven out into the street?"

"They promise they'll arrange a place for me to stay."

"And what about me?"

"You would come with me."

"Don't fall into their traps."

"That's what Holger says too."

"Says something different behind your back," Alma said after a while.

"You don't understand, he just talks to please Teodolinda, he's my friend."

"And would the pharmacist really help you? When it's time for him to leave for Lappeenranta, he'll ask for your last penny. Don't you remember?"

"It's not nice to say so."

"You yourself wept and swore then. And whether it's nice or not, you don't have to do what they want since the papers were drawn up right and proper."

"But you said yourself the papers at your house were drawn up all wrong and should be contested."

"That's a different matter."

"No, it isn't. You fail to see injustice here, but you do see it there."

"Did you see it that way when you did it?"

"I? Did I do anything wrong?"

Red spots came into the cheeks of the parson's widow.

"If you go and fiddle with the books, what else is it but admitting there was something wrong?"

The widow was silent for a long time. Alma clicked her knitting needles.

"You're a good knitter. I've always given you credit for that. Just look, you've already reached the heel." Alma switched knitting needles, and was silent.

And then another story began.

"It was in the autumn, like this, a beautiful afternoon, when Birger came home and said: 'What should I do now?' 'Do what your conscience tells you to do,' I answered. He didn't say a thing, just sat in the very rocking chair I'm sitting in now, I've told you about this, haven't I? He was waging a battle, I could see that all right, but I didn't say anything. Finally I said, 'What does your father want you to do?' 'The house should go to me; the sisters get their fair share.' Alma, do you think Elsa and Teodolinda left here empty-handed? No. You should have seen their dowries, you should have seen the linens their mother provided for Elsa, for one thing. But what happened? You know. After Birger died, that's when it started. First comes Teodolinda. 'This piano was promised to me,' she says. 'Take it,' I say. 'If it's yours, take it, I don't want to keep what's yours.' But she wouldn't take it. 'Play, Teodolinda,' I said when she came to see me after Birger's death, 'play just the way you played when we were young.' 'Why?' she says. 'Why should I play?' she says and looks at her fingers and then at me as if I'd stripped her fingers of their skill in playing, and she gives me a bitter smile. You know how she smiles, rarely, and always with bitterness. 'Why are you looking at me like that? What have I done to you?' I ask. 'Adele, give that piano to Teodolinda,' says Holger. 'But I've said she can have it if it's been promised to her.' 'If,' says Holger. 'She heard that you said "if," and you shouldn't have said "if."' She's always been like that. And the same story with that drop-leaf desk. 'Give that desk to Teodolinda,' said Holger. 'Of course, if it's hers.' 'If,' says Holger, 'why do you say "if" again?' How could I know what had been promised to each one. And then came Elsa. 'Dear Adele, Father gave me that little desk as a Christmas present.' That one there, Alma can see it, all right. 'My dear friend,' I said, 'take it since it's yours.' 'Why don't you take it, Elsa,' I said when she came over a second time. 'But you wouldn't even give Teodolinda the piano.' That's what they would always say, they'd come here and keep saying: Father promised, Mother promised, pointing at things: no, not Teodolinda, now I'm doing her an injustice. She just came that one and only time, looked at the piano a moment, and went away. "It was a terrible time," the parson's widow went on. She rose and started pacing back and forth, agitated. "One morning, after I had again stayed awake all night, when my heart was aching over everything, I walked to the pharmacy, went behind the counter and faced Teodolinda and said: 'Come, come, all of you, and take whatever is yours so I can finally be in peace.' But Teodolinda didn't answer at all, she just looked at me, you know how she looks at another person: like an eagle from the edge of a cloud, that's how she's always looked at me. I don't say hawk, she's not a hawk, not a hawk-owl or chicken-hawk either, but proud like an eagle. 'Go tell Elsa, maybe she wants something, I've already got what's due me.' That's what she said to me, but I knew as soon as she said it she was thinking of the piano. I ran towards the county doctor's house without a hat on my head, without a scarf, coat, gloves, it was God's miracle I didn't get pneumonia. There were people out in the yard. 'What's going on with you now,' says Elsa. 'Well,' say I. 'Come in, don't talk while you're outside, people will hear.' 'I won't come in, I have my pride too,' I said. 'But my dear, darling Adele, I can't go off with you in the middle of the day just like that, and soon it's going to be lunch time. How could you!' I had decided that everything would finally have to be set right, I'd thought about it all through the night. They hadn't dared come while the parson was still alive, but after he died it all started, as soon as poor Birger had been seen to his grave. Not the very same day. Only after a few years had passed, when I believed they weren't going to come, after all, when I'd forgotten to be afraid they'd come, that's when they came. It was a Saturday . . . no, a Monday because just the day before, Antti had gone off to school in the city. Afterwards, it came to me that they would have been ashamed in front of Antti. He is, after all, their brother's flesh and blood. It was like this, towards nightfall, just as I stood watching the sunset, you know I always watch it from that window, not from the dining room, because you can see the new parsonage from there, I never look that way . . ."

"No, you don't," said Alma.

"The sun was just setting beyond the islands. I am standing by the parlor window closest to us, looking straight at the setting sun, do you understand, straight into the sun, when I hear Elsa's voice. And when I turn around, Elsa is standing behind me and breathing like this, nervously huffing and puffing."

"'Well, what's going on?' 'I came to pick up . . .' 'What?' 'What was promised to me.' I sit, trembling in this very chair. She's brought a horseman and wagon with her, and she waves to the hired man: 'That and that and that and that.' Altogether she took eleven objects, do you understand, eleven. I sit and watch. 'This painting,' says Elsa, and takes down a seascape from the dining room wall. A picture of a warship, there are big waves in it, a storm at sea and the ship sinking, and she says Father had promised it to her. 'I asked Father, "When I grow up can I have that picture?" and Father said, "It's yours."' And the hired man carries out the ship. And Elsa stands, looks around her, goes to the other room and I can hear her snatching books from there, the best leather-bound ones. Herman, of course, had advised her. Elsa herself has never read a single book in her life. And the hired man carrying the books out . . ."

"And you just look on."

"I'm looking and trembling. I didn't say a word even though I knew they weren't hers. I tell you this: I am ready to swear before God that they hadn't been promised to Elsa. How could that have been possible?"

"She made it up right then and there."

"Yes, I've told you: she made it up. So is that what you think too? To speak plainly, I'm sure of it myself, I've thought about it on many a sleepless night. 'And this desk, I'll take it as well,' she says, and stands in front of the desk. 'No, I won't take it, after all,' she then says. 'It's dirty. What can I do with it now that dirty birds' eggs have been kept in it?'"

The parson's widow paused and looked at Alma.

"Do you understand . . . she certainly knew that an ornithologist doesn't put dirty eggs in drawers. That Elsa had the nerve to
say so. And she turns, like a hawk-owl her eyes light on the brocade
tablecloth, she yanks it off the table so that the book of Thomas à
Kempis devotions falls onto the floor, the book I read every day,
she had the nerve, and finally she stares at the rocking chair. I get
up and say politely, 'Do you perhaps want this?' She takes a look.
'No,' she says. 'That rocking chair rug was crocheted by Mama, but
you've got it all dirty and worn out, I don't want it.' That's what she
says and doesn't even say thank you when she leaves. And when I
go into the dining room and to Birger's study I can see that three
pillows have been taken. Two velvet ones, one made with cross-
stitching, and one chair that was at Birger's desk, made by Russian
serfs, decorated with ornamental carvings. It had come to Birger
from his uncle, who lived in St. Petersburg. Birger had once promised to leave it to Teodolinda as a Christmas present after his death.
Elsa was the one who took it. And that wasn't all, I almost forgot.
'Where is that brooch?' 'What brooch?' 'You seem to be wearing it
on your chest.'"

"Took it right off your chest," said Alma. "Some nerve."

"Just took it. Reached out her hand, said, 'It's my mother's. Birger
had no right to give it to you.'"

"Took it. Lord God Almighty."

"Like this. Loosened it right here, even though she didn't have
any right to that brooch. And that wasn't all. Two silver candlesticks,
five pairs of forks and knives, seven spoons, two ladles, silver all of
them. The next morning, in comes Teodolinda. I saw her coming
down the birch lane and thought: so now it's her turn to come. I
stood on the stairs to receive her and I thought I would say: take
everything."

"But then she didn't take a thing," Alma helped her along.

"No. Came in, went into the dining room and said: 'So Elsa has done some taking.' 'What?' I asked."

"As if you didn't understand."

"That's right, I was pretending. 'You're out of your mind, Adele.' 'Why do you say that?' 'You should have told her to clear out.' I didn't answer. 'Well, you see,' says Teodolinda, 'as a matter of fact, Father had promised that painting to me. I was the one in this house, not your husband Birger, who played with tin soldiers, and Father said to me: "My dear girl, you should have been a boy." And Father said: "Now tell me, what do you see in that painting?" "Will all the people drown?" "Is that what you're thinking?" he asked, and looked at me with tears in his eyes. "When I'm a grown-up, may I have it?" "You may. It'll be yours." But Elsa claims that Father had promised it to her. Before she came to see me, Teodolinda had gone over and spoken with Elsa and had disapproved of her stripping me of the things. 'Since you wouldn't take anything, I did,' Elsa had said to Teodolinda. 'But go ahead and take it if it's been promised to you.' 'No, thank you. If you think it's yours, then it's yours.' From that day on, they haven't been sisters to each other."

"Oh, my God, the greed in that woman."

"Is that how you see it?" The parson's widow smiled, stopped, then came back and sat in the rocking chair. "That's what I too used to think."

"No blessing on those things, that's what I'd say." "Oh, yes there is." The widow laughed. "The county doctor is a rich man. Teodolinda and Holger . . . well, let it be. What's this house but a sinking ship. It's a good thing Elsa was rescued."

"They've bought a fine new carpet," said Alma, after counting the stitches on her knitting needle. She was starting another sock.

"Well, I'll get a look at it when Elsa's name day comes around."

"And you'll step across that threshold. I wouldn't set foot in there."

"I'll set, I'll sit, and without letting on, I'll keep an eye on Teodolinda and observe that she'll never look straight at that warship."

"Who did the county doctor's wife take after, that she turned out that way?"

"God only knows, I don't. They say, and I know it for sure as well, that her mother was just like that. Her mother was like she is now, but tall, while the sheriff was short."

"The one who was against you?"

"Exactly. Her."

"Were you any worse regarded than she was then?"

"Yes, I was," the parson's widow said simply. "I did go to the girls' school in St. Petersburg, but my father wasn't a sheriff like Elsa's and Teodolinda's father, or a pastor like Holger's father, and my mother wasn't a fine lady like the sheriff's wife. I just don't understand who Teodolinda took after." "A proud woman."

"It's not the same pride as Elsa's pride. Teodolinda's pride is not of this world."

"Not of this world. What, then? She isn't a child of God, that's for sure, she's so proud."

"That's not the way it is. Teodolinda's heart has ached but it hasn't broken. God has not yet set up His dwelling in her. He hasn't, I know. But still, it isn't a pride of this world, it's a woman's pride."

And then the third story began.

Thirteen

The parson's widow had woken. Maybe some bird had flown over the house, but it was autumn, late autumn. She stared into the dark and there was an image she now realized she had gazed upon in her dream, in which Alma's brother, as if he were stubbornly rebelling against time, stared back at her with the shadow of the asparagus plant against his face, the "dream"—that was Alma's voice. The "dream" grew in a tub in a corner of the parlor, and yielded cuttings for wedding bouquets. And at that very moment the bird call was within her, the one she had heard in the dream, or else she had had a dream about something that had brought out that sound. "What kind of sound was it? Tell me." "Kung kung kung kung." She saw herself trying to act out a swan, a swan she had never had a really good look at and then only once, swans high above the house, not making a sound on their way south. Why, then, did I pretend, why did I try to act out something I had never seen myself?

But the man who looked like a thief who dwelled in the forest was looking at her, the shadow of the asparagus plant across his face, the shadow of the dream, more beautiful that way. And she repented: hadn't she sensed the embarrassment and shame on Alma's brother's face as she stubbornly kept repeating to him: "Tell me, show me how." And the brother hadn't told, had been embarrassed, ashamed for her. Well. He was lighting a cigarette and speaking in an embarrassed yet still polite voice, that voice different from Alma's or from any relative of Alma's, the voice in which, underneath the rough dialect, you could detect the greatest considerateness, a kind of manly modesty when he tried to answer her. And his eyes, averted from hers: "I don't know, I guess they may be." And she, acting out the mating rituals of swans, she who had never seen a swan except that once when they were flying overhead. "Swimming in clear water, two big birds." "And you didn't recognize them?" "Yes, yes, I don't know how." "A holy bird," she said, if not in reproach at least in a gentlewoman's tone of voice, she knew it all right, talking about things which maybe were strange, wasted on the ears of that peasant who looked like a forest bandit yet was still so refined. "Kung kung kung." "Did the sound come from the wings or the throat, that sound like the tolling of church bells, as if someone on shore were banging on an iron pot, as you said?" And Alma's brother, wanting to speak about something else, or at least hoping that she wouldn't talk about it anymore, silent, without a clue, in front of her as she tried out her miserable performance of a bird she hadn't even seen.

"I'm not an actor. I'm not as good an actor as you," she had said, and now the wood grouse had gone out of his eyes. He didn't look at me, thought I would say something sarcastic.

"Well, he didn't understand me," the parson's widow said aloud. "I was excited, much too excited," she said after a while. And still: wasn't there something else in Alma's brother's eyes? "You are a great actor." Hadn't he, after the discussion turned to other matters, hadn't he said: "Well, the sisters, they did some acting. Not me, certainly." And then she had heard how Alma, dressed as the maiden Aino, and the neighbor's boy dressed as the old sage Väinämöinen had stood in the grassy bay, with the brother laughing on the shore. Yes, they had started a young people's association. "Didn't you? You're such an artist." "No, not me." "Didn't he say it almost angrily, as if he were fed up?" "Well, he was feeling embarrassed," said Alma. "Come on, stop being silly, that's what I said also." "Silent stands

Ferenc Renyi, silent General Hanau too." But Alma, with brothers around her all of a sudden telling how, in the old days, they would read, sing, act, and this performance had been given only once, at the time when they'd founded the young peoples' association. "And these two stood in the water up to their underwear, all dressed in white, hair flowing, Alma here being Aino and the Rämänen boy V-äinämöinen. "Don't be silly," said Alma. "Frans was ashamed," the sister-in-law whispered to her. "If only they would come away and stop making fools of themselves," the wood-grouse brother had said, watching his sisters' performance from the sidelines.

"In open water, the lakes had already frozen over, but in Kurki-inen, the current keeps the water from freezing, I just happened to come across two big birds on the ice, I was fishing, just so happened I was carrying a gun." "And did you shoot?" "Yes, I did, shouldn't have done that, I hadn't understood, oh my God how the mate screeched and circled around." Mate. By that he meant the other swan which had circled above the village, screeching, the sound like a church bell, as if a bronze bell were being struck. "That clanging. Made me sick." "Did you see it?" They had seen it and not seen it—but the sound they had all heard, all except Alma, who insisted she couldn't remember. Of course she remembered, she only pre-tended not to, the parson's widow thought. But what if it was the sound of a wing, sound of flying, not a bird call—"kylk" it had called, clanging like a bronze bell. "For a long time it was flying in a circle, like this." The brother was making a circle of his arms. "Well, of course it might have been calling out in its grief, I then thought that there would never again be a day for me when I shot a bird, it sure robbed me of a night's sleep. The women had been afraid, well women, they were always afraid. They interpreted everything as an omen," the brother had laughed. "I took it away to be stuffed, heaven knows where it is. The kids would ride on its back, and it finally got carted off to the hayloft."

Why had he taken it to be preserved? Because he'd wanted a decorative object, or had he not known where to put it? Where would one put a strange white body which ... well, where had the dead swan been lying? In the kitchen, the front hall, the shed, the yard? Where had it been for that time? Was it taken to the taxidermist the next day, or after a couple of days? Maybe the one who shot the swan had decided to have it stuffed only after he realized that he didn't know how to deal with that strange white body, didn't know how to get rid of it. Even the dogs avoided it, considered it unfit to eat. Maybe the women of the house ... Alma's mother, if she had been told, maybe the mother had become agitated, been restless after hearing the bird's call in the night, had become terrified, maybe the mother had been shown the dead bird, it had been carried to her sick-bed in the dim room, a boy carrying a large bird in his arms, dragging the big bird by the feet. "Kung kung kung." The parson's widow had set her arms down along her sides. Wings dragging on the ground, maybe the neck, she stretched out her neck ... she saw Alma's brother wandering around the darkening yard with the dead bird in his arms, looking for a place to bury it, maybe with the cry of the mate of the dead bird circling around overhead in the sky, and the slayer—she said it aloud: *slayer*—had decided right then what to do with the white body which you couldn't bury because there was no place on earth for a bird that belonged in the heavens. The parson's widow said it aloud, she was making up a story of a swan which, shot down from the sky, had come across her path and into her life by such a strange route, and which would now have been a part of her collection if she had known how to proceed the right way and in time, and which had not been given to her although it had first been promised. Alma had promised, but to this day she hadn't kept her promise. And the parson's widow grew angry.

I don't hate your brother, Alma, for he already understood what he had done as he carried the swan down the village lane like a cross on his back as he went to the taxidermist, carrying the body of the swan on his back like a white coffin. The parson's widow saw a ship land at a pier, saw Alma's brother get on board the ship, a black steam barge, with a strange burden on his back, and though the widow knew no ships sailed in the winter and that it had been winter when the swan was shot, this is the way she always saw it: Alma's brother climbing aboard the black ship with a white load on his shoulder, the astounded silent glances of the sailors—for as the men saw him standing on the pier in the semi-darkness, they had thought he was carrying a coffin, and he had brought death to their minds—and Alma's brother, an awkward, sensitive woodsman, ever more troubled under his strange load, and as the story went, he didn't speak to anyone on the voyage, could not speak, he was becoming more and more tormented, and he knew he could never get away from the bird's "kung kung kung" calls until he could get the white body out of his hands. The ship was covered over with ice, the swan was frozen, its carrier's hands were freezing, icy leather mittens wound around the bird's neck were holding it; on the feathers, stains, icy dried-up blood, dirt stains which the taxidermist . . . she could see his blackened fingertips, could sense the smell which haunted him even in a dream. The parson's widow saw Alma's brother go to the taxidermist to pick up the bird he had shot. She saw him stepping into—every room where the swan had ever been was dim in the widow's imagination, so that the bird's whiteness stood out all the more clearly—stepping into the steamy room, covered with snow, frost clinging to his beard, eyebrows frozen, saw his eyes looking to the back wall of the room where the birds were lined up on the shelf: owls, wood grouse, black grouse, some smaller birds among them, beaks all pointing in the same direction, and in the middle of the shelf, above all others, his bird, the large white one, looking as if it were alive, washed clean of blood stains, its neck lifted, straight, waiting for its mate which, out of sight, was eating succulent grass on the shore. Alma's brother's eyes, delighted, relieved, his voice as he pointed to the bird and said: "I came to pick up this one." And how pleased he was to pay for it, how willing the fingers as he counted out the money into the taxidermist's hand. That's where the story ended. The parson's widow could no longer see how the bird had made its way back to the house, could not see it in a corner of the parlor, and could not see the degradation in which it was to end.

"You are a great actor." She remembered her own words. And as she said it she had realized that her own performance had been below par. She tormented herself, was overly harsh, for she hadn't even performed it, the mating dance of the swans, had only asked, did you see it, how did they do it, how did they bow to each other. Only once had she bowed her head, maybe twice, once craned her neck to show how the swans, hadn't she tried to mimic the swan's call . . . and still, hadn't she tormented Alma by asking, "Alma, did I utter that 'kung kung kung' then?" "Oh, my God, Missus, you always go 'kur kur hei hei hei,' how could I forget it?" "No, Alma, long-tailed ducks call 'hei hei,' the loon calls 'kuiiki kuiiki,' you mix them up, but now did I say 'kung kung' . . ." That's what had got Alma mad at her again last night. But she couldn't get away from it, though she was sure she hadn't tried to act out the swans' mating dance; but still, she had bent her head once or twice, had stretched out her neck once, yes, it was possible, exactly at the point when she had stretched out her neck, that sound of 'kung kung,' which she had read about in books but which she herself had never heard, had remained to torment her. Did the noise come from the wings when they flew, or did it come from the throat? she had asked.

She had certainly understood that Alma's brother, embarrassed at being asked something like that, and thinking he was being mocked in some way, said, lighting his cigarette that had gone out: "Don't really know them, don't know their habits, but the sound was mean, when it circled around and screeched, circled for days on end." "Well, I'll bet it disappeared in the river, who knows where it flew." "You're a great actor." But facing her sat an embarrassed, troubled artist who didn't even understand that he was an artist. The word was strange, alien to him, made him think he was being sneered at, and that's what Alma had thought too, before she came to know me and know I'm mad. Mad. Alma thinks I'm mad. She no longer remembered whether they'd had this discussion before they even spoke of the swan . . . her miserable attempt to act out a swan, if indeed she had even made the attempt, she hadn't, Alma had sworn to that . . . but just the fact that she could have, before it or after it, when Alma's brother turned into a wood grouse right before her eyes . . . if again the brother, embarrassed by her futile attempt, before he had changed into a wood grouse, so that she, in her attempt to best a perfect artist, she who could not even mimic the squeaking of a duck, had been mad.

The parson's widow tried to sleep, tried, but still the images, that story, the swan's journey from the open water to the hands of the taxidermist . . . should get some sleep, but she couldn't, she couldn't, when she thought again that the swan would now be in the collection if only Alma, in her stupidity, hadn't told them to take it up to the loft of the cow barn. She was sure that if Alma had gone with her that time they would have found it, but Alma, in her great stupidity . . . and she herself hadn't known to act at the right moment, either.

This is my fate, she said to herself. She never knew what she should have said, she always said it only afterwards, and now Alma wouldn't even consent to listen when she tried. To go get a non-existent bird, no, Alma wouldn't give in to that. And my insomnia tonight is all because you don't obey, I'll pay for any of your trips . . . she had even promised Alma the silver candlestick if only she would go for the swan before it was too late, but Alma had become horrified and had forbidden her ever to breathe so much as a single word to her family about it. As if I wouldn't understand, she thought. As if I wouldn't. But they don't understand that I would give all my finery, would give everything to the one who would bring the swan into my collection. That very swan: she felt, she was sure it had been God's will and intent that the hand of Alma's brother had been lifted to kill the swan—like Abraham's hand over Isaac. But Alma called it heathen, called it madness, Alma got hurt, upset, didn't want to listen, went straight to the pharmacy when I said: "It was God's will that your brother raised his hand, God's will that the swan was shot, for me, by the hand of Alma's brother, a message to my heart, to my collection."

And again, the parlor empty, Alma and Alma's sister-in-law, laughing, children they tried to keep quiet and out of the parlor, the parlor empty, she alone with Alma's brother, still trying to portray, her head lifted, bowing, still asking, pestering: "Was it like this, was it spring, were they courting?" But the swans had been swimming in open water, the open water of a current. And she, the parson's widow, a guest who had come to Alma's old home, in the middle of the parlor emitting from her mouth strange gurgling noises, lifting her head, spreading her arms, her fingers, and asking "were they bowing to each other like this, like this," and the shame that this memory of the event brought to her was so painful that her body kept repeating those ridiculous bows as if she were punishing herself, arms flailing along her sides with the fingers now spread, now tightly pressed together, back and forth, repeating the movements she had made when she'd been acting out the bird she had never seen.

But it wasn't true, of course. She hadn't made any of the movements she was now repeating over and over again, pacing back and forth in the room. Alma had sworn up and down that nothing like that had happened, that yes, the widow had raised her head once, but only once. But had Alma seen everything? No. And the parson's widow stepped towards the door, walked across the room, started towards the door, stopped in front of the door, thought a moment, yanked the door open and was on her way downstairs. She went in at Alma's door, went to Alma's bed, and woke her.

"Oh, my God, you're driving me crazy."

"Light the lamp, light the lamp so I can see in your face whether you're telling the truth," said the parson's widow. She fumbled for the matches on the table, managed to light the lamp. Alma had woken up, had thought the pharmacist had come and once again fallen on the stairs. She hadn't been able to fall asleep right after she'd gone to bed, but had stayed awake, crying, had finally fallen asleep, and when she finally realized that the parson's widow had awoken her in the middle of the night to ask the very thing she'd been after all evening, Alma became furious and said: "You drive me out of bed and it wasn't even the pharmacist."

"You lied to me. You lied, do you think I don't know, the night before last you were out fishing with the pharmacist although you told me you had gone to the old people's home, to butter up the director. Go to the old people's home, go on, go right away. Go ahead. Go, go. I ask you, and you, answer me now, did I demonstrate to your brother the mating dance of swans, did I show him how they do it, did I raise my neck, and you swore to me that I didn't do it, that I asked only whether they went this way and that and as I said it, I just bowed my head a little. How could I have done anything like that, I, who have never even had a good look at a swan? Why don't you come out and say that I did it, why? Why wouldn't I have done it? If you lie that you were seeing the director of the old people's home and were, after all, out fishing with the pharmacist, you are also lying about my bowing my head only once. Tell me, how could I have mimicked a bird I have never even heard, have seen a swan only once, flying over the forest in spring."

Alma was putting on her shirt and crying.

"I've told you that you said 'hoi hoi' only once."

"You're lying. You mix everything up, you do it on purpose, you pretend you don't remember that's what long-tailed ducks say."

"How could I remember when you always say 'kuiiki kuiiki'!"

"I do!"

The parson's widow slammed the door shut, ran down the stairs, mimicking Alma: "Kuik kuik kuik." For a long time, Alma could hear her venting her rage upstairs, pacing back and forth in the hall: would she, an ornithologist's wife, know only one bird call, would she ever confuse the calls of a long-tailed duck and a swan, let alone a loon and a swan? "For years I've had to teach her, free of charge, using the collection of Finland's finest ornithologist to demonstrate, and she will learn nothing in my house but to lie right to my face in order to get to sleep, her miserable animal sleep.

"Like cattle you sleep your deep sleep, but I stay awake because of your lies, if only you had said to me straight that it was true, that—I'm prepared to confess my performance was below par— I . . . supposedly imitating a swan, you should have told me the truth, you were all mocking me, I know."

The shouting upstairs turned into bursts of weeping and laughing, in turn. Alma could make out some words but she didn't understand what they meant. And she didn't listen, she had gone to the pharmacy to get some sleeping medicine for the parson's widow.

FOURTEEN

"The parson's widow is already asleep, you mustn't disturb her, Sir."

"You bear," said Holger, "you guard the lair well. Come sit with me. I just came back from the city. You know my wife. Do I have any business going home when I've just got back from the city? What do you think?"

"How do I know? But please, Sir, go away, the parson's widow is asleep."

"But you don't sleep, do you? You stay awake, you vestal virgin. Come here, give me your hand. So you won't come, you're being very proper. Well, listen, when I look at you I see someone who looks more like a man than a woman. Right here," said Holger, patting his hips, "you're like a woman, but there," he touched his chin, sketching in the air with his hand as if he were using a pen, "there, you're a man. You're of good stock. Where did you come from? Here, among us weak and miserable mortals? Don't go. Stay and talk to me. Well, why should you pretend? You know all right, well, don't tilt your head, your mane's just like a horse's, long, let me feel it . . . you pull back, well, put that club on the table, do you think I'm some robber? What? I'll tell you who's a robber." He pointed behind his back with his thumb.

Alma didn't know how to get the pharmacist out of the house. Now she sat down behind the table.

"Don't you want to talk with me? What, do you think I don't like you? You know I like you, well, have I ever treated you badly? Tell me."

"What are you up to now?" The floor was cold. Alma was sitting in her nightgown, barefooted, just the way she'd risen from her bed after hearing noises on the stairs, and there was the rolling pin she'd happened to take into her hand when she quietly crept to the front hall. She had heard the pharmacist's voice behind the door, and so as not to have the parson's widow wake up, Alma had opened the door to say the widow was already asleep and this wasn't a good time to come in.

Holger listened to Alma, his head tilted to one side, and he did not look drunk.

"You're looking at me," he said all of a sudden. "Shall I tell you what you're thinking?" When Alma didn't respond, he went on: "You do a lot of thinking, you think about us." He waved his hand. "Go ahead and think. It's good to think. There's no end to a thought. When you start at the beginning you won't get to the end, there's plenty of it. I know. Tell me why you left home. Don't you want to? I mean, wouldn't you like to go away? You turn your head aside but I say to you, don't leave Adele, she's a fine person. What do you think of me? You pretend not to think at all. I know you think, and I know I'm an old drunk. How old are you? You're already really fat. Look at me, am I fat?"

"No, Sir, you're not," said Alma.

She stirred, moved to a chair on the opposite side of the table.

Outside, the wind was blowing and rain was pouring down. "It's raining," said Holger. "Have you got rats here?" he asked.

"Haven't heard any. Mice we've got."

"There, we've got rats. Do you think that's nice? They attack."

"We had rats at home," Alma said.

"Were you afraid?"

"What's there to fear? Well, it made one scared now and then because when we went to the cellar we had to hang by our hands."

"Hang?"

"Yes, we had that kind of a crossbeam and you had to grab hold of it first and then let go and drop yourself down in the cellar. That was nasty."

"What made you leave? Did you get mad, or what?"

"I tossed the threshing flail out of my hands in front of the drying house and I've been away ever since."

The pharmacist, she could talk with the pharmacist when he was no more drunk than this. One could talk with him, especially at a time like this, when it was raining outside.

"Do you understand Adele? Of course not."

"It's not my business to understand. I just do my work, that's enough understanding for me."

"Why don't you go somewhere else?"

"Should I get going, then?" Alma's voice was aggressive. She was listening carefully.

Holger pretended not to hear. He had lifted his arm and was holding it across her shoulders.

"You know that Adele . . ." Holger knocked on his head. "You know, but you don't care, that's right. And don't go anywhere. Do you want me to find you a man?"

"I don't care for men," Alma said, and got up suddenly, walked to the window, walked back, this time to a different chair, one that stood next to the wall.

"You do care. You pretend. You look at me and think, that man sure wouldn't look like that . . . well, just take a look. Do you know, there was once a handsome growth of hair on this head. Just ask Adele. There was a time when this head had hair, all blond and curly."

Soon the pharmacist would begin weeping.

He was looking at his wrist, which bore a light scar.

"At first it wasn't the way it is now with Teodolinda," he said. "Now, don't act superior."

"What about me?"

"Yes, you think I don't understand that you know . . ." He described a circle in the air, circumscribing the whole family and the three houses in which they lived, in one gesture. "You're curious. But I don't tell you anything."

And after a moment:

"Have you heard I was the first one, before that Birger came along? Don't act as if you didn't know. The two of you here, you women, what do you do here, I'll tell you, you gossip from morning till night. My wife doesn't gossip, no, she doesn't. Teodolinda has learned to keep her mouth shut, she's out for revenge, you see. I come and I go, and she says nothing, but you know that Teodolinda makes me sleep in the cellar. You see, I go there myself . . . no need to, I say, no need to say it. I know it. I know my place, there are no rats here, none, and she washes my laundry. She's a good wife. Don't you speak ill of my wife. What? Don't I know what the two of you together . . . old harpies. There was a widow in Viipuri, a beautiful one. Teodolinda knows but doesn't say anything. I say: what if I go to Viipuri . . . she doesn't say a thing, doesn't answer. She doesn't live there anymore. Went away. Have you ever been to Viipuri? Answer me."

Alma made a gesture the pharmacist could interpret any way he wanted.

"So what did Viipuri look like?"

"A fine place, they have a tower there."

"Listen, you don't know anything about Viipuri. Tell me something more specific, define what you mean. I'm a drunk, yes, and that widow doesn't live in Viipuri anymore, she doesn't, and I don't go to Viipuri even though I say to Teodolinda that I'll head off for Viipuri and you take care of the pharmacy. A daughter of a Swedish-speaking sheriff, still, she speaks Finnish . . . Come closer. Are you afraid of me?" Holger said after a while.

"What should I be afraid of?"

"Do you think I'm a nice man? What?"

"Of course the pharmacist is a nice man," said Alma and sat down beside Holger. "But if you could please speak more softly, or the parson's widow will wake up."

"I'll whisper." And Holger whispered: "Have any of them come around here?"

"Any what?"

"Of Adele's visitors."

Alma didn't answer.

"Don't you know? But they will come, just wait, they'll come and walk on the porch and in the attic. Haven't you seen the one that's dripping with water, appears in a hunting outfit. Adele's visitors."

"The widow doesn't have visitors, she doesn't like having lots of people around."

Alma braided her hair and wound it up in a bun.

"Make me some coffee."

Alma fixed her hair.

"Adele will scold you if you don't make me some. She'll ask you in the morning: did you make coffee for the pharmacist? What will you say to that? Or haven't you people got any?"

"Oh, sure, we've got some." Alma went off to the kitchen. First she put on her dress and then started a fire in the stove. Alma listened. Strange that the parson's widow didn't wake up though she usually woke at the slightest noise. It came into Alma's mind that the widow was dead, lying with hands crossed on the sheet . . . no, those weren't the widow's steps, it was the pharmacist moving about in the dark parlor, and next, a thumping sound. Bumped into a chair and knocked it over, Alma thought, and now the widow is going to wake up. But it was silent upstairs, and the pharmacist's uncertain steps could be heard in the front hall. Could he be leaving? Alma wondered. She stood holding a log in one hand while the other hand held open the stove door. She was awake, lively, and would have been glad to make some coffee, for the pharmacist was really drunk. She could convince him to go home if only she could get him to drink some coffee, she could certainly manage that. But the steps came into the kitchen and now the pharmacist was standing at the door, looking at her questioningly, as if he were sober, his sparse hair hanging over his eyes, one hand in a pocket, the other shoved inside his jacket across the chest, he stood just the way he did when he faced a customer at the pharmacy.

"Come talk with me."

"I'm making the coffee now."

"I don't drink coffee."

"But you yourself told me to make some."

"I won't drink it. Come."

And Holger sat down on the bench by the side of the stove and looked.

"What are you doing there? Go on inside."

"Do you think . . ."

"What?"

"I just asked: do you think?"

"What should I think?"

"You don't think wrong at all, you know. It was you I came to see."

Alma put the log back into the wood box and went and sat down next to the water tub.

"There's a storm, a storm."

"You're drunk. You go on home now, the parson's widow will wake."

Holger leaned his head on the water tub. "Woman," he said. "Woman," he repeated as if he were beginning a speech.

"Don't knock over that tub now."

"Is there water in it? Let me have some, I'm thirsty."

Alma scooped water from the blue tub which looked black

in the dark and the water in it was black. She took a glass from the cabinet and filled it with water, but Holger wouldn't take the glass. Instead, he dropped to his knees next to the tub and started drinking, drank water straight from the tub, making slurping noises. Alma, standing, was now watching the slurping man from a black corner on the other side of the kitchen.

"Sit down. Let's talk."

Alma sat down.

"When I tell you to do something, you obey right away. Haven't you got a will of your own?"

"The parson's widow will hear."

"I'm quiet, I'll sit quietly."

Outside there was wind and rain, and branches of the maple tree swayed under the window. Now and then the rain beat harder against the window panes. The silence continued, and Alma thought of the night noises. She concentrated on listening, thought the pharmacist had fallen asleep: his head drooped on his chest, eyes closed, legs sticking out straight. Alma wondered whether she should move the sleeping man onto the floor, carry him to the sofa in the parlor, or go away, when the pharmacist stirred and said softly, with his eyes open: "Come here."

"Come here."

"I'm not coming anywhere. I'm here, but you'd better go home, you're tired."

"Don't be afraid. If Adele hears noises she'll think they are visitors, and maybe I'm one of them, after all," he said after a while. "One of Adele's visitors."

Soon he'll begin to cry, Alma thought, but the pharmacist moved his head.

"You know that it's for you that I'm sitting here. It amuses me."

"What's making you laugh? Even though you're as drunk as you are, you shouldn't laugh at people who are beneath you."

"What's going to become of you, old hag with a hooked chin? You won't become like Teodolinda, my wife, and you won't become like Elsa, that spouse of the quack. You're a selfish person, yes, you are, a selfish person, and Adele won't drive you mad, you don't catch madness, you'll turn into a tough, sturdy old woman, you won't grow old like Adele and me, before our time. No, when you leave Adele, you'll take on someone else who'll boss you around. You'll be an old maid if you don't get married right away, but you won't, you have the kind of chin that won't let you get married. Don't get angry, well now you did get angry. Don't you understand that I admire you, it amuses me that you're the best man Adele ever had."

Alma asked about the two women, the sisters-in-law of the parson's widow.

"My, aren't you clever," said Holger. "But I won't tell you anything, anything at all. You're waving your mane in vain. You don't know how my wife Teodolinda has had to suffer. You're wise not to take a husband. But it hasn't always been like that. What? Shall I tell you?"

Alma pretended not to hear. If he went on like this, she would hear, she would find out something new. To be sure, the beginning of the story was just the same as before.

"The sheriff had two daughters and a son. That son was the parson, his name was Birger, husband to this Adele. Well, you know that, but you don't know everything. Some say Adele is mad, but I say Birger was mad, but he could preach, oh how he could, you don't even know, he made me cry once. I cried, you see. I'm crying even now. These sheriff's daughters were proud, both of them. Pride, I say, that's all, but Teodolinda has the right kind of pride, that woman doesn't complain . . . but you go over to Elsa's place, just listen to her. I don't go to Elsa's, I don't go except when I'm sober. They celebrate name days, they do it out of pride, to show

how things are with them and how they are with us. No one cares about Adele. You too despise Adele because you're a silly peasant woman . . . Not bad, not bad, though Teodolinda's nose is long like her father's, proud, these sheriff's daughters, these two, and at that time they still had something they could pride themselves on. Well, their father was a drunk. So away went the fortune, all of it, now they say I drink. Elsa, never have liked her, took after her mother. And this Herman came along and took Elsa, he didn't know how things were. Papa's money all gone, Herman really got taken in. Teodolinda was taken in when she took me, because I wasn't the right man for her. You pretend not to know all of this, but I know Adele. Adele chatters on about everything. Birger did reproach her for it. And I'll tell the truth: Teodolinda hasn't been a woman at all, you don't know and I'll say no more . . . This house is the same, here we danced and played, we were young, Teodolinda was not what she is now, and Elsa knew how to blush and sit nicely, sipped her coffee with her finger lifted, has never known how to do much else, but Teodolinda was a learned woman, she's read a great deal, but you wouldn't understand any of that. Have you read *The Kreutzer Sonata*, or *War and Peace*, *Anna Karenina* . . . the pharmacist reeled off names that slid past Alma's ears until she heard . . . 'if I had studied,' said Teodolinda, that's what she used to say, and now she doesn't say anything. 'And where would you be?' I said. 'I would be alone.' You see, she meant me. 'But you are alone now, too,' I say. But all of that's in the past. It's over and when I speak to her she doesn't answer, the worst thing is that she never says anything, not ever. A bottle, a bottle," repeated the pharmacist, "a tightly corked bottle, high-necked, but I know what's inside. Poison. Do you know that when a person is alone, that person is filled with poison, don't you believe Adele isn't, Adele is a bottle of poison, Adele has poison in her. Pulls out the cork, lets her God in, plugs the cork back in, can't do anything about it. Herman a bottle, Elsa a bottle, poison in every bottle but I am a free man, I go to the city, tell them to pull out the cork, see, I talk, I let it out, do you hear me talking, even though you are what you are, you're not yet a bottle of poison, but you'll turn into one, you won't make it through life, I know you've already been poisoned, Adele has poisoned you. Teodolinda had the poison already in her, you see she had a dream, the devil knows what about, people shouldn't have dreams, and now it's turned into poison . . . Elsa was cream pastry, it was all the same whether it was Herman or someone else who ate her, Elsa wouldn't have turned into anything other than what she is, just take a look and you'll see, a little round chicken's head, the rear end of a hen, trailing behind Herman, quacking. You think I'm the worst of us, but you're mistaken, it's Herman, just you take a peek inside him, everything you see is empty, the man hasn't either rejoiced or mourned and he calls that kind of life sensible . . . Teodolinda no longer mourns, the cork is tightly plugged, the bottle sealed, the wine that was in it has soured, it won't explode, no, like the jars of jam in that hell of a cellar, when I thought they were shooting at me when the bottle burst open. . Teodolinda makes berry preserves every autumn and the bottles ferment in the cellar, but Elsa's bottles don't ferment, Elsa knows how to make preserves, go take a look, in that house they look after the household in quite a different way from ours. 'You should learn from your sister,' I used to say. I don't say that anymore. Did I tell you about Adele? Adele has taken out the cork, it burst open when Birger died, you know, Adele went mad, they say, it isn't so . . . well, crazy. And no wonder. Things didn't turn out well for the sheriff's children and it's not my fault, Teodolinda took me at Elsa's urging. You think Adele is innocent. She's not, I tell you. She held her own, this house and lot are hers. Birger said: 'Let's divide up the rest among the sisters.' Adele said: 'No.' I know. First I had my eye on Elsa, the small roly-poly one, red cheeks, and I could have had her but I didn't find her voice appealing, she twitted and chirped, in other words, she was a hen. I looked at Teodolinda, dark, proud, very different from her sister, tall, thin, long nose like her mother's but she had breeding, you don't know, you should have seen her, no. She wasn't so appealing, but the voice, like that of a foreign governess, like a Frenchwoman, a white dress, always neat, steady voice, steady gait, she read books, I thought at least she was clever. 'How do you like Nietzsche?' I would converse, I would say: 'How do you like this book?' That was *The Kreutzer Sonata*. And then a light came into her eyes, she talked for a long time and very excitedly and I proposed—just like that, without giving it much thought, I was already over thirty and Mother said I should get married and settle down, and I thought she was right. Teodolinda had the same erect carriage she has today, I saw my life ahead of me, together with Teodolinda, and life has been together with Teodolinda, that it really has been. But then I went to Viipuri."

"You've already talked about that. I'd like to go to sleep now. You go home too, Sir. The parson's widow will wake up."

"Has already woken, is listening to us, pretends to be asleep. I don't care about her, it's you I came to see. Listen, it wasn't that one anymore but another, a small round one, I've never liked tall women, tall women scare me, she was small, a little woman, a real wench, not like you or all of you harpies around here. Young and pretty, white teeth. What else could I have done? Teodolinda didn't care for me or I for her. Well, Teodolinda didn't care for me and I went to Viipuri and took that other one, and went again to Viipuri and took a third and a fourth . . ."

"You're lying, you're talking nonsense."

"All right, you guessed it. Have I talked about this before? Have I? Well, no, all I had was the one and I did love her. Teodolinda knew but didn't say anything. She was proud, took after her mother. But Elsa got wind of it and Herman and Elsa came to our house and said you must make a decision, Teodolinda will leave you if you don't make a decision. 'What decision? What do you mean?' I said. 'Don't act as if you don't know,' said Elsa, and Herman told me not to go on pretending. You see, it was an offense to their honor. 'It's not a long way to Viipuri,' they said. I let them talk and then I said, 'Is it true, Teodolinda, have I neglected you?' 'Holger goes to Viipuri on business,' said Teodolinda. 'How can you bear it?' said Elsa, weeping. But my wife Teodolinda stood by me and didn't complain, she never complains. And since then, the sisters haven't been sisters to each other . . . But everybody knew I had someone in Viipuri. And that one said, I can't bear it, I can't take it anymore. We were sitting on a bench in Monrepose Park when she said, 'I can't bear it,' and she wept and I gave her a handkerchief so she could wipe the tears from her eyes. And then she simply left, went away. She wasn't like my wife Teodolinda, she was just a small, round ordinary woman, a bank clerk . . . Could I have left my wife Teodolinda for some bank clerk? Answer me?"

"How would I know, and you sure don't seem to have left her since you're sitting right here now."

"That's it, you're right. But the pharmacy is mine, did you hear, the pharmacy is mine!" Holger said angrily, and slammed the side of the water tub with his fist. "Please be quiet now, I didn't say it wasn't."

"There's a spring storm out there."

"The snow will melt in the rain."

"It'll melt, that's for sure, but a heart doesn't melt. Do you believe me?"

"Sin doesn't melt," said Alma.

"Sin? I can hear in your talk that you're Adele's disciple. But what are you staring at the door for? Are you expecting the parson's widow? She won't come. But you, come, come right here next to me, it's so lonely here."

"Come on." Alma sat motionless, without making a sound, her gaze fixed on the door, past the pharmacist's face.

All at once Holger got up, came towards her, grasped Alma by the waist with both hands. Alma tried to wrench herself free, the grip of the hands tightened, the drunken man's breathing poured over Alma's neck and slobbering lips were groping for her mouth, forehead, neck. Alma was struggling to break the grip of the hands and kept repeating in a whisper: "What do you want from me? Let me go! The widow will wake up. Let me go!" But Holger shoved Alma against the wall with the weight of his body. "The tub will tip over," Alma managed to say, but the lips were again on her mouth. Holger had pushed her into the corner past the tub and the china cabinet and was trying to knock her to the floor. "Woman," Holger said. "Woman, woman," he spluttered and bent her head back. Alma let out a muffled sound: it felt as if the hairpins in her bun were pressing through the skin in her neck, but right then, hands, a man's hands, no longer the pharmacist's but a man's, pushed their way through the neck of her dress and down, she felt the hand squeeze her breasts, both breasts, first one and then the other. As if uncon- scious, Alma sank to a sitting position when the hands pressed her further, the man kneeling on top of her knees.

FIFTEEN

Holger was stacking prescriptions, saying this was the way it had to be done, each edge lined up precisely against the next. "You're careless," he said to his wife, "the edges have to lie neatly against each other. If only I were a doctor," Holger sighed. His wife paid no attention to her husband's talk, but just went on wiping the pharmacy counter with a damp rag. "It's a good thing you're wiping it clean," Holger went on. "They bring in bacteria, all kinds of diseases going around again." His wife put down the rag.

"Is that where it belongs?"

His wife took the rag out of the drawer into which she'd slipped it, and took it to the kitchen. Holger went on talking. Year after year he had had to wrap up the same medications, put the same mixture into bottles; from one year to the next he had seen the townspeople walking along the birch lane away from the pharmacy, bottle under an arm. "I wonder whether they've gotten any better?" he thought. "If I were a doctor . . . So, you don't want to talk with me," he said after a while. "In the old days you'd say to that, and what then? And I would say, if I were a doctor you'd take care of the pharmacy all by yourself, and I would write the prescriptions. Won't you even answer me anymore?"

"As far as I know, there's no special disease going around. I wipe the counter, just the way I do every day," said Teodolinda. "And Herman's a good doctor, you shouldn't talk." "Is that medicine effective?—the one fortified with vitamins and iron."

"For unspecified illnesses it is, you know that."

"You're Elsa's sister. Oh, yes, the sheriff's daughter."

"When customers come, you'd better stay in the back rooms."

"I'll stay, I'll stay." Holger went off, whistling.

"For goodness' sake, here comes Alma," said Teodolinda.

"Who?"

"Alma."

"So it is." Holger pulled a flask out of his pocket, took a swig. "Adele's she-bear," he said, and kept on looking at the one who was coming, the one slowly approaching along the birch lane.

"Do you think she'll come in?"

Now Holger saw fit to be silent and just looked out.

"You go talk to her."

"Talk to her yourself. What do I have to say to her?"

"Adele has become difficult."

"She'll surely come in. Don't pay any attention to her."

"She's been gone a year, hasn't even written to Adele. Wonder where she's been."

"Don't ask her anything. We'll find out. I'll go into the back room. You come too. It's better if we don't pay any attention. But do put some coffee on, and serve her some when she comes in."

They both went into the kitchen.

"You're nervous," Holger said, looking at his wife, who was beginning to make some coffee.

"I'm thinking of Adele. It'll be a pity if Alma won't even go visit her."

"Of course she'll go. The same thing has happened before. One has to know how to handle her. Let me take care of her."

"Now she's in the yard."

Alma had reached the yard and stopped at the well. You could see the well from the kitchen window. They pulled further back from the window, surreptitiously keeping an eye on her, and saw how Alma set her round veneer case next to the rock and sat down on the edge of the well. Now she was looking toward the wall of the graveyard, a gloomy expression on her face.

"A strange creature," Holger said. "Goes off with her traveling case and comes back with her traveling case."

"That's just the way she sat one whole morning in Mikander's yard, when Mikander thought she was a gypsy."

As they both peeked out the window again at the same moment, Alma was pressing down the broken lid of her traveling case and tightening the leather strap over it, clothes were spilling out from under the lid. Alma kept shoving it down with her palm, moved the box between her legs. And then she just sat in that unattractive position, as Holger would say later, and stared at the door to the woodshed.

Soon the round traveling case was left by itself on the well cover, and not long after that, Alma's heavy steps sounded on the stairs. The doorbell rang.

"You go first," said Teodolinda. Holger drew himself up but didn't make a move toward the door. He was still looking out the window. "Left her traveling case there, a peculiar sight, all by itself like some kind of Pantheon."

"Be quiet. She's already inside."

Holger got moving.

"Good day," said Alma.

"Good day, good day, and how are you? Sit down, my girl. Were the loonies nice to you?"

"I didn't go there," Alma said reluctantly.

"Oh, yes, you went to Viipuri."

"But you know I don't know anyone in Viipuri."

"Good day, do come in," Teodolinda interjected. They exchanged greetings and went single file into the dining room.

"Thank you," said Alma and took the glass of juice that Teodolinda gave her and said it was a terribly hot day, it had been so hot on the bus she was on the verge of suffocating. She had come here from the city by bus.

"It was nice of you to come see us. Where are you headed?"

"I'll go look after the pharmacy," said Holger, and he left the room.

Alma looked into the pharmacy wing through the open door and when she recognized the woman who had come in on an errand as the shopkeeper's wife, she moved to the other side of the table where she couldn't be seen from the pharmacy.

Teodolinda, after a moment's hesitation, went and closed the door. "I guess everything's the way it was before," Alma said, referring to the pharmacist. Right now, she was free of anyone's service and her voice carried a hint of arrogance. She didn't fail to notice that after that, Teodolinda wasn't as polite and friendly as she'd been just a moment before.

"We've been well, all of us."

Holger returned and started to get Alma talking. At first, Alma gave vague answers, wouldn't say where she had spent the past year.

"I went to the city, I looked at boats, thought I'd go to Kuopio."

"You didn't go. Did you miss the boat?"

"What would I do there? That's what I thought then."

"Well, and where are you headed now?"

Alma answered that she had a mind to take a trip somewhere. She said she had decided to come see people here before she left. "I may go to Kuopio after all."

"Recently, the parson's widow has been sick off and on."

Alma acted as if she hadn't heard.

"Aren't you going to go see her?" Holger lit a cigar. "Teodolinda has had a lot of trouble with her, as you can imagine . . ." Holger knocked on his head.

"Oh, Holger, please don't. Miss Alma doesn't really have to go see Adele. After all, she's free to do as she wishes."

"I'm free, all right. That's just what I said to myself when I stopped working and left."

"Did you spend a long time at home?"

"Long enough. It would be nice to be in Kuopio. I thought I'd at least go visit, but then I thought, why should I waste money? The boat trip costs something, and I let the boat leave without me."

"Well, well, boats leave, boats leave."

"Berries will be ripening soon," Alma said after a while.

"Oh, yes, I think I saw Adele out walking with a berry cup in her hands when I went fishing the other day."

"No berries are ripe yet," Alma snorted.

"Well, you know her. She walks along the edge of the meadow with a little mug in her hands, looking for wild strawberries. She finds one or two and tells you she's gone berry-picking." Holger gave a little laugh but Alma didn't respond.

"Will you have some more coffee?" asked Teodolinda.

"One or two strawberries could already be ripe," Alma said in a tone they didn't expect.

"Of course they could be, with July coming on soon, a warm summer."

"Unusually warm, unusually warm," said Teodolinda.

"They did all the planting and sowing real early this year. I put in a flower bed for my sister, planted a little arbor for my sister-in-law, and made one round flower bed around the flagpole, a rectangular one under the window, and for each of them I planted a vegetable garden."

"I'll bet you got good wages for that," said Holger. "We never got the flower seeds planted," said Teodolinda. "I mean the nasturtiums and marigolds." "Wages. Where do I ever get wages? I just go on serving people as long as I can. I guess my wages will be paid some day."

"Poor Adele hasn't had any luck with her vegetable gardens. She tried to do some hoeing in the spring but got a headache."

"Couldn't someone go help the parson's widow?"

"My sister and I tried to arrange some help for her, but it was so difficult."

"Not a single cabbage plant?" asked Alma.

"No, not a single one."

"Not a single one," added Holger as he sat fingering his cigar, scratching his neck, and looking directly past Alma at the wall.

"Is the parson's widow still angry with me?" Alma asked after a while.

"No, not at all. Why would she be?"

"Wonder if I dare go say hello," said Alma.

"Well, why not?" said Teodolinda.

"When we parted like that . . . I wonder how she is. Have the birds been aired?"

"Hardly, hardly. Sometimes she sits on the steps of the veranda, holding some bird or other in her arms. That's how she gives them an airing. People look when they go by . . ."

"But one can arrange for the airing to be done so that people don't see," said Teodolinda.

"I took them out to be aired on the back porch, lugged each and every creature through the kitchen and gave them a brushing on the back porch. That was embarrassing enough."

"Yes, we know, we know everything. She's difficult," said Holger.

"Wonder if I might go over."

"Why don't you go take a look?"

Alma still sat there, looking as if she was wondering whether or not to go.

"I'll go," said Teodolinda when the bell rang, and in an instant she was gone. Three customers had come into the pharmacy at the same time.

"Summer people," said Holger. "Young folks, relatives of Paananen, the shopkeeper. You can't imagine how bitter the parson's widow is now that Antti has made friends with them. Adele will never forgive Paananen."

"Well, it wasn't my fault," said Alma, "but of course I got the blame that time when we had the argument . . . maybe I'll go, after all."

"Of course it wasn't . . ." Holger glanced at the closed door. "Wait a moment until Teodolinda, until my wife comes back. We'll send a little present along with you. A little medicine, you know, the liquid kind . . ."

As Alma picked up her veneer traveling case from the side of the well, the pharmacist and his wife were looking out the window and the pharmacist said: "Like a building, some Pantheon. Just look at her carry it."

"That argument they had?"

"They went out to pick berries, came back enemies, each one from a different direction. Each gave her own explanation. I didn't understand either one. This red-headed woodpecker here said Adele had raked her over the coals with the kinds of words she couldn't repeat. Adele said that Alma had been irritating her. When she had said, 'It's three o'clock,' Alma had snapped at her, asking how she knew. When Adele had said it was four o'clock, Alma had gotten angry again: 'How do you know?' and that's how it had gone until it was eight, nine. Adele naturally traced the course of the day from the lengthening shadows, the position of the sun, bird songs, you know all those skills of hers from her outings with Birger, and it's exactly that that Alma can't stand. Finally they were both standing on a high rock, and Adele claims there was a murderous look in

Alma's eyes. During the night Alma packed her veneer traveling case and in the morning she left."

"That wasn't all. All spring long Adele complained to me that she was displeased with Alma."

"And that's what you told Elsa and Elsa told Alma. That was all that was needed."

"I have never been able to understand Elsa's openness . . ."

"You mean commonness."

"There was no reason for Elsa to go tell."

"If you only knew what's inside that Pantheon . . . look, she's taking a shortcut, she's climbing over the wall of the cemetery, apparently doesn't have the nerve to go along the road."

"Spoons, I guess . . . Or maybe she didn't take them because she got angry."

"Would that woman be so out of her senses that she wouldn't take any silver with her? In that traveling case she's got not only the silver but a plaster cat, without legs, the galoshes of your late brother, Sunday school magazines, postcards . . . Don't you remember? I told you. Adele had secretly examined it during the night. The red-headed woodpecker was asleep. Adele was awake, and checked the traveling case. I told you how Adele laughed when she told me what was in the case. It's all just like before, this is the third time. When she leaves again, she'll have more of Adele's things. Adele gives them to her, she's not stingy, and that's what made Elsa furious when she saw that your mama's sugar sifter was in Alma's case. And then the red-headed woodpecker came here, blasting Elsa, demanding that I answer: is she a thief, is she? Oh, my."

"There she is now, walking through the graveyard with her case. I only hope no one comes along. She just might get mad and go back, there's still a bus to the city this evening."

"Adele has become difficult indeed. She can't stand Elsa and she simply doesn't want my help," Teodolinda said. "You've seen her kitchen. I tried to tell Antti that we should get a cleaning woman for her, but Adele felt insulted and told the woman to go away. Poor Antti, it's got to be dreary for him to be there alone with his mother, and Adele doesn't let him go into town to be with people his own age."

"Antti goes off, all right, don't you worry about it. He doesn't give a damn about Adele and he's right about that. You women make these questions of authority too complicated, you can't handle Adele. I walk in the door and don't give a damn about how she looks at me. I sit down and say to her: how about making some tea? I don't think it was tactful of Elsa to hire Alma to be in her own service. She should have understood that something like that would deeply offend Adele."

"It was Alma herself who went to Elsa after the quarrel and asked if she could stay. You know, she would have been on her way to our house but I guessed they'd had another falling-out and I told her to patch things up with Adele. I could guess what would come of it. If only Adele could be sensible now."

"Tomorrow they'll be the best of friends. Adele does have a sense of humor."

"Yes, when she chooses to."

"She's clever, very clever. You mean those spoons. Of course that woman took the spoons with her. It was just to annoy the two of you that Adele gave them to Alma. That's her kind of humor. The one who was really stupid was Elsa with her going and checking the veneer traveling case and then coming here, bellowing about the sugar sifter . . . I wish you'd believed me, Adele had given it to her. Adele got twice as much pleasure out of it because she'd managed to trick Elsa and at the same time got Alma to leave Elsa's house. Don't you remember? Adele herself called Elsa and told her to look whether the spoons and the sugar sifter were in the veneer case. And then, just remember . . ."

"That's just like Adele, in such bad taste. I've never understood it. It's something children would do. Besides, I don't get involved. I could tell right away it was one of Adele's schemes."

"What if I called Adele?"

"Is that really wise? Maybe a surprise would be better."

But the pharmacist was already on the telephone: "Hello, Adele. Look out the window, guess who's on the way over."

Sixteen

"You're walking around barefoot," said the parson's widow.

"So I am. I can't afford shoes." And as soon as she'd said it, Alma knew that now, now she would talk straight and she also knew the widow knew it. For the parson's widow turned to look at the glass door of the bookcase, and in the glass Alma could see her own reflection. In that image she saw arms, dress, blue-checked apron, light-colored scarf, a Christmas present from the parson's widow. The strings of the apron barely reached around her. It was a hand-me-down from the parson's widow, who was getting thinner day by day, and who wouldn't grow fat no matter how much she was fed. And then there were all the relatives saying that Alma wasn't even fit to cook for her. That woman, the doctor's wife; hadn't she asked whether Alma took the trouble to cook twice a day, with the widow so thin?

"Your sloppiness is getting more and more obvious."

The parson's widow had fixed her gaze on Alma's broad, bare feet—filthy, she must have been walking outside again, and come in without wiping her feet. Alma had reverted to her old ways, walked around as if she were still walking the grassy banks of her home village, and no amount of talking did any good. Martyrdom, the parson's widow thought, martyrdom. Alma was punishing herself, pretending to, anyway, but all of it was really directed at her, the parson's widow. She wants me to tell her: you're going to catch cold, so that she could say, "Who cares about me?" But I won't say it, I won't, because Alma never catches cold. From one year to the next she just goes on being hale and hearty. Only her character has changed. If that, even; hasn't she always been obstinate and pig-headed?

"Why do you want to quarrel, Alma? You do want to, I can see it."

Alma made a clanking noise against the chair and pretended not to hear.

"Day after day you've been like this . . ."

But Alma didn't reply.

"Have you had bad news from home?"

And what had made Alma become talkative before, loosened her mouth this time as well.

"Well, where is my home, anyway?"

"This is your home. You should know that."

"What am I here? Nothing but a maid."

"If that's the way you want it, that's the way it'll be." Furious, the parson's widow started upstairs.

"But you won't even speak to me," Alma said just as the widow had reached the landing at the top of the stairs.

"I don't speak to you?" The parson's widow looked over the railing, straight at Alma, who was standing in the hallway, her back turned.

"That's right, you haven't said a word to me for days."

"Haven't I?" the parson's widow repeated. She quickly came down the stairs and now stood behind Alma. "I? Who is it who's been walking around here without speaking for four days not . . . yes, four days, for four days you've been brooding about something."

"I've been in this house for fifteen years, and now I don't know where I should go."

"What's this about where you should be going?"

"I'll be able to get a job at the poorhouse, as a cook if nothing else."

The parson's widow was about to say "You've tried it there three times, and everybody knows what a troublemaker you are. Go ahead and go off to the poorhouse."

"The poorhouse will take me when I can't go on anymore." This was just like Alma, one minute she threatened she was at death's door and demanded they take her body to the cemetery of her home parish; the next minute she'd say, "Plop me down any old place," and at still another time she'd say, "I'll live to be an old woman." The parson's widow had grown tired of these conversations, so very tired she no longer bothered to respond. Through them, Alma was begging for sympathy, which she, a healthy, headstrong woman didn't need at all, and as the widow thought about it, she said aloud.

"But you've already been at the poorhouse." During the silence that followed these words, the parson's widow could see Alma packing her belongings in the veneer traveling case as she'd done on three separate occasions over these years, no, three was not enough, she couldn't recall how many times, packing up in silence, wandering around the house with the air of one on the verge of departure, expecting me to plead with her to stay, but I haven't ever, I haven't asked her to stay . . . slowing her steps at the parlor door to give me the chance to say, "Don't go." But I never once said it, not even the last time she left. Her departures—hand extended, "Goodbye now, don't remember me badly,"—when it was repeated a third time, it had made her laugh. Holger had been on his way over, coming down the birch lane. She had looked out the window. Holger had said hello, asked, "But where are you headed?" Alma had walked past him without answering, scarf over her head and veneer traveling case in hand. She had stepped to one side, to the edge of the ditch to let Holger pass, and Holger had come into the parlor where the widow was sitting: "Where is your bear off to? She was so furious she didn't even give me the time of day." "Off to the poorhouse." "I see," said Holger and burst out laughing. They both laughed. But Alma couldn't bear to be reminded of it. When she had returned a week later, she said she'd only come back for a visit. The first time, she had stayed at the poorhouse for two months; the second time, a week; and the third time, a few days, but that time around, she'd gone over to the next village. "So where are you going now?" "Haven't really thought about it." "Wouldn't you like to stay here?" And Alma, at first with an air of thinking it over, had said the next morning: "I guess I could stay a little while." That little while was now two years ago, and once again there would be the packing of the veneer traveling case, and before long the tightening of the scarf around her head . . .

It had become a game people laughed about, but Alma didn't know that. Every time she left the poorhouse she had extensive and valid reasons. Unbearable people; they made her clean up the nuthouse; and when Alma had seen a man who shook his fist at a window from morning to night and talked to himself and swore, she'd had enough. "Has the bear come yet?" Holger asked. "Be quiet!" and it made them both laugh. And when Alma brought a tray of coffee into the parlor, Holger said: "Well, good day to you. I guess you were on a trip." "Don't know if you can rightly call it a trip. I'm sure not going to clean a loony-bin, you go crazy working with the crazies." The matron of the poorhouse said there was no getting along with Alma, she would start to boss people around, and she'd insist on her sense of order in the ward for the mentally ill. The poor miserable people would become anxious at the mere sight of her. She treated them as if they had their wits about them, insisted they sit on the edges of their beds. "Don't you understand? No sitting on the floor," she had said to a woman who didn't even have any awareness of the changing seasons. "They'd roll on the floor in their blue linen dresses. Just as soon as I managed to get a clean dress on her, she'd get it all dirty. 'Can't you get it into your head that you're not going to soil it!' but she'd start to scream. Oh my God, I covered my ears and thought, I'm not going to spend one more day in this place. Never mind how crazy they are, they've got to understand that you don't go and get a dress dirty right away like that." "You were right about that," Holger had said to Alma. "Did she listen to you?" "What do you think? A loony is a loony. She just screamed. I tell you, it's the devil that's got into them. I saw with my own eyes how they're possessed by the devil." "And you cleared out of there." "I sure did." After Alma carried the coffee cups to the kitchen, Holger was almost choked with laughter.

"I'll go to another poorhouse," Alma said. Once she had found her way to the poorhouse, she was perpetually on the verge of leaving. It became like a disease. There's a red building to the left, a long one. The shorter one is the main building. There they are, the mentally ill in their little coops, the matron saying: "Watch out. Make sure you face them whenever you're cleaning." Alma could have put up with the male loonies but the women were too much. "Why?" asked Holger. "They screamed and tossed their heads around like this," Alma said, and gave a demonstration. "How did you happen to think of going there in the first place?" "Of course, they deliberately made me look after the loonies," and Alma portrayed the matron as a woman who stole money from the county and lived high on the hog. Alma didn't stop saying bad things about the director of the poorhouse, not until the parson's widow asked: "What did you say about me there?" At that, Alma had fallen silent. Once she had asked, to end an argument: "I guess you think I belong there." "Where?" "Where you go spend your holidays." "Where?" "The long red building." Alma had understood and become silent.

Where was she now thinking of going? Never again to the poorhouse.

Shopkeeper Mikander, Alma thought. What if she went and asked for a position at the place which had whisked her here? And then she remembered the shopkeeper had died. It wouldn't be easy to go offer herself, but she had to get out of here and go somewhere, because, no, not yet another time, no going after birds.

"I just won't go chasing birds."

"Is that what got you all upset? But you know, you don't have to. I simply talked about it with you." "But if I'm a maid, don't I have to do what I'm told, even if it doesn't make sense?"

"So you mean I'm out of my mind, and my place is in the red building, right?"

And once again Alma had left. All day long she didn't utter a word in reply, was silent until nightfall, didn't speak in the morning, and gathered her belongings before noon. The veneer traveling case came down from the attic, different bundles emerged from every corner. She kept putting them into a salt sack and into birch-bark knapsacks and boxes. But Holger had seen her going and he had taken a short-cut through the woods to intercept Alma on the road. She was standing in front of the store, waiting for a ride. "Where are you headed? Going home?" No answer. "There's no point arguing with Adele. Just listen to me. She's a bit childish, you know. I do understand, well, let's go back now." Silent but already yielding, Alma put the veneer case down on the road. There she stood, with the sacks and boxes on one side and the veneer case on the other. "Well, how about turning off the road now. Or, you could come to our house." The pharmacist had coaxed her, and so, after he had started walking ahead, she had stood for an hour or two among the alder bushes, thinking, and then circled around the back of the graveyard so that people wouldn't see, had climbed over the graveyard wall with her sack and boxes and then waded through the wet grasses to the pharmacy. Teodolinda had acted as if she didn't know a thing about the whole matter, and to this day Alma was convinced that she had given up leaving that time out of the goodness of her own heart. "Heaven knows where I'd be now if I'd left that time."

"That urge to wander comes over you the way it does for the gypsies."

Alma had become angry, but Holger knew how to talk her out of it, to appeal to how indispensable Alma was for all of them.

"You sure do know how to talk and trick me into doing things."

"Who has tricked you?"

But Alma was yanking a rug out from under a leg of the sofa. She didn't answer, and the parson's widow said to Holger: "Don't talk like that. Alma will get her feelings hurt. She's not stupid." "Funny, funny," laughed Holger. The parson's widow remembered that day.

"I won't go there." Alma banged the leg of a chair. "I tell you, I'm not going to go there, not to that hag."

"Do you mean the matron of the poorhouse?"

"You know what they made me do? Empty bedpans for loonies."

"But you went there yourself."

"Well, there are plenty of jobs in other places."

"Sure. I'm not telling you that you can't go."

And Alma:

"Sure, sure. Fifteen years I've been working in this house and that's all the thanks I get."

"What's the matter now?"

"All I'm saying is that it's fifteen years and a person gets no thanks when she leaves."

"But you haven't left."

"I'll leave all right, when it comes to that. One can sure be a maid somewhere else, too, once you've taken up maid's work."

"Well, how about making some coffee. Let's talk about it to-morrow."

By afternoon, Alma had forgotten the whole thing, or at least she no longer talked about it.

There were times when she thought about going home, but she

knew they'd say she'd had a quarrel again. She'd have to work for her sister-in-law and her sister, and she'd be the least independent person there. She'd certainly experienced that. Who had construct-ed the lilac arbor and put in the flower beds for her sister if not she? Who had weeded the potatoes, who had woven the rag-rugs if not she herself? She'd told the parson's widow about it with bitterness in her heart: there would be no going home. "It wasn't home any-more since Mother wasn't alive." Mother said to me when she was alive: "Don't you go off to other people's places. You don't get along with people well," but I wouldn't listen to her. After that, Alma had returned to the city, had circled around the casino, no, not to the casino, she hadn't even dared to go ask. How she had even got such an idea in her head? The boats sat in the harbor, boats going off to different districts, different cities . . . for a moment she had thought of getting aboard the boat headed for Kuopio, but in a flash she had understood: what would she do in Kuopio? The water was lapping against the pier, and as she looked at it, her feet, as if by their own will, started walking and she found herself at the station, then on the train, on her way to the parson's widow, just for a visit, she had thought. Of course I can go for a visit and say that I forgot my shoes; that was true enough, and the parson's widow had pretended to believe it. "Oh, Alma, you left your shoes behind. Is that what you came to get?" "Yes, I left my shoes." "Please sit down. How are you?" And so she had told, first briefly, then going into everything.

"The train brought you back." She heard the voice of the par-son's widow. "I'm sick." The widow had a fever, and she had stayed on to take care of her; she would leave later. When the widow was well again. Neither one of them talked about leaving. That was five years ago. The owl looked down from the top of the cabinet . . . five years ago, a Sunday morning, she had burst into tears when she saw the owl. It was as if she had come home . . . it looked at her like a living creature, spoke to her, had missed her. For some reason, the owl was the only one of the birds she had grown fond of, its head was round, it was alive like a child, the size of a small child when she took it in her arms. Poor thing, has anyone looked after you while I was away, poor thing, all dusty, when she brushed against the tip of the owl's beak, a fleck of dust had stuck to her finger and that had made her burst into tears. It was like leaving a child all alone. But today she hated the owl especially, it looked like the parson's widow. Didn't the widow care for it better than she did the others? Why, she didn't look after the snipe at all. Alma was looking at the snipe: spindly legs, long bill—it looked like the pharmacist's wife. In her eyes, each of the birds had begun to look like someone or another. Hadn't she looked at the wood grouse and hadn't it brought to mind her brother Frans . . . when you spend time with a madwoman you yourself go mad: think how the birds have got such a hold on her. Fifteen years had passed. Alma was thinking of that as she opened the parlor window, fifteen years, and it was autumn again, time to seal up the windows. Had it been like this, her hands just like this fifteen years ago when she had opened this window for the first time? Fifteen times she had sealed up these very windows while the parson's widow had paced from parlor to bedroom and back again, just the way she was doing now, keeping an eye on her to see that she was stuffing enough cotton batting between the double windows.

A boat was gliding towards the shore, and you could see the islands, Lappi Island, and over there, Muha.

What she had missed most when she was among strangers, she now realized, were these white boats that carried you home and away from home.

SEVENTEEN

"Did you notice the expression on Elsa's face?" the parson's widow asked the pharmacist. "Of course you did. Bring the tea service over to the table," she said to Alma.

"Sit down, Holger. Did you notice? Elsa tried to count the spoons, one, two, three. I saw how she tried to count, and whenever I knew she'd got to three, I said, 'Have some cake, Elsa.'"

"Don't make me laugh," said Holger.

"I deliberately put out all the spoons from different sets, just as you told me to. She probably stayed awake all night pestering Herman. 'Listen, Herman, the spoons don't match. Only two of the spoons Mama got as a wedding present were out. Where has Adele tucked away the others?' And Herman gets mad and says to Elsa, 'For heaven's sake stop counting spoons and let me sleep.'"

"But why did she look at the tea set?" the parson's widow asked, casting a sly glance at Alma, who was carrying tea to the table in a silver pot.

"I don't know," said Alma.

"That even happened last time. The only pieces from the tea service that I set out were the creamer and the sugar bowl. I could see Elsa was thinking, where are the teapot and the large plate?"

"There is some joy in this life of ours, after all . . . I can't remember any more of it," Holger said. "It's from some poem."

"Alma, do you think . . . but sit, please sit down next to the pharmacist. Do you think I invited Elsa and Herman over for a visit for my own sake? Do you think they would come? No. I call up and say, 'Elsa, my dear, could you come over for a visit, you and Herman? Holger and Teodolinda will be coming too. Today is the anniversary of Birger's death. Could you come over and share a moment with me in his memory?' And I had to laugh when I put down the receiver. I know Herman will get angry and start waving his arm about like this." The parson's widow swung her arm and slapped her palm against the table.

"No, he does it like this," Holger said, and banged his fist on the table. "'Again, damn it! We were over there just a little while ago. You people are forever dying and being born.'"

"But Elsa says: 'We have to go. I want to see whether the tea ser-vice is still all there, complete.' It's the tea set Elsa will come over to spy on. Her little chicken-head, as you call it, Holger, is just about to burst with her thinking of where the teapot is and where all the platters are. You haven't betrayed me, Alma, have you?"

"As if I didn't know the doctor's wife."

"That's why I gave you another spoon. Did you see, Holger? Elsa pretended not to notice, but did you see Elsa's neck?"

"Oh, Missus, you shouldn't give them to me when they're look-ing on," said Alma.

"But if I don't give them to you while they're watching, when I'm dead and gone they'll come and ask for them. They'll list how many spoons there should be. How would you prove, then, that you got them from me as gifts?"

"But not even then."

"Now-now-now-now," uttered Holger. "Don't worry, I'll swear to that . . . Would you allow me," he said, and took a small flat flask from his left pocket.

"Just a splash, Holger, just a splash."

"No, no," said Alma, and pulled her cup away from the bottle.

"Last time, when it was Birger's birthday, do you remember, Alma, I hid the tea service and told you to pour tea from the old enamel pot. Did you notice, Holger? 'No, thank you,' said Elsa and wouldn't have a second cup, and her neck was glowing red as a sunset."

"Well, well," Holger sighed, and tapped the table with his fingers. "Sunset time has come for Elsa too."

"Did you notice how she tries to hide her years! When Antti, it certainly was mean of him, asked: 'How old are you, Aunt Elsa?' what did Elsa answer? 'I'm forty.' She turned red as a beet and started to talk about her aunt who had emigrated here from Russia."

"Now, now, Adele."

"I admit," Adele said, "Teodolinda didn't approve of that. I understand, they're sisters in spite of everything."

"Teodolinda is tactful," Holger said with dignity, and took a flask from his right-hand side pocket. "No, not for me, and keep in mind, for you only on the condition that you don't go . . ."

"Now, now."

"Do you remember when Herman came into this town? I looked out the window when he and Elsa were walking along the road together. 'From a big manor house.' Elsa said. A rather small farm, it was. Well, they did send the son off to school. Herman's sister didn't marry well, she's poor, I've heard, but does Herman help the sister at all?—no. Herman has made Elsa greedy too."

"Now-now-now-now," Holger said in a sing-song voice, his tone rising on the third syllable.

"Alma, where did you put that spoon?"

"Back in the cabinet, just in case . . ."

". . . you know, if I die, they'll come to inspect things. And when I do die, hold your own."

"Stop this talk of dying, you're not going to die," said Holger.

"No, no, perhaps I won't just yet. That's something only God knows. What about the wood grouse, Alma? You forgot to bring him in."

Alma went to fetch the wood grouse.

"Not on the table," said the parson's widow. "Haven't I told you, put it on the floor. I have taught you that, haven't I? It must be set out as it is in nature, and you can well see that it's in its mating dance position. Holger, you wouldn't believe what a remarkable artist Alma's brother is. Alma has told me about it, and I've also told you about it. Well, well, my husband Birger, as good an ornithologist as he was, he didn't have the kind of amazing ability, God didn't give him the kind of animal soul that he gave your brother. No, my husband wasn't the sort of artist your brother is. I say so even though it's the anniversary of poor Birger's death. But wouldn't you like to perform it for the pharmacist?"

Alma gave the pharmacist an imploring look, but he was listening to the parson's widow, gravely nodding.

"You don't want to," said the parson's widow. "Well, I won't force you to. You succeeded once, but I do understand it had to be a pale reflection of how your brother performed it. Yes, yes, he really is an artist. We are only two ordinary people, a couple of helpless women. Please pour the pharmacist some more coffee."

"Well, well, you vestal virgins." Holger was mimicking the parson's widow's sighing tone of voice. "But tell me something, talk with me. Look, the sun's setting, the shadows of night are creeping in."

The pharmacist stroked the balding top of his head.

"Alma, you go on and tell. I'm in such low spirits today."

"Yes, a spoon, that's what Adele has given you. Once again you've received a wedding present. Amuse Adele and me, us two sad people."

"Holger, you should know that I've decided to give Alma one piece of silver each year. Well, I know it's dreary for her with me here. I know I'm a bit strange, a lonely old woman, guardian of moth-eaten old birds, as you have said."

"Adele, Adele," said Holger in a scolding tone.

"Yes, yes, it's the anniversary of poor Birger's death, and before long it will be Onni's. So many dead . . ."

"Cheer me up," said Holger. "Cheer me up or I'll go, you know where. Please cheer me up. Why do you both just keep on sighing?"

"Your turn, Alma. Tell the pharmacist something."

"What do I have to tell?"

"Don't be shy," Holger ordered. "Don't you remember how the shepherd boy David delighted the heavy heart of King Saul by playing his harp?"

"Tell from where you left off, when Antti came back from the city," said the parson's widow.

"I can't remember any more."

"When you were all looking out the window."

"Why go into that? What's past is past," Alma said reluctantly.

But the widow's eyes were already shining.

"Tell how they were coming down the road and you looked out the window and were able to guess."

"Well, there had been talk about it in the village. We knew about it all right, just didn't know it was so far along," Alma said, still reluctantly.

"What?" asked Holger.

"Don't interrupt. This is one of those stories that can't bear any interruptions, and you, Alma, begin at the beginning." "How do I know what's the beginning!"

"Why don't you start where you were carrying the bed. That's not the beginning, but if you start with that, even though it's the end of the story, you can get back to the beginning. Now listen, Holger. This happened one autumn night."

"But it was summer then," Alma said.

"You said before that it was autumn."

"If I say autumn, you'll say summer . . . I guess I should know better because I carried it on my own back."

"All right, good. You'll just start with when you said, if it comes to that, I can carry these, even on my own back."

"That's not how I said it, and I haven't told you I said it that way—instead, I said, even if we have to carry these things to the bottom of the lake, we're going to haul them away."

"And so it took place in the summer."

"Late summer, the end of August. I remember, because that autumn it turned cold early."

"So it was. The sky was dark, the night cold, the moon covered by clouds, that's how you've told it, but after all, start from the point when you are all standing by the window, and tell the pharmacist everything that had happened before that."

"There had been some talk in the village," Alma said reluctantly.

"What are you talking about? You're not going to start arguing, are you, my dear ladies? Softly, softly, Adele."

"Don't you stick your nose into this," the parson's widow said, her eyes shining. "And you, Alma, start with the shirt. Tell the pharmacist just the way you've told me. It started with your brother standing in front of the mirror every day, combing his hair, and insisting that you get him a clean shirt. Go on."

"That's right, he demanded a clean shirt."

"And you said he had just now got a clean shirt, and then your brother got mad. And that's how you guessed."

"Did I have the strength to wash and iron shirts every single day . . . ?"

"'Who's doing all the work around here,' you said," the parson's widow went on in a voice that sounded as though she were beating time.

"Yes, who did all the work if not me?" Alma said bitterly. "Mother is lying in bed, paralyzed, one brother has left home and whenever he did come home he wandered off in the woods, shooting game birds, one sister off and married, the other brother doing a bit of this and a bit of that, went off fishing, the fields leased out to others, and everything on my shoulders."

"You milked the cows, you did all the work."

"Who was there but me? And I worked, I'd learned to work."

"And you did it willingly because home was still home for you then. But go on."

"She had come to do some sewing. The mistress of the neighboring farm was her aunt."

"But there were already rumors going around the village. And you guessed."

"Should have guessed even earlier. That's what those nightly outings were all about. He came home in the wee hours of the morning, clattering about the doors of the shed, slept in the daytime. 'Where did he go off to now?' Mother said. 'Maybe off fishing,' I said. But I'd already guessed. And one time when I was going out to the island to pick blueberries, the boat wasn't in its place on the shore. 'We hear your boat's on the Rämälä shore,' people said. He went by boat, didn't have the nerve to go along the road. As if I hadn't guessed," Alma snorted.

"Guessed but didn't say anything."

"You forgot the feathers."

"What feathers?"

"The bloody feathers behind the drying shed," the parson's widow answered sharply. "You told me earlier that it was you, you yourself, who noticed bloody bird feathers on the heath behind the drying shed. Don't you remember? You guessed that your brother had shot a bird but he sure didn't bring it home, he took it to the other place, to the house where that woman was staying as a seamstress, at her aunt's place. That's where the bird was plucked, roasted, and consumed by better mouths, exactly, that's exactly how you've told me before. My, my, but you forgot to mention it now. But what was this particular bird, you haven't been able to tell me that. You tried to make me believe it was a mallard. Alma, dear, ducks do not walk around on a dry heath, you yourself said it's quite a way to the shore from the drying shed. But let it go this time, just go on from the point when they came."

"They came just like that, came down the road one day."

"That road's beautiful, beautiful," the parson's widow said dreamily. "Rye fields, hay fields, rye and hay on each side. Holger, you can't believe how beautiful a village road is, how the field of rye waved like an expanse of water in the wind, like a river, widening to still water in the front yards of the houses. Holger, you don't know how beautiful a road. Alma, do you remember when we walked from the pier through the village towards your home, and the swallows in the yards were pricking the air as though they were weaving nets, and there were the sheds for the seine nets on the shore where the boats were kept? You cannot believe, Holger, you should see it all, but go on, Alma, stick to the story. So, you were standing by the window."

"My sister, she was the first one to see, she looked out the window, she was sitting behind the table and talking with Mother. She had dropped by for a visit home, she was already married then, but she did come by to see Mother every day. It was afternoon, like this, and home was still a home for both of us, but when that woman came . . ."

"Stick to the story. Go on with what happened when you saw them coming."

"Sister looks out the window . . ."

"You said that already. Let me tell. 'Who are these people?' says your sister. And you go to the window and say 'Who are they?' And you answer: 'Who else but them, that woman, she's coming now, and the mistress of the Rämälä farm, and third, your brother.' And you got all upset. Go on."

"Mother started crying."

"And they've already come to the rock," continued the parson's widow. "I remember the big stone that Alma calls the rock. At the edge of the field there's a big stone, like the back of an animal just getting up, the back off the ground, head and feet still deep in the earth. That's just where they're coming, and you're in a hurry. Go on."

"Mother started crying," Alma continued.

"No, not yet. She didn't start crying until your sister, after she'd gotten over the shock, started cleaning the house. Don't you remember how much you had to get done before they got into the house? Don't you?"

"We put some clean clothes on Mother. We did our best to keep her clean, but she was paralyzed, couldn't use her hands. We had to feed her like a child, so of course her clothes got stained. Mother was trembling and crying and said it was the end of her life, and it felt like the end to me too, when I saw that woman there near the rock. And when they came into the yard, my sister says, look, she's got a watch dangling from her neck."

"And when you saw the watch, you finally understood home was no longer going to be a home for you. 'That watch,' your sister said, grabbing up near her heart, and you felt the woman was thrusting it ahead of her for you to see."

"What was it coming toward us with a warning bell hanging from its neck? I don't understand."

"Holger, don't play stupid. You understand perfectly well what this story is all about. Alma's older brother, not the one who can act out the mating dance of a wood grouse, but the one who doesn't have that skill, had become engaged without letting on to his paralyzed mother or to his sisters, and Alma here is trying to tell us how they felt when they looked out the window at their new sister-in-law, to whom their brother, the fiancé of the woman in question, had bought a gold watch as an engagement present. It's this timepiece we're now talking about. And this very woman, I've seen her, has a distinctly small build, yet she does have remarkably big breasts, and I can very well imagine the kind of impression she must have made as she was approaching the house, her watch on a chain, swinging over her breasts. I can well believe your heart was gripped with pain at the sight of it, Alma. But there are many details you have forgotten or deliberately left out that absolutely belong in this story."

"What?" said Alma. "They just came in and there wasn't a thing anyone could do about it."

"You just go on and tell everything honestly. Don't you remember: you burst into tears. Tears of frustration, that's what you said to me. But your sister, who's older than you are, was smart enough to behave more sensibly. She started sweeping the floor, tidying up. You've told me you were cleaning as though your lives were at stake so that your brother's fiancée wouldn't see the disorder in your house, because it was all a mess, don't you remember: the table hadn't been cleared, things lay scattered about, you yourself were in tattered clothes, that's what you told me, out of spite, you went around in tattered clothes so that your brother, the one who'd just got engaged, would see that not a single penny was going to be wasted until it was all settled about what you sisters would get. All the things had not yet been apportioned, what would go to each one hadn't been put down in black and white, your older sister hadn't got her share from home and would come and weep about it to your mother, and you would always quarrel about these things, and now this brother of yours goes and gets himself engaged behind your backs. Secretly, because he didn't dare tell you anything about it beforehand, because you and your mother had decided you'd rather tear everything into bits and pieces than give up any power to that woman. That's what you've told me. But how did it go?"

"We lifted Mother into the rocking chair, I've told you that before. We got her all dressed in clean clothes."

"No, in a flowered blouse."

"But you're getting caught up in details," said Holger.

"You go ahead and laugh," said the parson's widow with dignity. "You don't know how I feel when people change details all the time. What's all right for one story isn't all right for another."

"Poor Mother wept, and it's no wonder," said Alma.

"You forgot about the hymnal."

"What hymnal?"

"You've said you put a hymnal into your mother's hand. Why?"

"Mother was a religious woman."

"So why do you mention it only now? When I saw my mother-in-law for the first time, she had on gloves and a parasol in her hands."

"What's that got to do with anything?"

"This story has been ruined. But let it be, I don't insist you begin at the beginning. Tell about when you carried the things. But tell it from the beginning."

"Who knows what the beginning is . . ."

"First went the table . . ."

"First we took the bed, the one Father died in."

"No, the table."

"The bed, as if I would ever forget, I was the one who carried it. Painted yellow, a wooden bed with a side that slides out, the very one in which Father died. 'Now that woman is coming into the house. This is the end of my life,' Mother cried. 'Here are the things that belonged to your late uncle, still not designated for anyone in particular. When that woman comes, she'll take everything. Whose are those things?' Mother wept, asking my brother, 'Whose

are they?' My sister came by and cried, 'Whose are these things?'
Said she hadn't gotten so much as a bed from home. 'Whose are
these?' I asked my brother, but he didn't say a word and that's how
we knew he was already under that woman's thumb. 'No member
of the Lahikainen family is ever going to sleep in the bed your father died in,' Mother cried.

"And you said . . ."

"Yes, I did. I said, we're going to take these things to the bottom
of the lake and now they're on their way. 'The devil with them,' I
said, and snatched the blooming balsam under one arm and the
feathery asparagus plant under the other. 'I do have the courage,' I
said, and on the run I whisked them out behind the cellar so they'd
be there, waiting in the grass. The men had gone night-fishing and
I thought we'd carry out the big things first and still have time to
carry out the smaller ones later. 'If you're not strong enough, I'll
carry this on my shoulders,' I said, already furious at my sister. But
she's just sitting there. The husband had made her that way, she'd
learned to submit to her husband's will. 'If you can't manage it, I'll
have to carry this on my shoulders,' I said angrily. I tugged the bed
from a corner of the main room . . ."

"Half a bed," said the parson's widow.

"Mother said: 'Take it, take it away, it's better that way. I was
already carrying half of the bed on my back when my sister comes
after me. Well, pick it up, I said, and we were lugging it along like
some old coffin, holding onto it by the sides. 'Get behind it,' I said
to my sister, 'the legs are scraping the ground and there'll be tracks
on the road. Hold it higher.' We carried it to the blacksmith's shop,
lugged it all the way down to the gully, put it down there. We were
exhausted! A heavy bed, made of good thick boards."

"You said, 'Let's rest a bit,' the parson's widow continued. 'Let's
rest,' you said. And you were out of breath. It was dark."

"Yes, it was dark, and there we were with the bed made out of good thick boards, the bed Father had died in. 'Let's rest,' I said, and we were all out of breath."

"And you went back to get the other half of the bed."

"Yes, that other one."

"And you carried it there."

"Right, and then the table and the flower stand and the candlesticks that I'd snatched from the parlor, because that woman was coming and the wedding was to be in a couple of weeks. 'It's now or never,' I said, and Mother said the same thing but my sister was afraid it was against the law. She'd been married long enough to be afraid of men. 'What if he takes it to court?' That's what she said of her own brother. 'We haven't got anything in black and white,' she said. 'We have your uncle's word,' Mother said."

"Ah, now I understand," said Holger.

"And what then?" said the parson's widow excitedly.

"And what then?" Holger asked as well.

"That woman came, didn't say a word at first, just kept looking around."

"And then she started . . ." said Holger.

"That she did. The house seems to be missing the bed from the back wall of the main room, and the table and candlesticks from the parlor as well. That's what she was saying to her husband, you see, and also hinting to me."

"So what did you do?" asked Holger.

"Pretended I didn't hear. When people came by the house, that woman, my brother's wife, would say that there sure used to be a wooden bed, painted yellow, and with it a round table painted black, right along the back wall of the main room. It seems they've vanished. Don't know where to. I didn't say a word."

"Did you keep silent for a long time?"

"No. One morning I said there sure wasn't going to be any new coat bought for me from the fair, like there was for some people here, and my sister said, one day when she'd come by the house to look in on Mother, she sat on the bench in the main room and said right there, no, no, there's been no new coat for the little one, that's for sure. No new coat's been bought for her. I was the youngest of the children, they called me the little one before that woman came. 'Take the little one to town, buy her one if there's enough money,' the sister-in-law says to that. 'There will be no more peace for the dead in this house. They used to let the dead have peace and honor in this house in the old days,' my mother says to that."

"Listen closely, Holger."

"The sister-in-law says to her husband: 'Was it the dead who carted the things away? You hear . . . could it have been spirits that came by for some stealing?' Then our younger brother, too, got mad at that woman and told her off."

"Tell the pharmacist everything. Tell it just the way you've told me. Then your older brother got mad and took his wife's side, tell about that. You picked up a piece of firewood that was lying in front of the wood stove in the main room, and flung it down on the floor, right at the feet of your sister-in-law, and then your brother came and grabbed you by the hair and you attacked your brother, and your sister began to cry and your mother began to cry and you began to cry, and your sister comforted you and said, don't you cry, Sister will sew a new dress for the little one, and your older brother didn't know whose side to take and in the end he got mad at everybody, at his wife too, and he went off fishing and stayed out all night. You don't know, Holger, what this sister-in-law of Alma's is like, the one we're talking about: little, fat, black hair in a tight bun, pretty head, just like a heifer's but without horns, slippery and sly as a snake, I know that type of woman."

"You mean Elsa."

"Just remember the time Elsa came here to pick up her things," the parson's widow said pointedly. "Go ahead and ask Teodolinda how she felt when Elsa took the picture of the warship down from the wall even though their father had promised it to Teodolinda. The sofa cushion, the one with the cross-stitching, oh my, this story Alma is telling us here, has such a familiar ring to it. Alma did the right thing. And how could they have managed to get the bed out of the house if they hadn't done it the way they did? Not everyone is as brazen as Elsa, who came with her horseman to cart off the things in broad daylight. Alma acted wisely."

"Very wisely," Holger said, and blew a thick cloud of smoke from his cigar. "It certainly would be a tough job to get that kind of bed back into place along the rear wall once it had been carried out like that."

"Sure, how could you get it out of there if not that way? That woman was coming. 'Did you have to go and take the things away like thieves?' asked the brother. It hurt his feelings. 'You wouldn't have let us take a horse,' I said. 'And would you have been able to bear seeing the things carted off by a horse with everyone looking on?' Brother couldn't say a thing to that."

"The bed moved along in the night, swaying as if it were being carried by invisible hands. How mystical, how enchanting," said the parson's widow. "But you haven't yet told the pharmacist everything that happened that night. You see, it just so happened that Alma's brothers hadn't gone night-fishing, after all. Instead, they'd gone on a drinking binge at the very house where that feared woman, the one engaged to Alma's brother, was staying to work as a seamstress at her aunt's place. And what happened? The brothers were on their way home when they caught sight of people coming along the road toward them, and they ducked into the woods. And they looked out from their hiding place and saw what their sisters were up to."

"Yes, they saw," said Alma. "And later they admitted it would have been better not to have seen."

"Your older brother, the one who was looking at his sisters going along the road in the black night, the engagement ring on his finger, his hair mussed, shirt dirty, cursed out loud."

"That's what they said he did."

"And the cursing wasn't aimed at the sisters as much as at himself, at the deed he was committing: perhaps he understood he was bringing into the house a woman who was going to eat his sisters out of house and home. And you walked through the dark night, one holding up one end of the bed, the other holding up the other end."

"That's just what we did. 'Where are they taking it to?' my older brother said. 'Maybe they're taking it to the lake,' the younger brother answered. He's the one who told me about it afterward."

"And that's when the older brother swore."

"So he did."

"The brothers could hear their sisters' breathless march. You must remember, Holger, that the hill rises steeply at that point, the bed is heavy, the sisters' breathing would carry to the brothers' ears through the darkness. Their drunken stupor evaporated, and what they saw wasn't pleasant, what they were there to witness. 'They've already hauled off one half of the bed,' said Alma's younger brother. As you may remember, Holger, we're talking about a wooden bed, the kind you pull out at the side, and the half they were now carrying has only two legs, so this is the inner half of the bed, the half you pull out, take note of it, the legs were scraping the ground. Alma has told me you could see cracks scraped into the village road by the bed legs until the rains came, and people would look at them and wonder what in the world they were but no one would tell, no one would answer any questions at all. This thing with two legs was swaying in the hands of the people carrying it, you can't believe how enchanting I find this point in the story. 'Let's rest,' the brothers hear their sisters say. They recognize the voices and understand everything. 'They seem to be getting tired,' says one brother, the younger one, the one who wasn't yet engaged to be married. Can you imagine, Holger, what an impression that night journey of the bed had to make on them: a bed moving along in the dark as if it were all alone, by its own volition, senselessly. The drunkenness had evaporated, their heads cleared, their pleasure destroyed, well, it was an unpleasant feeling, do you understand?"

"I understand, I understand."

"Even if the brothers had seen their sisters carrying trees, let's say trees five meters tall, torn out of the ground by the roots, that sight would not have had a more stunning effect on them than this bed-carrying."

"Yes, yes. Women will carry birch-bark baskets for picking wild berries, and they'll lug pails and other senseless loads around, but for sure, far more rarely do they carry beds, and in the dead of night no less. Oh my," Holger groaned. "But did they have the right to remove the bed from the corner of the main room just like that?"

"Now you don't understand it at all. Elsa was doing the same thing. When something's been taken away you can't get it back, though this story of Alma's isn't at all the same thing as what Elsa did to me. Elsa took something that belongs to Teodolinda and me. Alma and her sister took what was theirs. And how would you have dealt with a situation like this?"

"I would have made sure I had a horse."

"But no. You see, if the bed had been carried off on a horse cart, we wouldn't have this story."

"Their drunken stupor vanished all right," said Alma. "They'd gone into the woods when they heard us coming. Planned to scare us. 'I guess your heads cleared for sure,' I said to my younger brother when we later talked about that night. 'I guess you sobered up when you saw what we were carrying off.' 'I guess we did sober up,' he said. 'Strange,' that's what he said. 'It was strange to go home and not find that bed along the rear wall, the one that had always been there.' And it was strange for me too. It still feels strange when I go home. People, too, kept asking where in the world that bed along the back wall had got to. But none of us said a thing to anyone."

"Strange. Holger, you must understand how I felt when Elsa arrived with the horseman to take away the things in broad daylight. Elsa took revenge on me over those things she had asked for after poor Birger died, took revenge in full view of the parishioners."

"There's all kinds of revenge. Didn't you take revenge on Elsa when you ran to the house of the county doctor without a coat and hat in the bitter cold, and then to our house, didn't you get revenge when you said, in the hearing of all the customers at the pharmacy, that Elsa had come and robbed you? Just tell me."

"You're right," the parson's widow said after a moment's thought, and laughed aloud like a child.

"But the things I'm talking about here belonged to my sister and me. Our uncle died without having married, and the things belonged to him. And that woman was on her way. That woman would have helped herself to everything."

"But who was the designated heir? You yourself just said the deed hadn't been drawn up and your mother was still alive. Therefore, everyone stood to inherit. Your brother, the one who had gotten engaged, was also an heir. According to the law, you didn't go about it exactly right. In other words, you took the law into your own hands. It shouldn't have been divided up until after your mother's death."

"What do you think happened after Mother died?"

"This sister-in-law of Alma's wouldn't even let these daughters have their dead mother's clothes. Go ahead and tell, Alma."

But no more sounds would come out of Alma. In deep gloom, she stared straight ahead.

"Sometimes swift action is better than legality," said the parson's widow.

"You would know," said Holger. "You knew how to do it."

"I did know how," said the widow, ominous red blotches appearing on her cheeks. "If only Teodolinda had known to act more quickly, the picture of the warship wouldn't be hanging on the wall of Elsa's dining room right now."

"Teodolinda doesn't complain, she's not standing guard over your silver. I find these inheritance matters so tiresome. Tell me something else."

The women were silent.

"Tell me some dreams. Let's talk about dreams. Dreams, that's what I like."

The women were silent.

"Come now, why are you offended with me? Am I drunk, dear ladies?"

"Tell about your mother's dream, tell about the boat leaving," the parson's widow said to Alma.

"No, no," said Holger. "Not about anything that's departing. I always feel such longing when I see something going away. I can't bear to look at a departing boat at all. When I go to Lappenranta, I never go to the pier."

"Bring the pharmacist some hot water."

Eighteen

"I love birds."

What kind of remark was that? It was a confession, I love birds, that was all one had to hear, the woman facing her saying something like that with hands on her hips, saying it as if it were a good thing. Love, love but get out of my way. Mad, mad, get out of this room. Alma was speaking in her thoughts—it came on like a disease—she would have wanted to beat, tear, smash something to pieces. She was overcome by pity for herself, to have been put here, to have to live with someone who, with fiery eyes, came on as if to suppress her. Why did she have to work for someone like that, she, who was a worker whose type and value you couldn't find anywhere, to work without seeing any results, from spring to spring chasing after birds—was that sort of work fit for a human being? And now she was standing before her, her face radiating that disgusting smile that seemed to know everything.

"I know what you think of me. Go, if you want to, but I know you won't go anyways," the parson's widow said. "I, I'm afraid of people, I'd like to love people but people have so much evil in them I don't have the courage to go among them."

And—that's where she started it this time, Alma thought.

"Are lifeless creatures better, then? You set yourself up as a religious person, and you can't even bear to have people near you," said Alma, and knew how pointless it was to say it. The parson's widow stood in the middle of the room with her back turned to her and her arms folded across her chest as if she were shivering from the cold, her mended cardigan wrapped around her flat-chested upper body, her back suddenly bent, as if she were protecting herself with her arm, protecting the side of her chest where her heart was beating, it was beating irregularly, with a rapid pulse. Alma had had to test the pulse rate so often that she knew, and she was no longer able to take pity on this woman whose every fit of madness she had had to see over these past years.

And now she's over behind the sink, she'll talk from there and soon will be pacing around the room and then she'll either burst into tears or she'll just sit there staring ahead of her until Alma can't take it anymore, but in order to keep herself from hitting that creature, she goes out, heads down to the sauna cabin on the shore, walking with measured steps, takes a pail in one hand, and in that way masks this as an ordinary trip down to the sauna shore. Perhaps she too cries: throws herself face down on the sauna benches and cries—for what will become of her life when . . . where would she go, who would she turn to? At home they were now planting potatoes—the smell of manure, the opening of furrows, yellow flowers on the banks of ditches—oh, how she could have wept, how, in her turn, ask her: what about me, I would like to go and be among people, but I'm a stranger here, a servant, no one cares about me, if I'd stayed home I might now be a farmer's wife—no, no—none of that, not even a thought, all thrust out of her mind. "Alma . . . please forgive me."

If she hated anything, it was this begging for forgiveness—she would have liked to shout and mimic that "forgive me, forgive me" and that which the woman was now saying:

"I feel so bad in this world, I don't hate anyone, I don't wish anyone ill. Isn't it true that I speak well of people—isn't it true, Alma—but I feel so bad . . . I don't have any friends, I used to have some when I was younger, but everyone has turned so strange, they're not the same people—maybe I've changed—I don't have the strength to keep up with people. Did Alma notice how my sister-in-law looked at me—well, Alma, I certainly notice everything. People think I don't understand, but I'm aware of even the slightest stirring of emotions and that's been my misfortune. Do you know, Alma, it's not good for someone to be like me."

Alma let out a laugh and then started to weep aloud.

"What are you crying about, Alma?"

But she only cried harder.

"You have it good, Alma, since you don't grasp everything that's going on in another person's mind. You go through life with your good sense under control, you suffer less than I do. When I was younger, I couldn't look people in the eye because I always knew what they were thinking and it made me ill, because what I saw they were thinking about me was not always favorable. I became ill and lay at home with a cold-pack on my head, I had a headache, a headache, how many headaches I have suffered through in my life. People are far worse than you can guess, Alma, no one cares for anyone, don't ever grow fond of anyone or anything . . ."

"But you did have a husband, Missus."

"He never cared for me. Whenever I had a headache he would say: 'Behold the birds of the heavens, and leave your heart under God's care.' 'Give me some medicine.' 'No,' he would say. 'Pray,' he would say, and refused to give any to me. But did he himself pray when pains seized him? No. He'd say to me, 'Give me some medicine,' and I would remember and say: 'Pray. Leave yourself under God's care.' No one has ever looked after me. You can go, Alma, you feel bad being with me—I know, when a person is the way I am, it's not good for anyone to be with her . . . I know that something evil radiates from me to other people—I'm restless, so restless I pray in the morning and later in the day: dear God, give me a tranquil mind, and do you know, that's what is said about temptation in the

Our Father, 'Do not lead us into temptation but deliver us from evil,' I say that ten times over but it doesn't help, I haven't learned to resist temptation. Do you know what temptation is—everything that makes your mind restless. I'm unable to be tranquil for even a moment, oh, I wish I knew where there's peace of mind—you tell me what it's like. If I think: today I won't get a headache, I'll be calm, I soon remember, and the sense of peace is gone. I believe that God hates me . . . and then again, I believe I have always been a child of God, always, and that he torments my anguished mind for that very reason. I'm in anguish, Alma, there is no God, well, what if there isn't, then—maybe everything is in vain, my struggle, my prayers, just think what theater, what theater all of this is, good God, I say to myself, maybe I'm only acting, and you all look on and laugh as I'm acting out, fighting the good fight. 'Do you love the birds at all, Alma, the only thing that gives me any peace of mind is when I watch them fly—do you think I don't know that they die too, that they're the same sort of birds of prey as people, they oppress one another—I certainly do know that, but they haven't done anything to me, that's why I love them . . . But my husband didn't even love birds, no, you're wrong, he studied them, you don't understand how I felt when, at this very table, he first skinned a bird, a poor little bird, and then, shall I tell you . . ."

Alma knew what the parson's widow left unsaid: that the husband had wanted to and his wife had refused him. Alma's eyes turned toward the bedroom door and she felt sick—she didn't want to listen and yet she had believed and been horrified. But now.

"Why is it that some people have to suffer in this life and others just get through it?"

"Have to suffer—it's not like that, Alma. I used to ask the same thing: why do I have to suffer so much?"

"Tell me, Missus, have you had an answer yet?" Alma asked maliciously.

"No, I haven't. I haven't. I only suffer. But do you know, Alma, what's the worst thing, the very worst?"

Alma didn't bother to ask what. They had had these conversations so many times:

"The worst suffering is not for the people who know why they suffer but for those who don't know why they suffer."

"And does the parson's widow know?"

"You see, I've lived through this life and suffered as much as anyone, but I still ask: why?"

"But perhaps the parson's widow really does know."

"Shall I tell you? I pity those who don't know why they have to suffer, that's the worst kind of suffering. When one knows why, it's much easier, much easier when at least you know, it is easier."

"Well, does the parson's widow know it, then?"

"I do," the widow said simply.

Alma didn't ask for more, but the widow began to speak. Her thin face was turned toward the evening, she was looking out at the lake and the horizon. Alma hadn't seen the parson's widow so quiet and uncomplicated in a long time. It was as if she were another person, almost a stranger to Alma.

"I used to question, I questioned God a great deal. Alma knows I have attempted suicide—yes, you know that, I know you do, my sisters-in-law have told me. You were brought in to watch over me way back then so that I wouldn't . . . I guess it's pointless to say that I was aware of it all and I guess I enjoyed it in my own way and never uttered one word about it. And then, I have abused drugs, you'd be the one to know that, Alma, and the times I forced you to go begging to the pharmacy, and that night, too, when I wept here in this room because you wouldn't go, all of it, I remember all of it, and it's true, I confess that sometimes, even still, when I can't get to sleep the temptation builds—if I only took all of this, that would be the end. My sleepless nights . . . I don't complain, I don't say this

in the same way as I used to, my sleepless nights, during my lifetime
I've tormented many people, you, for one, with my insomnia—oh,
I know, don't interrupt me. And it hasn't been on my mind only
once, but many times. All at once an end to everything—and why?
Because God wouldn't answer me: Why was I the one who had to
suffer?"

"Don't other people suffer? I know some who are much worse
off than the parson's widow."

"Alma, don't interrupt me now, I'm just coming to that. Of
course I know that all people suffer, but does that make my suffering any less? No. My suffering diminished when it became clear
why I suffer."

"And why?" Again Alma's voice was mean.

"Because I am a child of God." The parson's widow stiffened her
back and looked Alma straight in the eye. Alma had to turn away.

Child of God, child of God, isn't anybody else here just as much
a child of God? Did the parson's widow have to act as if she were
the only one who was in the right and that it was she and she alone,
and no one else could possibly be. Besides, how could she know
she was the one?

"Alma, you're thinking, how do I know for sure, isn't that right?
But I do know, it took a long time and it still isn't altogether certain,
it's certain only at some moments, but at those moments I have
a strong certainty, a knowledge that is so strong that I no longer
doubt it when I return to my old self, I don't doubt but say to
myself: if I can only go on living until the time when knowledge
will be granted to me. It's only a matter of having the strength to
go on, Alma."

"How does one know it?" Alma asked. "How in the world does
one know?"

"It's difficult to explain. Sometimes it comes at night, sometimes
during the day when I'm resting on my bed, it's as if it filled me,

my body is light, I am as if in the air and I know: now it is in me. God is in me, I am in God, and when it is like that, there is nothing more for me to suffer in this world, it takes everything else away. Well, Alma, do you think I'm not just like anyone else? You know I'm bitter, I'm mean, I am a very bad person, I don't love people. It's true: I've never learned to love anyone, but at the moments when God is in me, all people, everything that lives and breathes in the world is unspeakably dear to me. At first I thought I was only deceiving myself, and I still feel at times that I've thought it up only to ease my own mind. What could you be, I said to myself, you, bitter, mean, full of evil thoughts, and how you root around in them, like digging in filth, I dig up everything that's been done to me in this life, in this house, including everything you've said to me, Alma. You don't know how I've dug up even those things you haven't said to me directly but have told other people. For one thing, I haven't even forgiven that time when you called me a wagtail, Alma, and that's nearly ten years ago. Can you understand it, Alma? I don't understand it myself, I wonder to myself how it's possible that you call me a wagtail and then I lose control of my nerves, my health, I stay awake nights, I hear your voice calling me a wagtail. I keep asking God about it, I keep asking whether someone who won't let go of such trifles could possibly be a child of God. Good God, I think, and I thrash about on my bed, and I hate you. Do you know why?"

"Well, I guess the parson's widow got mad at me back then."
"No, I didn't get mad, that's just it. If only I had gotten mad, I would have called you by the name of some bird I consider silly, let's say a lapwing, you with your hair in that bun, to tell the truth, it has always made me think of a lapwing, and you are just as pigheaded and strange as a lapwing, you do remember the bird that held the tip of that point of land as its territory all summer long, and there was no way of scaring it off. Do you remember, we kept

clapping our hands, and all it did was fly off to one side a little and then it would be right back. When you went away from me again that time and then later came back, I thought I would say: you are nothing but a lapwing, but I didn't say it, and see, that's just it, I never say anything, you see, I am unkind to myself, not to others, isn't that right? Compared to me, you are a happy person. When you get mad, you find words right away, but I have never been able to think up anything to say to anyone. It's only later that I think of what I should have said."

Nineteen

"At some point in the night, early Friday morning, isn't that right?"

"Yes," said the voice on the telephone.

"I'll tell her."

The voice faded. The parson's widow went on standing there, and looking. The red glow of evening beyond the stand of fir trees on the shore, more beautiful than it had been so far this winter. A bird gliding slowly above the fir trees. "A hawk," the parson's widow said aloud. Alma's brother, sitting there swarthy as a gypsy, like the hero of a folk tale. "There'll be a spot for you in heaven," the parson's widow said, and folded her hands. Died in the hospital, thus dead, Alma's wood-grouse brother, she thought. But in place of the image that she tried to evoke, a black-haired man arose next to the "dream," the big asparagus plant which grew in a wooden tub in a corner of the parlor in Alma's home. "There'll be a spot for you in heaven," the parson's widow said in a calm, commanding voice. The image vanished. "Soul, you are free." And just then she heard Alma's footsteps.

"So, Alma, your brother is dead."

For the first time, she did this. The hand of the parson's widow lit timidly on Alma's shoulder, and in an instant, as if the light touch hadn't occurred, the widow had already flitted to the opposite side of the room. She stood there, studying the pattern in the wallpaper. It had once been green, a leaf of a lilac bush, but was now brown.

All of this had happened before. She moved along the wall to a place by the window.

"Are you still crying?"

The parson's widow turned to look but Alma wasn't crying. She was kneeling on the floor, her head leaning against the sofa, repeating, "Thank you, thank you."

"What are you saying, Alma?"

"I am thanking God for taking that burden away from me. I am giving thanks, even though you are crying."

"How can you say that? That's not why I'm crying. Your brother was a great artist, that's what I'm crying about. Please, to honor his memory, please show me . . ."

Alma stared at her, disbelieving. She began to weep like a child— in a sacred moment of her life she was being asked to portray . . . a bird. But the parson's widow had already spread her arms, silhouetted against the red glow of the sunset. "Like this, Alma? Tell me, am I doing it right? Was it like this?" The widow acting out a woodgrouse, her thin neck arched, her head a black silhouette against the window: "Was it like this, Alma? Tell me, am I doing it right? Is your brother's soul in me, tell me . . ."

And it wasn't until Alma's footsteps had faded into the dark that the parson's widow, her neck still arched, eyes closed, realized that Alma had left the room.

"Have to get to the pharmacy, the pharmacy," Alma kept saying to herself as she walked toward the pharmacy, taking the short-cut across the field: she felt as if the parson's widow were at her heels, like a spirit. Alma hurried along, holding herself back from running, towards the pharmacy, towards a circle of light. No matter whether they're home or not, she would spend the night there. She knocked on the door. It was opened for her. When they asked what was up with her, what had happened, she wept and told, with tears running down her face, that just when she had returned from here, after cleaning the pharmacy . . . for two days she had been here, cleaning, to get the house ready for Christmas visitors, and Teodolinda and Holger listened and couldn't understand why Alma was telling them about that because they knew it very well and Alma had left their house just a short while ago. But they heard her out, and the pharmacist raised his hand when his wife was about to ask something.

"How could she do something like that?" Teodolinda said when Alma had finished her story.

"Please don't cry anymore, Alma," said Teodolinda.

"Adele didn't mean any harm," Holger said.

"Here she is," said Teodolinda.

"She came after you. Calm down, Alma, that's a good girl." Holger spoke to her as if to a child.

"Where's Alma?" The parson's widow stopped at the door. Alma was silent.

"Come in," said Teodolinda.

"No, thank you. I just came to see where Alma is."

"Well, Alma's right here," Holger said, and let out a sigh. "Please sit down. Let's clear up this matter."

"Adele, why couldn't you understand just this once," said Teodolinda.

"I've grown old," said Alma.

"What's the matter with Alma?" asked the parson's widow.

"Leave Alma alone," said Holger, suddenly irritable. "Let her rest."

"Well, we're all old," Teodolinda said. "But she has the strength to keep going."

"Yes, Adele has the strength to keep going, you're able to keep on, Adele, but please, just let Alma be for a while."

"It's over, all over, he has it good now."

"Think of that, Alma," said Holger.

"Alma's tired," the parson's widow said. "I know Alma's tired."

"Let Alma be," said Teodolinda. "Can't you understand that you mustn't torment Alma?"

The parson's widow fell silent. She sat immobile on the sofa, right in the middle of the sofa in the parlor. How could she tell them she had sat all evening worshipping the setting sun. When the sun had gone down beyond the grove of firs, the sky had been strangely clear, like a thin stretched-out sheet of copper above the forest on the opposite side of the lake. The parson's widow had seen a bird fly past the tops of the firs, then vanish as if the sky were water into which the bird could dive. And as though the heavens had clanged at the touch of the bird's wing, the clang still hanging in the air like a bird, nameless birds, black bird-shaped images, celestial satraps. And she felt that as she waited and remained silent, the answer would come, expectation would be fulfilled.

If Alma had been at home when the telephone rang, perhaps everything that had happened would not have happened.

All were silent, the parson's widow sitting on the sofa, in the middle of the sofa with her hands in her lap. Alma went to pack her things. She would leave now, to go help with the funeral arrangements. Teodolinda saw her to the vestibule and spoke with her there. The parson's widow would stay here overnight. She didn't answer when they asked her what had happened, or when they asked her how she was. Because the parson's widow and Alma had to be kept in different houses tonight, it was better for Alma to go and for the widow to stay, said Teodolinda. She made a bed for the parson's widow and managed to get her into it.

At night she spoke with her husband, and in the morning they both took her home; Alma had already left.

"What did you do to her?"

"Yes, Adele, what was it?"

"I prayed for him."

"For whom?"

"For her brother's soul."

"But what did you do to Alma?" That was what Holger wanted to know.

"Leave Adele alone," Teodolinda said. "She doesn't even understand it herself anymore."

"You're blaming me, isn't that right? You're blaming me. What's the matter?"

"Did you have any visitors?"

"You know there are no longer any visitors. Alma's driven them all away. You know that."

The parson's widow's gray head was shaking. "You're thinking I've done something bad to Alma, aren't you?"

"Oh, let her be," said Holger.

"Where's Alma?"

"You should know that Alma has gone to her brother's funeral."

"Why didn't she tell me?"

"Once in a while, you should think of someone besides yourself," said Teodolinda.

The parson's widow started and became frozen, immobile.

"Don't you agree?" Teodolinda asked her husband. But he shook his head sadly. She shouldn't have said that.

"Calm down, Adele," he said.

But the parson's widow wouldn't calm down. Instead, she suddenly stood up, stepped over to her sister-in-law, and said, "Just say straight out what you've got against me!"

"I have nothing against you, but you shouldn't have . . ." Teodolinda tried to explain that Adele should have treated Alma differently in the moment of her grief.

"What should I have done?"

"What did you say to her?"

"I prayed."

"What did you ask of her?"

The parson's widow didn't answer.

"She's sick, leave her alone."

"Adele's a selfish woman."

"I only asked her for a favor."

"What did you ask her?"

"She wouldn't do it even though she knows it's too late now."

"What did you ask her?" Teodolinda asked yet one more time.

"I asked her but she didn't want to. She's never agreed to do it even though I've asked her nicely. Now it's too late."

"What's too late?"

The parson's widow didn't answer.

"You must understand that Alma was tired. You shouldn't have asked her for it, at least not now."

"Adele, you've never been able to pick the right moment, that's been your mistake all along. You don't understand that you can sometimes be downright cruel in your self-centeredness, you don't understand that . . ."

Teodolinda stopped because the parson's widow had jumped to her feet and was staring at them both with utter fury in her eyes. Her head rose, her arms grew taut along her sides, and stiffening up in that position with her head held high, she stood in front of the window, staring straight ahead. Then her mouth opened and at first no sound would come out, and then:

"I asked but she didn't want to, she did it out of spite so I would never see it, she doesn't want me to see it. Alma is a mean, jealous woman; she doesn't want me to see it."

"You're mistaken," said Holger. But now he didn't ask her how her little birds were doing, because the expression on the widow's face and the position of her arms had frightened him. "You're mistaken," he repeated, sighed, and wondered what they should do now.

"No, I'm not mistaken, you know that. It was pure spite on her part."

"Her brother is dead. Can't you get it through your head?"

"For years, I've kept asking her for it, and now I asked if she couldn't show me just this once, but she didn't want to."

"But her brother is dead."

"If Alma had shown me even once, her brother would go on living through me, but Alma didn't want to and now it's all too late."

"Nothing's too late, Adele. Alma will show you when she comes back."

The parson's widow didn't answer. She ended the conversation. Teodolinda went to the kitchen.

"I'll make you some coffee," she said.

The widow didn't answer.

"Are you going to have some coffee?"

Holger had gone back to the pharmacy. Teodolinda was left alone with Adele.

All day long the parson's widow sat in the same position in the middle of the sofa, her head slightly raised, her eyes staring out into emptiness.

Teodolinda telephoned the pharmacy and said, "You can take a turn and come here. Can't leave her alone."

They called Herman, and Herman and Elsa came over. In the evening they managed to get her to get up from the sofa and go upstairs.

And this is what Alma had to cope with when she got back from the funeral. The final madness of the parson's widow, it was called. Forever after that night, she walked with her arms dragging down along her sides and people believed that the madness was precisely that she had turned into a bird. She believed she was a bird in order to prove to people that she hadn't wronged Alma when, that night, she had asked her to perform a wood-grouse mating dance in her brother's memory. People said that the widow spent every night getting drunk with the pharmacist. This rumor started when someone who had stopped by the pharmacy at night, a person who had come to the back door to pick up some medicine, had seen Holger with a glass of medicine in his hand, right there in the middle of the night.

"Don't let her catch sight of you, Alma."

Teodolinda had rushed to meet Alma, but it was too late: no sooner had Adele caught a glimpse of Alma than she had at once set herself in that accursed position, bewitched, as Alma called it. The parson's widow was bewitched, and Alma yielded to that madness, at last yielded to the madness that the parson's widow had been begging from her for twenty years, and that night, letting out a scream, she spread her arms, flew, plunged, thumped like a wood-grouse, like a wood-grouse in a mating dance, said Holger, who looked on and bore witness to this terrifying scene, the scene to which the county doctor, his wife, and Antti, the widow's son, all came; they were gathered at the pharmacy that night because it was Christmas.

Alma's brother had died before Christmas and Alma had returned from the funeral in time for Christmas; she came from the train carrying a suitcase, a small bag, other people said, and it was this bag that she had flung onto the kitchen floor when she saw the parson's widow right in front of her insisting on the same thing, and Alma, shouting at the top of her lungs, had thumped down, said the son and daughter-in-law of the parson's widow, shouting and stomping they said she had fallen unconscious, others said, hysterical, said Herman, in the grip of senseless hysteria, said Elsa, an old woman tormented in her period of mourning, said the villagers, collapsed right in front of the parson's widow, blood-curdling

shouts, a screaming which then turned to howling, barking, ringing, gurgling, as if a cork had been pulled from a bottle, said Antti,
a champagne bottle, said Holger, making the most terrible racket,
said the doctor's son, she went mad in the company of a madwoman, said the shopkeeper and his wife, touched by God, said the
parson (for in the midst of all Alma's noises, that's what the parson
had been told, amid all her fierce fury people could hear her utter
"forgive me, forgive me" over and over) when the parson's widow,
transformed into a bird, had screamed in full voice: "Beg forgiveness, you know for what, beg forgiveness for your brother's sake, his
soul demands it through me, you know that, Alma," and to that, Alma's screaming voice which—as all who heard it testified—was like
the screams of one descending into hell, terrifying, and over and
over, "forgive me, forgive me" . . . and then the parson's widow, in a
human voice and all at once sounding in her right mind, had said:
"Go to your resting place, soul," and Alma was lying on the floor
and the doctor was shouting: "Get out of here, all you crazy people,"
and the parson's widow was saying: "Herman, I am all right, I don't
need your medicine. Get up, Alma." And Alma, they said, rose from
the floor and with unseeing eyes staggered toward the sofa where
Teodolinda, the only one who had remained calm through this
dreadful scene, had told her to sit.

"Alma, rest and listen to me."

And in the morning they went home together, Alma and the
parson's widow—Antti and the daughter-in-law had fled back to
the city during the night—they went home to the widow's house
and ever after that, there was no more talk about them in the village.

TWENTY

"So where should I go, then?"

Alma didn't have to look at the pharmacist's wife. She knew. She had learned all right, and out of consideration she had come to know when Teodolinda didn't want anyone to look at her, and this was one of those moments. Teodolinda's eyes were dry, and still she was crying. Her crying wasn't like the crying of the parson's widow, or of the pharmacist, noisy, wet, full of sighs, but like this: face turned toward the window, towards the edge of the forest, arms pressed to her sides as on a statue, head held proudly.

"Why don't you think about staying on? With us."

For the first time, Teodolinda said: with us. Alma had already guessed that what Teodolinda meant by "staying on" would be for her to stay at the pharmacy.

And she pitied the poor woman.

"But I have to go—they asked me to."

"Both of them?"

"Antti. Antti asked me. And who's going to look after the birds?"

Teodolinda understood. Alma was mourning for the birds. Her grief for the parson's widow had turned into grief over the birds. Where would they eventually go? Alma didn't want to hear any talk about the collection being divided up, with each family member taking some of it and giving the birds a place in their homes. Alma had her doubts. "You're right. You're right," Teodolinda repeated. "You are quite right."

Silence.

"And later on, in the future?"

"I'll go somewhere."

"What about the birds?"

"Of course. I'll take them with me. Antti doesn't really care about them."

"Couldn't you just let me have them?" Teodolinda turned to face her. "In Adele's memory . . . But you're thinking that I will die, aren't you? But you know, you'll die too. Where will they go then? What did Adele say?"

The parson's widow had never said a single word about the birds, and besides, Alma knew that the widow had trusted her, had bequeathed the birds to her. Teodolinda should know that, and also that there had been a fight with Antti right after the funeral, when Antti had started to think about which birds he would take and which he would leave.

"Yes, you told us about it. And what you did was right. I think that's what Adele would have wanted."

"Everything's just the way it was," Alma said.

"But that's impossible. Where will you go? Where will you find room for them? You know there isn't enough room in a cramped city apartment."

Everyone knew that. Alma had set one condition: if they wanted her to become Antti's maid, she would go, but not without the birds. All the birds, all the birds' eggs. She had to be allowed to bring the entire collection of the parson's widow, but no one understood that, not even Teodolinda, and Alma had found out for sure that no one understood. The pharmacist would laugh when he was drunk, he laughed when he came to visit, he'd knock on the door; and Alma would let him in day or night, because the spirit of the parson's widow, that's what he told herself, the widow's spirit wants me to let him in and to listen through the night when he talks about the parson's widow and now and then he takes me for the parson's widow herself.

"Adele, my dear, you're doing the right thing, the right thing."

"Is that so?"

"Yes, it's so. It's so."

"One egg broke, but it wasn't my fault. It was Antti's fault. He was handling the box carelessly and the box fell. No, not Antti, but that woman."

"That woman," said Holger. And laughed.

"What are you laughing about, sir?"

"That woman," Holger kept saying. "You're incorrigible," he said, and Alma didn't push the pharmacist's withered hand off her knee but let it rest there.

"Why should we pretend? Why?"

"Why should we?" And so they sat all through the night. Every so often Holger would drift off to sleep, wake up and mutter to himself. It was all so familiar, and so comforting.

"Where are you going?" Holger said, starting when she tried to creep away; each time, the pharmacist would wake up like a child, and that's what he was, a child. A child who belonged to the parson's widow and to Alma, a poor dear child. All night long, and it was as if the parson's widow were with them there, a third person in the dark. Whenever it grew dark, the parson's widow would make it three.

"Set out a third cup on the table."

And Alma, surprised: "Why?"

"For Adele."

The pharmacist's hand rose in the dark and pointed to the corner of the sofa where the parson's widow used to sit wrapped in her shawl, right next to her owl's image, her legs pressed tightly together.

"For Adele."

And from then on, Alma set three glasses on the table whenever the pharmacist came over.

"*Skoal,* Adele."

"*Skoal,*" Alma answered. And Alma knew that Teodolinda knew and she had the feeling that the others—Antti, the doctor, Elsa, everybody—knew that after the parson's widow had died, Alma had learned to drink up the glass the pharmacist handed her. Now it was to her, just as it had been to the widow in the old days. Year after year she had been guarding the secret, in her horror had been arguing, threatening, tyrannizing the parson's widow, trying to fight against it: but the widow had been drinking, not like the pharmacist, not until she was out of her senses. And come to think of it, had she ever been in her senses? What was it for her to be in her right mind? She was always the same. But in the company of the pharmacist she was happy, happy and laughing.

It had taken a long time before Alma had understood, after many nights of listening, after years of listening to the talking and laughing she could hear going on downstairs all through the night. Alma did not laugh. Did not talk. She took a glass, emptied it, and when it was refilled she took it up and emptied it again. But while the parson's widow was alive, Alma would never take a single glass, except for medicine. The widow's voice: "But Alma, you know it anyway. Why should I keep it a secret? Holger taught me a long time ago, and who am I to say, 'Holger is a drunkard'? Why, I drink too. Tell me, am I any the better or worse because of that? I don't go to take Communion, and people wonder why I, the widow of a clergyman, don't go to Communion services. Holger comes to me. He hands me a glass. I think: it is a cup. A dark room, my birds, and my suffering congregation, Holger. 'Do this in remembrance of me.' Do you see: tears well up in my eyes. One night when I was thinking about it I heard a voice and I saw something like a smile, and the smile said, 'Do this in remembrance of me, even though you do as you do.'" Horrified, Alma had thought it was madness, blasphemy, and had fled so she wouldn't have to listen. "Do this in remembrance of me." And on the night when the pharmacist had said, "Set a third glass on the table," Alma got drunk with him, and weeping welled up in her and she understood what the parson's widow had said: "Do this in remembrance of me." That the three, the three of them, that it depended on the spirit in which the glass was emptied, that you didn't need a church for it, only love.

But these matters were secret, none but the three of them knew. The pharmacist who, lying on the floor, drunk, weeping over his wife who didn't love him and whom he had never loved. The parson's widow who hadn't loved anyone, only her birds, the widow weeping over being unable to love anyone individually and that she wasn't the kind of person the pharmacist could love. "I would have loved you, Adele, and I do love you, I have always loved you, but you are mad, Adele, you know that yourself as well." "Of course I know that. Anyway, you shouldn't have loved me." "Do you forgive me for not proposing to you back then? Do you? You see, I could tell right away that you were out of your mind, and I let Birger have you." "But Birger was mad," cried the parson's widow, and then she laughed as though she would burst. "Yes, yes, he was." "And that's why I didn't love him. I knew he was mad, knew it right from the start, from the day he proposed to me and shot at his sisters when we were out on the rocky islet." "Now, this Alma here, she's not mad." "Then why are you sitting here?" "I'm keeping watch over you so that no one will hear you." "You're so damned selfish." "Leave Alma alone." "I will. You know I will. It's just a habit. You know me, Adele, don't you? I don't really cheat on you. It's just that my hands go on and fiddle about all on their own. Woman's flesh is nice, soft. You, Adele, have never had the flesh of a real woman. You're always wearing that terrible dress, and that maid of yours, she's filthy too, but oh, what tenderloin!"

There were no words to describe the indecency of the parson's widow. Night after night she sat up with the pharmacist, convulsed with laughter at his bawdy stories.

"I never stop marveling at you, Adele. You're an oasis in this desert. When I don't have the strength to go into the city, I come here to your house. I am an old man, an old man. Sometimes I pull myself together and go to the city. I decide, I decide, last week I decided to go to the city. Well, did I go? No. And you know, what would I do there anyway? I can't even make it up those stairs. Everybody knows that, and this Alma here, she knows I used to be a lecherous man." "But Holger, what if you told Alma straight out: she might even become afraid of you before long. Well, you've never really been lecherous, you're all talk. If you only had been, you wouldn't talk . . . Well, all that was . . . oh, yes, don't get angry, that plump little one in Viipuri." "But I loved her. Remember that." "You loved, you loved. I'm not going to deprive you of the only happiness you've known in your life."

"Alma, please bring some water." And water pitcher in hand, Alma went into the parlor. "Do you enjoy watching the two of us?" "She doesn't say anything. Well, she'll learn, she's loyal. Where in the world could you possibly find such nice people as this Adele here, your own parson's widow, and me, the town pharmacist? You haven't yet come to realize what rare people you've had the chance to see. Only this Adele here, she understands what I am, and I am the only one who completely understands Adele. See, she's laughing. I'm the only one who can make dear Adele laugh. We are amazing when we're together. God can see, and looks on approvingly. You see, we're God's children."

"I'm going to cry a little. I put my head on Adele's knee, and I cry, I cry. Adele, go ahead and laugh. You aren't laughing because I'm crying, you're laughing because you think I'm so nice. Did you ever love me? For one day, that one day. And I didn't even notice you. I always thought you were kind of different when you'd walk past the pharmacy with your mother, a little slip of a girl, tall and thin, with a curved back, and a bit cross-eyed—that I did notice about you. Everything else about you has grown old: hands, feet, teeth, you still do have hair, but you hide it under a scarf, and never mind your hair anyway. But the eyes. Do you see, Alma? Have you ever seen eyes brighter than the widow's? Take a good look."

But the parson's widow had died, and now it was only the two of them, Alma and the pharmacist.

Twenty-one

It was a beautiful autumn day when Alma came to visit Holger and Teodolinda. The pharmacist and his wife, that's how Alma used to refer to them, but with the parson's widow always having talked about Holger and Teodolinda, Alma too thought: I'll go see Holger and Teodolinda. After all, they'd asked her over, had sent word that she should come visit some time. They were living in the very house they had lived in all their lives, as long as Alma could remember. It was a beautiful autumn day. Alma got off the bus at the store and walked the rest of the way. She walked towards the pharmacy that she had sometimes circled, running in the snow in the dead of night when they wouldn't give the widow any medicine and the doctor wouldn't renew the prescriptions. And right over there, from those windows where Holger and Teodolinda had looked on as she'd kept circling the dark house, banging on the door, they had watched without turning on the lights, pretending they weren't home.

Alma had other business to look after as well; she hadn't come only to visit Holger and Teodolinda. She had come to pick up the things. It was four years now since the parson's widow had died. Alma had gone to look after Antti's household; Antti had divorced, leaving his wife and child, and then remarried. Alma had stayed on with the former wife. When Antti had divorced a second time, the second wife had come for a visit, and these two former wives had become friends. They were just waiting for the third to join them. There already was a third, but Antti was still married to her. Alma had looked after Antti's household, and after Antti had left, Alma had stayed on. She had been able to bear it when the second former wife would come around, there was something to talk about, about Antti, but when they had taken in a young girl, a dark-eyed young girl, Alma's nerves got on edge. There were just too many women. And she didn't like guests, not the kind of guests that would come around. With them, you never quite knew what they were, and when she'd ask who someone was, it might turn out that she was a doctor, but there was no way of guessing that's what she was. As far as Alma was concerned, life had gotten out of control.

Holger was in the yard when Alma arrived.

"Oh, it's Alma!"

And Alma was surprised that the voice and Holger himself had grown thin.

"It's me."

"Let's go in," Holger said. "Teodolinda's inside."

"Thank you."

We're really old friends, many times over, Alma thought as they went in.

And Teodolinda came and gave her a friendly greeting.

"It gets cold just as soon as the sun goes behind the clouds," Alma said. "Of course it would do that, the end of September already, and October coming soon."

Teodolinda agreed.

Holger's eyes still had their old sparkle, just as in the old days, even with him grown so thin.

And Alma was surprised when Teodolinda started to make some coffee right away and to set the table, just as she would have done for a guest.

"I could do that," said Alma.

"Alma's going to be the guest now. I'll make the coffee. It'll take only a minute."

After they had finished their coffee, Teodolinda said:

"Now I'm going to talk about these matters for the first time. Until now, I have listened. I've listened for decades about Uncle Onni, and then about the fire. I haven't spoken out, not even among members of the family, because ordinarily there's no point talking about things. There's always someone in the family who lets it out, and then it's on everybody's lips. Now I don't mean Alma. Alma knows, all right, Alma's heard everything from the parson's widow. But that's precisely why I want to talk, so that Alma will know that not everything Adele said was quite true. Adele wanted to see things that way because, to put it bluntly, Uncle Onni was strange, and because some believer, some famous preacher, had predicted that Uncle Onni would die on a particular day, and because it did happen on that day, then ever after that, everything followed naturally, the supernatural, that is."

Alma nodded.

"And it's true that on that very day Uncle Onni did go out hunting and got a cut on his hand which led to blood poisoning, but that doesn't prove anything either way. It just came from his handling half-rotten eggs and not from the prediction. But be that as it may. The fire is another thing entirely. People have said that the sexton had been beating the top of the piano with an alder branch when it was already in flames and that the fire was about to burn it up right there in the yard and that the lacquer had already begun to turn to gas, that's how you've always explained it, Holger, to gas. But the sexton never did beat the top of the piano with an alder branch for the simple reason that, wonder of wonders, I was right there and I took care of it—as soon as they got the piano outside, and that did happen at the very last minute, they carried it to the shed so it would be safe. You know, a piano can't take any humidity. And I told the sexton to fetch the straps that are used to carry coffins, you know, those coffin belts, and then the men said you can't lift the weight without the straps that carry pianos, and even then you'd have to have four men."

Teodolinda was waiting to see whether Alma had understood.

"And I asked what those straps were like, and rounded up four men from those who were running around the yard, one carrying a gum tree, another something else, no one with any idea of what was valuable and what wasn't, and when they tried to get out of it by talking about straps, it came to me that of course we had them, strong straps, and I told the sexton's son to go get them. And finally, it was with their help that the piano was carried out. Then the roof caved in. And there it is, Alma. Just take a look and see whether there are any traces of fire on its lid. No, and there never have been, it's all nothing but talk. But I've listened, I haven't said who took care of it, it was the only thing that was rescued in a sensible manner. Isn't that the way it is?"

Holger agreed that it was.

"This is the first time I'm speaking of these matters and I won't speak about them ever again, but because it'll soon be thirty years since the fire and, I guess, some fifty years since Uncle Onni died, and there's been so much talk about them, it's time someone says what's true and what's not. It is true that a fortune teller had come to Uncle Onni and it is true that, in a way, the prediction was fulfilled and he died, but we all have to die. And it is true that the parsonage burned down. But everything else, only idle talk. Idle gossip to disgrace our family and, whether she meant to or not, Adele did her share. I'm speaking out now. And Adele wasn't alone, that's true, the sexton's wife was the worst, she was the one who said that the parson's wife sat on a rock, her hair a mess, while the parsonage burned, like a gypsy woman with a shawl wrapped around her shoulders, and that they had had to force her feet into shoes and had to dress her forcibly as well. But that's not the way it was. After all, I was there and saw everything."

"Sure, there's been a lot of exaggeration," Holger said.

"Now you agree. You didn't use to, but that's the way it is. Because Adele wasn't that foolish even when the parsonage was burning, though she was expecting Antti and maybe wasn't quite herself. But no one had to dress her. On the contrary, she did everything people told her to do, wrapped the shawl around her shoulders, put her shoes on. Someone brought them to Adele. It may have been the sexton's wife, I don't know, and maybe she got angry because her care wasn't appreciated enough. She was the one who started all those stories. And that's how it is, once a story starts going around, there's no point trying to correct it. It goes all around the world just the way it got started. Nothing's going to change that."

"It's like us people."

"Don't make light of it. That's how it is," Teodolinda said. "And yet. When we left the site of the fire, it was morning and it had begun to rain. They said that Birger had been the last to go. Bare-footed, when really he had galoshes on, all alone, the last one, though he was right there in the midst of us. And the most common claim was that he was walking around in his nightshirt, but he was wearing his clerical robe even when I got there, and I was, after all, one of the first to arrive on the scene because I realized what was happening just as soon as I heard the tolling of the church bells. Trailing after the others, bare-footed and alone, in his nightshirt, birds dangling from his hands. The only thing that has any truth to it is that he did have some bird or other in his hand, but you could hardly notice it. And they said that the parson's wife was led around like a senseless woman, which is very much exaggerated."

"It certainly is."

"In a word, all of it is nonsense, such inaccurate talk that even what was factually correct wasn't really true."

"Certainly not accurate, or very badly exaggerated."

"And simply nasty."

"But Adele herself said that as they were leaving, Birger had held a bird in his hand, upright, as if it were a living, representative specimen. But what kind of bird it was, I can't remember. Yet be that as it may, when you consider the circumstances, and especially Adele's condition, she and Birger both behaved sensibly. Certainly there were things I would have done differently. I would have organized the rescue operation. Just as in the pharmacy, you can get by with fewer people when you arrange the working times sensibly."

"Yes," said Holger.

"But no matter. The ruins of the parsonage have been cleared away. They haven't been there for decades."

"The only things growing there are fireweed and nettles," said Holger. "That's how you can tell there was once a house there, an inhabited site."

"Well, I wonder how Antti is doing now," Holger asked when the women were silent.

"Just as before." Alma gave a snort.

"Still problems with the girl students."

"I guess so. I don't know."

Alma started asking about buses, fussing over her departure. There was a time to arrive, to chat, to take care of business, and to go away.

"What are Alma's plans now?"

"I'll go on to my old home town. After that, I don't know. Well, because I've got that plot of land there."

"Do you plan to settle there, build a house?" Holger asked.

"What money would I build anything with?"

"Don't you have any money in the bank, Alma?"

"Well, I don't know. With that road and all. Everything's so different there now. It's not like when I was young."

"But it's good there's a road into town."

"And where can an old woman go anymore? Just go where cars and trains take you."

"But Alma's not really old."

Holger winked at his wife and said to Alma, "How about Alma staying here for a couple of days? She should go through the things."

"Yes, the parson's widow did promise me some things. But there's nothing on paper."

"But we don't have to do these things according to papers. Alma will get what was promised her."

"I've sure learned in those dealings over our farmhouse that if there's nothing on paper, you don't get a thing. But thank you, anyway."

"Why don't you stay on for a couple of days? You know, there's an empty room for you," Teodolinda finally said.

"Yes, let's do it that way," said Holger.

Alma stayed on.

Stayed on as she had before. Had come for a day, stayed a week, just to get her things sorted out, stayed a year. "Wartime marriages," Holger said one day not long after Alma had come, when the talk turned to such things, "wartime marriages," he said, as if the war, and not marriage, had been the pointless and imprudent event, not the getting married, whatever the time. "I could see right off that nothing good would come of it. And Teodolinda said, just as soon as she'd seen Antti's wife, that nothing would come of it. I didn't be-lieve it right away. But as a woman, Teodolinda saw right away that they'd rushed into that marriage without careful consideration." And Alma listened to a new tone in Holger's voice. It was Teod-olinda's voice, echoing through.

"That's how it was," Teodolinda agreed.

"Antti was too young."

"Is he any more grown up now?"

"Well, I guess not. Antti will always be Antti."

"No more birds here either," Alma said. "And to think how many there were and how they had to be taken out to be aired."

"Yes, Birger's birds are gone," Holger said. "And I remember Uncle Onni's birds from the time I was a child. He was a taxidermist. He lived in St. Petersburg but in summer he'd always come visit the old homestead. He was the one the birds belonged to, and Birger inherited them from him, and what people called Birger's madness, maybe for good reason, came down from him, the birds, and maybe that's why so many strange things are connected with Uncle Onni's death, for as we know, his death was certainly peculiar. Some believed it and some didn't, for it did go beyond all understanding. I too have thought about these things, and I cannot tell. I've wondered where Antti's restlessness came from. I guess it's from way back."

"The parson's widow always said it was from Uncle Onni."

"Sure, of course she would, because Uncle Onni was Birger's uncle," Holger said, "and maybe that's the way it was."

Teodolinda was silent. She had been quiet for a while now, and one could tell it would be a while again before she spoke.

"Antti still had one bird when I went out there four years ago," Alma said, "and it was old, the owl. It used to belong to Uncle Onni, Antti said. Maybe he was right. The owl stayed behind in the home after Antti left; it stayed in its nest. Wife, child, and owl. There wasn't much else left there, anyway. Wonder what would have become of them if the wife hadn't been an elementary school teacher. Antti already had so many children to support. It was an old bird, shedding feathers, and Antti's wife said, 'Let's throw it out.' But Antti wouldn't let her. But when he took off and went chasing after that other woman, the wife got mad and shoved the bird onto an acquaintance of hers as a present, though I can't really say whether it was a suitable present anymore, but she gave it away because, as she said, all of Antti's family was looking at her through its eyes: the parson's widow, Uncle Onni, everybody."

Holger listened.

"I wasn't there when it was given away. And when I asked where it was, they first told me it had been lent to a science student. But that was a lie. She had simply given it away. And a year ago, when I saw that acquaintance of Antti's wife, a married woman younger than she, and I asked her, so, where is the bird now, she told me. Because I knew this woman was no student but already a mathematician, that's what she was. And she told me she had gone through many changes in her life, but that she had always carried the bird with her, as a memento. I can't understand what kind of memento it could have been for her. Well, she did visit us once, visit the parson's widow, when Antti's Ritva spent a summer there to get away from Antti. He was already on his second or third woman at that time. I could tell that that woman had seen the parson's widow, and of course, she'd heard everything. But now, when I happened to ask her about the bird, she didn't have it anymore, she'd given it away. Who did she give it to? Where? To some painter, an artist who looked like an owl, and who kept it as a model."

"The owl?"

"That's what she said. It was Antti's, it belongs to the family, and his wife had no business giving it away. And the woman understood that and promised to get the bird back. I guess she got a bit offended, and when I asked about it later, she said she'd asked that painter about the owl but he didn't have it anymore. He'd given it away to somebody else, somebody with a Swedish name, somebody who'd asked for a crow owl. That's the end of the owl, for sure. And Antti, he didn't even make it to his mother's death-bed. He was chasing some woman then, too."

A literal translation of the Finnish title of this novel would be *Hers Were the Birds* or *His Were the Birds,* and in fact both versions have appeared not only in translations into various languages but even in different English-language references to the book. This is not surprising, for in Finnish the gender of pronouns is not designated. Thus the word for "he" and "she" is the same. One word also indicates the possessive "his" and "hers," as is the case with the objective "him" and "her." The gender of a character is revealed only by references to "the woman," "the man," "the boy," "the girl," etc., or by the contexts in which the character appears. Most often, a Finnish reader would have no trouble identifying a character's gender, and in the few instances where there is ambiguity, that was clearly the author's intent.

In this novel, Vartio surely intended to leave open the question of whether the birds of her title were "his" or "hers." A good case could be made for either one, for the birds had originally belonged to an Uncle Onni, had then been inherited by the parson, Birger, and on Birger's death had passed on to his widow, Adele. Birger and Adele had each tended the bird collection so fiercely that either one could be considered to have earned the possessive pronoun of Vartio's title.

Our decision to call the English translation of the novel *The Parson's Widow* was made not simply to avoid the pronoun issue but to reflect the fact that Adele's story is the focus of this book. It also reflects her social status, for the parson's wife is at the top of the hierarchy in a rural village, and as a mark of respect the inhabitants often refer to her, and even address her, in the third person and by her social status rather than directly, by her name. This is especially true if they are in a subordinate position, as Alma the maid is to the parson's widow. Likewise, it would be customary for Adele to follow the same convention in speaking with her servant.

This usage, which one finds in several languages, accounts for forms of address in *The Parson's Widow* that may strike many readers as strange. Indeed, the use of these indirect forms is considered archaic in Finland today. That style of usage is, however, important here, and any variation can indicate subtle shifts in relationships, as we see in this example from the first chapter of the novel.

"And now, as it always happened when the parson's widow, whose Christian name was Adele, spoke so intimately with Alma, referring to the parson as Birger, to one of his sisters as Teodolinda instead of 'the sister of the dear late parson' or 'the pharmacist's wife,' and to Elsa instead of 'the dear late parson's other sister' or 'the county doctor's wife,' and all together called them the late parson's sisters. You could hear in the widow's voice that although she had brought them close, right here in the kitchen, they were still unreachable, just as she herself was, even though she was sitting at the kitchen table drinking coffee. But little by little, though she didn't change her manner of speaking, it began to go more easily, and the distance between 'the late vicar' and 'Birger' slowly wore down."

The servant Alma answers her with this speech: "The parson's widow is getting all excited for no reason, and won't be able to sleep."

AILI AND AUSTIN FLINT

SELECTED DALKEY ARCHIVE PAPERBACKS

FOR A FULL LIST OF PUBLICATIONS, VISIT:
www.dalkeyarchive.com

SELECTED DALKEY ARCHIVE PAPERBACKS

FOR A FULL LIST OF PUBLICATIONS, VISIT:
www.dalkeyarchive.com